Not My Kind of Hero

OTHER TITLES BY PIPPA GRANT

For the most up-to-date booklist,
visit Pippa's website at www.pippagrant.com.

Tickled Pink Series

The One Who Loves You

Rich in Your Love

The Bro Code Series

Flirting with the Frenemy

America's Geekheart

Liar, Liar, Hearts on Fire

The Hot Mess and the Heartthrob

Copper Valley Fireballs Series

Jock Blocked

Real Fake Love

The Grumpy Player Next Door

Irresistible Trouble

The Girl Band Series

Mister McHottie

Stud in the Stacks

Rockaway Bride

The Hero and the Hacktivist

Not My Kind of Hero

PIPPA GRANT

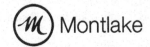

Text copyright © 2023 by Pippa Grant
All rights reserved.

Published by Montlake, Seattle

www.apub.com

Amazon, the Amazon logo, and Montlake are trademarks of Amazon.com, Inc., or its affiliates.

ISBN-13: 9781662513329 (paperback)
ISBN-13: 9781662513336 (digital)

Cover design by Caroline Teagle Johnson
Cover image: © Preto_perola / Getty; © kiuikson / Shutterstock

Printed in the United States of America

To the cow spirit who welcomed my family
to our new home. And also to Earl.

Chapter 1

Maisey Spencer, a.k.a. a single mom who can't stop second-guessing all her life decisions

This is fine.

Everything's fine.

I have it all under control. Three days from now, we'll think back on this, and we'll laugh until we cry.

Just like we have about a dozen other things in the past few months.

"Mom, *it's a bear*. What do we do *about a bear?*" Juniper, my sixteen-year-old daughter, punctuates the sentence by crawling onto my back and clinging to me for dear life.

For one glorious moment, I high-five myself. We're bonding! She's forgiven me for uprooting her and moving her from the only life she's ever known in Cedar Rapids to Wit's End, my uncle's old hobby ranch in Hell's Bells, Wyoming.

I was right.

This is exactly the fresh start we both need.

Champagne! Party balloons! Celebration!

Junie loves me, and once she starts school and makes friends and we get settled here, she'll forget she initially didn't want to come, and everything will be fine.

Moving truly was the solution to all our problems. We're home free.

The bear lifts its head and looks at us.

Happy feelings all gone.

Maybe this isn't our year to be happy.

Or our decade.

"It's outside, honey. We're safe. It won't get us."

I shift, adjusting her on my back so I can grab her legs and make this teenage bonding moment more ergonomically correct. My back isn't as young as it used to be.

Especially after childbirth, I hear my own mother say in my head.

"The window is open!" Junie screeches.

"There's a screen." I don't think I'm screeching back.

I think I'm being calm.

I am the competent, confident voice of *this will all be okay* reason.

The bear squints at us with murder in its eyes, and okay, yes, now I'm shrieking.

Junie squeaks out a terrified noise and tries to climb onto my shoulders.

The bear snorts in our direction, then goes back to eating—something.

"Shut the window!" Junie yells.

The bear lifts its head again.

I reach for the windowsill, and something twists in my lower back.

Not today, old lady body, I grunt silently to myself. *My baby girl needs me.*

Okay, I need me too. And I'm not *that* old. I was practically a child bride, and Junie came along shortly thereafter. And I'm in good shape.

But the bigger point—she's right. We should have glass between us and the beast. And the bear is a bigger threat than any back twinge.

Plus, if we intend to live here as happily as I used to when I would visit as a kid, I probably need to figure out how to deal with bears.

"Oh my God, Mom, can it *go through the glass*? Is that a black bear or a brown bear? What's it eating? Why is it here? *Why did you move me to a place where I'll get eaten by a bear?*"

Awesome. The window won't budge. "It won't—*ungh*—eat you—*argh*—on my—*oof*—watch. Not today, baby girl."

"*Mom.* Quit calling me *baby girl*. I'm not a *baby*, and I don't want those to be the last words you ever say to me!"

I heft all my weight into making the old wooden window scoot down in its frame.

Nothing.

I can fix this. I can. The past sixteen years of my life were dedicated to Junie's dad's handyman business.

Yep. Sixteen years.

I practically rolled off the delivery table, kissed my newborn baby on the head, and said, *Hand me a drill—you've got some loose boards in this shelving unit over my hospital bed.*

The final episode of the sixth season of *Dean's Fixer Uppers* aired on the Home Improvement Network not all that long ago. We spent this final season pretending everything was fine, despite the divorce proceedings going on for the entirety of taping, plus some *other* things that I don't want to talk about.

But the point is, I've fixed hundreds of sticky old windows.

I know how to do this. I'm competent. I've been doing it for a long time. Great track record and all that.

But this one will *not* move.

Apparently much like my relationship with my daughter.

"Okay. Okay. We'll fix this a different way." Have I mentioned that my heart's basically in my throat? I'm only playing brave on the outside and trying a lot of distracting self-talk on the inside so I don't make Junie's freak-out worse.

Did I know we might see bears if we moved here? In theory, yes.

Did I think it would happen within a week?

No. Freaking. Way.

And definitely not fifteen feet out from the old ranch-hand bunk-house on the other side of the ranch, which is still way too close to the house that Junie and I will be living in, at least until she graduates from high school.

She wraps her arms tighter around my shoulders. "What's it eating?"

"I don't know, sweetie."

I sound like my own mother, grunting as I dig my phone out of my pocket, keeping one eye on the bear, who's not coming closer but who also isn't leaving.

Can bears climb fences? Will it eat the neighbors' cows? *Is* that a brown bear or a black bear? Actually, where's the small herd of cows that Uncle Tony's tenant says were left behind?

Is this a murder bear?

Did it murder Uncle Tony's cows?

My *I don't know, sweetie* is really *I'm not going to tell you that that's a cow carcass right outside my window.*

Yes.

A dead cow.

That was *not* on my research list for what we'd need to know when moving to a ranch.

But it's clearly a problem for today.

Right after the *live* wild animal.

"Bear bear bear," I mutter as I balance my daughter on my back and keep one eye on my phone search and one eye on the bear happily chowing down.

Also?

Ew, bear. Just *ew.*

If this is its normal diet, that thing must have the immune system of a god.

"Cougar!" I say triumphantly as my internet search identifies a bear's natural predator.

Kind of.

This website says bears this size don't really have any natural predators, but if they do, this is my best shot.

"Mom!" Junie tries to grab my phone, and since she's taller than I am, with longer arms, she nearly succeeds. *"Don't you—"*

Before she can finish her sentence, I hit play on the YouTube video I've just found and dial the volume all the way up.

A lilting tune starts, and then a total silver fox starts talking. "Men, do you have trouble getting it up in the bedroom? I used to, too, until I found—"

"Mom!"

"Skip the ad!" I shriek at my phone. *"Skip the ad!"*

Junie and I are twisting and turning in the end room in the bunkhouse, which is getting hotter by the minute.

She's trying to take my phone while still clinging to me like she's small enough for piggyback rides.

I'm trying to skip the damn ad.

As I'm twisting and turning, I catch sight of the bear staring at us through just the screen window.

Why is the bunkhouse on ground level and not elevated?

Why why why?

This murder bear will eat us both in our sleep before we've made it a full two nights here.

And if it doesn't, I get to learn who to call to dispose of a cow carcass.

Is there someone you call out here for cow-carcass removal?

This is not what I want to do today.

My finger connects with the right little words on the screen to skip the ad on the video as Junie gasps again. "Mom, there's a—"

A mountain lion's roar explodes out of my phone at full volume.

A horse neighs.

"Mother," Junie gasps, drawing the word out into approximately eleven horrified syllables, which sounds impossible until you have a teenager.

The mountain lion sound roars out of my phone again, and this time, when I look up to see if it's scaring the bear, I see what Junie sees.

There's a man.

On a horse.

No, not on a horse.

He *was* on a horse, and now he's flailing on the ground, getting out of the way as the horse rears back, neighing like—

Well, like a mountain lion is after it.

The horse lands, its front hooves mere inches from the man's back, then leaps over him and takes off at a dead run toward the trees that line the creek at the edge of the ranch.

The man rolls.

The bear turns to look at him, and I swear, there's barely ten feet between man and beast.

"Oh my God!" I squawk.

"Run!" Junie yells at him. "Run for your life!"

My phone roars with a mountain lion roar once again.

"Off," I tell it. *"Turn off!"*

"Turn it off," Junie yells.

"I'm trying!" I yell back.

Twenty feet away from my window, the man leaps to his feet, straightens his baseball cap, and waves his sun-kissed arms at the cow-eating bear. I suppose I shouldn't judge the bear, considering I eat beef too.

Just . . . not exactly like that.

"Get out of here, Earl. Go on. *Git*," the man cries.

The bear snorts.

I finally succeed in shutting off the mountain lion video on my phone.

The man waves his arms again, making his T-shirt ride up and show off a flat white stomach with a happy trail dipping below his belt and ridges right above his hip bones. His jeans are plastered to the hard planes of his thighs, his feet clad in cowboy boots, his shirt sleeves hugging his solid biceps that might have tattoos on them. He's moving too quickly for me to tell, and really, that's not the important part here. Also, I can't see his face under the hat, but I can make out a copper beard.

"Did he just call the bear *Earl?*" Junie whispers.

She's gone still on my back.

I'm frozen too.

There's a man having a stare down with a bear over a dead cow right outside my bunkhouse.

A burly man who's clearly afraid of nothing—not runaway horses, not bears, and probably not hormones either.

All three of those things are currently making me rethink my life choices.

We are very permanently and irrevocably off relationships with men, I remind my nipples, my vagina, and my brain.

Be that as it may, the view is currently incredible. Please pass the popcorn, they reply in unison.

"Don't make me get the sheriff, Earl," the man says.

My ears shiver. His deep, rumbly voice is actually making my *ears* shiver.

It's clearly been too long since I've taken care of my own needs if a man can make my ears shiver almost before the ink's dry on my divorce papers.

But in my defense, he's taking on a bear for us.

Also, my marriage has been formally over for almost a year, and theoretically a lot longer than that. We kept up appearances to meet the contractual obligations for Dean's show. Some for Junie's sake, too, until she bluntly told me she'd overheard Dean making plans to hook up with the star of one of our rival shows.

The number of times I've wished I had skipped filming to go to her soccer games or to take her shopping for back-to-school supplies or to just *be there* to hear how her day was at school . . .

I don't blame her for being so snippy with me.

Between leaving her for weeks at a time to be raised by nannies, my in-laws, or my mother—which is another thing I need to address—and the normal teenage hormones, I'm lucky she talks to me at all these days.

"Tell me you are *not* drooling over this," Junie says entirely too loudly as I note that this man does, in fact, have a tattoo peeking out from beneath one of his shirtsleeves.

The bear studies the man once more, looks at Junie and me, snorts like he agrees with my teenager that I'm *disgusting*, and then swaggers in the other direction, taking his sweet old time.

It honestly reminds me of Junie on the nights she's supposed to do the dishes.

You can make me, but you can't make me do it fast, that swagger says. *I'm still a damn bear, and I can still eat you in your sleep. Don't you forget it.*

I feel Junie swing all her attention back to our unexpected hero a moment after I do.

She doesn't climb off my back.

I don't shake her off.

Not when I'm gaping as the man pulls his baseball hat off, looks around—I presume for his horse—pulls a disgusted face, and then turns fully to the window where Junie and I are gaping at him.

He reaches us in about ten long strides, even with having to walk around the carcass. Despite just being thrown off a horse, he's not limping—not even a little—and my gape gets gapier with every one of his determined, confident steps.

His cheekbones are chiseled over his beard, his eyes hooded under a strong brow, his lips full, and his hair thick and mussed. I can't tell what he has tattooed on his upper arm, but there's definitely ink there. I'd guess he's somewhere between thirty and thirty-five—maybe a couple of years younger than me—and there's no doubt he is *not* happy to see us.

When he stops on the other side of the window, his hazel gaze flickers from my face, to my shoulder—undoubtedly taking in Junie, who's still hanging on my back—and then back to me. "Mrs. Spencer?" he drawls in that deep baritone that's no longer making *only* my ears shiver, despite the subtle curl in his lip like he, too, thinks just as much of me as my teenager does.

"Mai—" I start, then have to stop and clear my throat as I realize he knows who we are.

Junie makes a disgusted noise like she knows Mom's having a little bit of a reaction to being in the presence of this much male-ness.

And *reactions*, while healthy and normal, are the last things I can afford to act on right now.

I shake my head and smile at the cowboy who just saved us from the bear. "Call me Maisey."

Then I wipe the smile off my face.

It's too soon to look eager. I am *not* here for dating, no matter what kind of inappropriately timed reaction my body's having.

Not until I've gotten back on track with being a good mother and then reconnected with who I want to be and remembered how to love myself first.

However, it's perfectly legit to smile at the man who just saved us from death by bear, so I smile again. *Don't be coy, Maisey. While he out-beared a bear, he is not your new hero. Do. Not. Be. Coy.*

"Thank you so much for scaring off that bear. That was—you were—just wow. Not that we can't handle a little wildlife, but we got in late last night, and we weren't prepared to have that big of an animal this close, this fast, but you just rode in and—wow. Thank you. Will your horse be okay? I didn't mean to scare it. We didn't see you coming. This is my daughter, Junie. And you are . . . ?"

Dammit.

Pretty sure that was coy.

No worries, though. This man is completely immune to whatever it is I can't seem to stop myself from doing, if his flat stare and stubborn jaw set are any indication.

"Flint Jackson," he says.

9

I make a noise that probably resembles something a dying cow would say.

This?

This is Flint Jackson? The man who rents the gatehouse and who's been managing the ranch since my uncle died? The man who's sent regular updates for the past few months about what's broken, what's been fixed, and what I owe him for his services?

The man whose emails suggest that he has the personality of a brick wall and likes to complain that *those whippersnappers need to get off my lawn*?

He doesn't say anything else.

"Seriously, Mom?" Junie mutters as she slides off my back.

"Mr. Jackson." I'm stuttering. On top of working as a handywoman since I was a teenager, always surrounded by men from all walks of life, I spent the past six years filming a television show and delivering lines and improvising as the comic relief under nearly every circumstance you can encounter when filming a home-repair show—except finding a bear eating a dead cow on set, that's definitely new—and I have never stuttered the way I'm stuttering now. "I thought you were much older."

I thought you were much older?

Someone please take my mouth away from me before it says something else stupid.

"He looks plenty old to me," Junie says. She tilts her head, reaches into the window jamb, and pulls out an eighteen-inch-long one-by-two that's propping the window up.

The pane slides shut on its own, landing with a thud hard enough to rattle the glass.

"Oh," I say softly.

"Yeah." The scorn in Junie's voice says it all.

That's the first thing I should've checked when the window wouldn't move.

I knew to check that.

And Flint Jackson is standing on the other side of the window that might or might not have protected us from the bear, staring in at us like we won't last four days here.

I pry the window back open, which takes more effort than it should, considering how easily it fell. There's some baggage to unpack in this window.

Or possibly I'm sabotaging my own window-opening skills because I'm so mortified by all this.

"Sorry," I say to Flint on a grunt as I hold the window open. "We're still learning our way around, but don't worry. Next time, we'll be more prepared for the bear. We've been studying how to live out here. Intellectual knowledge and practical knowledge are two different skill sets. We'll get there."

"I'm moving in with Grandma," Junie mutters.

"You can't move in with Grandma, and you know it," I mutter back.

"You know this isn't the main house?" he says.

"Oh, yes. We know. We're looking around. Seeing what needs to be taken out, what can be upgraded. Taking stock. As you do."

His cheek twitches. "Taken out and upgraded," he repeats flatly.

His doubt that I can handle this *should* alleviate this unwelcome attraction to his testosterone.

It does not.

Doesn't matter, I remind myself. *You are in control of your hormones, not the other way around.*

I think.

I hope.

I smile at Flint again, and this time, I'm fairly certain my smile is pure friendly-neighbor smile. "Would you like to come in? Or join us at the main house for coffee and pastries? We can go over the accounts for the ranch, and you can fill me in on anything new since your last email. I hope you don't mind if I ask a few questions. But just a few.

Overall, Junie and I are ready to manage this little ranch on our own now that we're here."

"*June*," my daughter says. "You can call me *June*."

His gaze flicks to her once again. "High school?"

She rolls her eyes.

His lips twitch.

The man's lips twitch at my daughter's eye roll.

What does that mean? What does that even *mean*?

"I get to start junior year at a new school with total strangers," she says. "Isn't that *awesome*?"

"About as awesome as getting thrown off a horse that's scared by a nonexistent mountain lion," he agrees.

Junie snorts.

She *snorts*.

Flint looks back at me. "Gonna have to take a rain check." He delivers it drier than the desert, which makes Junie snort *again*. "Got a horse to track down."

He tips his baseball cap to us, turns, and strides away, and I'm too stunned by his abruptness, his crankiness with me, and his completely opposite good humor with Junie to do anything but—

"Don't you *dare* stare at his butt," Junie mutters to me.

Yeah.

Anything but stare at his butt.

And I wish I wasn't staring. I truly do. But I can't help myself, nor can I stop it now.

Flint Jackson, who I thought was at least sixty-five years old and computer illiterate, based on his emails, who probably knew my uncle Tony better than I did, at least in recent years, who just saved my daughter and me from a cow-eating bear, and who clearly thinks I'm nothing but a nuisance, hands down has one of the best butts I have ever seen in person.

Junie makes another disgusted noise.

It takes everything I have to ignore it. "Great job finding why the window was stuck. Want to head out to the barn with me and see if we can find a shovel? Pretty sure there's not a dead-cow pickup service out here, so we're gonna have to bury it. Oh! I wonder if Uncle Tony still has his tractor. You can practice driving until we get your permit switched over to Wyoming. Doesn't that sound great?"

The brown eyes she got from her father look me up and down, then up and down again, and I'm pretty sure it's not that she's adamantly opposed to ever driving in her life after that little fender bender she had with a tractor during the single driving lesson Dean tried to give her on a backcountry highway before she was old enough to apply for her permit two years ago. "You chose this life, Mother. I didn't. Good luck. Don't get eaten by a bear."

I beam at her. She *doesn't* want me to get eaten by a bear. This feels like progress after the silent treatment I've gotten for most of the past two weeks since I told her we were moving to Wyoming.

She knows *all* of why we had to move. I know she does.

And I know she's probably glad in a lot of ways to be here, too, even if it hurts that none of this is her fault.

None of it.

But she gets the consequences anyway.

Lost friends. Getting cut from the soccer team back in Iowa. Side-eyes anywhere we went in town.

I'll do my damned best to make this a good new home for us, but we're here out of desperation more than anything.

We couldn't stay in Cedar Rapids.

Not after *all* the scandals.

And honestly?

Uncle Tony's old hobby ranch wasn't tempting merely because it's *away*. It was everything I needed in the event that I have to homeschool Junie while we grow our own food and I work on changing her legal name so no one will ever know who she's related to, so she can at least start college on a positive note.

This ranch holds so many happy memories for me. I *loved* visiting when I was a kid.

I hope I can provide the same for her that Uncle Tony gave me. A safe escape where I felt loved everywhere I went and where I knew I could count on him.

"I'll do my best to stay alive for you, honey," I tell her.

She rolls her eyes and walks away.

I get it.

I screwed up. Rebuilding this will take time.

Which is pretty much the entire story of my life right now.

Chapter 2

Flint Jackson, a.k.a. a man who wishes he'd stayed in bed this morning

Parsnip is in a mood as I steer her back to Wit's End, once I've finally found her hiding in the sparse woods by the creek, but it can't be helped.

There's no way Maisey Spencer can handle what needs to be handled with that cow, and if I don't deal with it, it'll only get worse.

Which is why Parsnip and I are headed back to bury the danged thing for Maisey and her teenager.

Might as well. Gonna hurt tomorrow already from getting thrown, so it's not like burying a cow will make it much worse.

"Simmer down," I tell my palomino quarter horse, who was really Tony's old palomino quarter horse, which I won't be telling Maisey. Care too much about the animal to leave her fate in the hands of a woman who hasn't been to this ranch in twenty years and whose most recent claim to fame was *not* getting run over by a lawn mower that she should've heard coming on the series finale of that stupid show she did with her even more stupid ex-husband. "Wasn't a real mountain lion.

Don't see those too often around here. And if it was, it would've gone for the cow first."

Probably.

Fact that the bear was noshing on it suggests it's past its prime and has probably been there for a few weeks.

At least.

Gross-ass animal.

I probably should've found the dead cow sooner, but I've been spending more time helping Kory next door and less time checking out all fifty acres of Wit's End on a regular basis. Ride the fences and check for breaks so we can fix those? Yes. Check in on the mostly empty house that Maisey had cleared out by an estate-sale company instead of tackling herself? Of course. Ride out to the closed-up bunkhouse just in case a wandering cow met an untimely death over there?

No.

Parsnip snorts and keeps trotting. We round the corner of the single-story, dirty off-white building, expecting to see nothing but a cow carcass.

Instead, there's a denim-clad, heart-shaped ass sticking up in the air while its owner bends over and inspects something on the dry, cracked ground near the dead animal.

Unfortunately for me, I watched enough of *Dean's Fixer Uppers* to recognize that ass.

Camera loved to zoom in on her at that angle anytime she was bent over doing any of her handyman work.

'Scuse me.

Handyperson work.

Tony didn't like to let me forget it either. That man was damn proud of her, no matter what stupid stuff she did on her show and no matter that she never had the time to come visit.

Or even the decency to show up for his funeral.

When Parsnip and I get close enough to her, two things click in my brain.

One, that cow is definitely old Gingersnap, who always loved pulling what Tony called *a jailbreak*. Kory told me he hadn't seen her in a while after the fence went down a month or so back. Just assumed the old lady had finally found her freedom and was living her best life however she wanted.

Figured we'd eventually get a call that she'd broken into someone's house a hundred miles away, because that would've been just like Gingersnap.

Instead, apparently she was here.

Wind didn't pick up the scent, and I've been in and out the past few weeks enjoying the last bits of summer vacation, helping friends in town with various projects, and getting ready to start the school year.

That second thing that clicks in my noggin? Maisey's holding a measuring tape.

Not just *holding* a measuring tape but using it to take dimensions.

"You planning on listing it on eBay, or you trying to figure out how deep to dig the hole?" I ask while I pull Parsnip to a stop beside her.

She jerks upright and squints up at me. I know full well the sun's blinding her from this angle, and I also know full well she does, in fact, know how to use a shovel.

Seen her do it enough times on that show.

Never out here on dried-up ranchland, though. And never *well*.

Am I being an ass?

Yes.

Do I have reason to be?

Beyond the fact that she got me thrown off my horse this morning, yeah. Got a few reasons.

Given that she inherited a ranch that should've been left to the town, has been a hoity-toity pain-in-my-ass landlord over email for the past year, missed Tony's funeral, and showed no interest in coming here at all until she randomly emailed two weeks ago, with all the exclamation points, telling me that she'd decided to move out here with her daughter and embrace hobby-ranch life, yeah.

Yeah, I think I have reason to be.

Last thing we need is a city slicker and her daughter getting themselves into trouble this winter—or before, apparently—and expecting all the townspeople to bail them out.

Last thing *I* need, that is.

I know how this goes.

Flint will handle it. He's close. Reliable. Capable. He'll make sure they don't die of stupidity in all the elements they're not used to out here.

Sorta like I just got thrown off my horse helping them chase off the world's least scary bear.

Freaking Earl.

"Mr. Jackson." She smiles at me as though she's genuinely glad to see me, but I know that smile. It was on my television every week from the time she started her little show until Tony left us. Her straight, brownish-blondeish hair, bright-blue eyes, white freckled cheeks, and Cupid's bow mouth shouldn't take me by surprise, but they do.

Probably because she looks every bit as fresh right now in the heat rising around us as she does when she's all made up for the cameras on her show.

And that's irritating.

Is she out here measuring for a hole under the full morning sun in *makeup*?

What's the point of that?

"Thank you again for your help this morning. I'm happy to report that I've now had two more cups of coffee. If that bear walked up into my yard right now, I'd be able to handle it on my own without screaming. Much. Probably. Whew. Is it hot out here? It's the elevation, right? Makes the sun feel hotter? Easier to lose your breath until you get acclimated? I forgot that part."

"Understandable, seeing how long it's been since you took the time to come out here."

Her smile drops all the way, and the closest thing I've ever seen to a scowl forms on Maisey Spencer's face.

I momentarily feel like a heel.

But Tony used to worship this woman, while she never made the time—*ever*, not in the six years that I've been back in Hell's Bells—to get out here and see him. And calling him?

Nope.

I'd ask on occasion while we were watching that damn show, usually after she tried to hammer something with the wrong end of the hammer or dropped an open bucket of paint on original hardwood floors in an early 1900s fixer-upper. *Talk to her lately?*

And it was always the same answer. *Nah. She's too busy for a crazy uncle like me.*

Shocked the hell out of me when he left her the ranch. Always wondered if he'd known his time was short, if he would've changed that and left it to the town and the school like he always said he should.

Considering how much he hosted for the town out here and how much he let the school use the land, it was honestly shocking that he hadn't left it to us.

Too late to know now.

"What's your plan?" I ask her with a nod at Gingersnap.

Maisey straightens and looks around, tucking her tape measure in her back pocket before she squints up at me. "Not sure yet. It was such an impulsive decision to move out here, I haven't had a chance to really think about what I want to do with the ranch yet. I'm sure I'll figure it out in time. Or the universe will give me a little nudge in the right direction."

I make a noise, startle Parsnip, and have to remind myself to breathe as I calm the horse again. Jesus Christ. "The universe gonna tell you how to prepare for a hard Wyoming winter too?"

She blinks.

And my brain goes blank.

Completely, totally blank in the face of that very wounded, very taken aback blink.

"I know it's a little different from city living in Iowa, but I have faith we can figure it out," she says, not nearly as confident as she was a minute ago.

Good.

Underestimating life out here is a good recipe for trouble.

But that waver in her voice?

It's doing something to me that I do *not* like.

I grit my teeth. Last thing I need is the world's most unknown and inept reality TV star getting under my skin with wounded blue eyes and a waver in her voice.

Parsnip whinnies, and I get a grip on her again. "I meant, what's your plan with the cow?" I say.

"Oh." She swipes her forehead and looks down at the animal baking in the sun amid the scraggly brown grass.

Need rain.

Probably won't get it.

She shifts a glance at me like she's judging my mood—*fuck*, I hate being the asshole—and then returns her attention to the carcass. "Once Junie got over the bear, she got upset that we weren't here in time to save the cow from his—her—its fate. So we're having a cow funeral this afternoon."

"A . . . cow . . . funeral."

"Have you ever ruined a teenager's life, Flint?"

The question would amuse me if it came from any other person. "Few dozen times every school year."

The woman does *not* hide her feelings. I see it the minute everything clicks into place. "You're *still* a high school teacher. When Uncle Tony would talk about you—"

I interrupt her with a low grunt. If she's about to call me old again, I have a name or two I can call her as well.

Also—when the hell did she talk to him?

About *me*?

"Never mind," she says. "Right. So you're familiar with teenagers. Are you familiar with teenagers whose mothers ruin their lives by moving them seven universes away from all that they love and hold dear, permanently scarring them for the rest of their lives, since they definitely don't have access to telephones and email and forty-seven varieties of social media to keep in touch with said friends until they all live out their dream of reuniting and sharing a house when they go to the same college in *two whole horrible, terrible, awful, never-ending years*?"

Don't wobble, I order my lips. *She's not funny. She's not amusing. She's going to ruin the ranch with her ignorance about what it needs and cause a lot of trouble for you in the meantime, and you should take a hell of a lot of pleasure in knowing that she has someone in her life making her suffer the way she's about to make you suffer.*

If she were anyone else delivering that line, I'd let myself chuckle. Because, yes, I know a little something about ruining teenagers' lives.

Do it daily.

And I go back every fall because *I get it.* I vividly remember being a teenager. I relate to what they're going through, no matter what *some* teenagers seem to believe. I can especially relate to what June's going through. I moved in with my aunt here in Hell's Bells at the start of my own junior year and never felt like I found my place in high school.

Being a safe place for teenagers to be who they are and feel what they're feeling gives me a purpose in life, and I wouldn't want any other job.

Or any other home now that I've resettled here.

And I don't love it solely for the view of the butte at sunrise and the bluffs along the creek at sunset that I can get from the gatehouse I've rented from Tony since I came back to Hell's Bells. Or for taking a dip in the creek on a hot summer day after working with the animals at Kory's place, or on a roofing project with a friend, or doing any of the dozens of other big and small tasks that I help out with around town most days in the summer and most of my free time on weekends through the school year.

I love Hell's Bells because it's home now. More, I love the ranch because Tony always welcomed me to bring groups of students out here when they needed to blow off steam or learn to ride a horse, or what it's like to herd cattle, or just to run free and blow off steam in a place with the occasional building to hide in when they needed some space to be alone.

The school has unofficially used Wit's End, which sits about a mile outside of town limits, as a teaching ground for the next generation to learn about being stewards of the land.

Might inspire a new generation of ranchers.

Or it might inspire someone who can figure out how to save the earth.

And while I'm worried about the future of Hell's Bells and the kids, she's traipsing in here and announcing we're having a *cow funeral* because that's what her teenager needs.

The *very worst part* of all this, though?

Hell if I'm not on board.

It's what the teenager needs.

"You know where to find the shovel?" I ask.

She wrinkles her nose at me. "*Shovel?* Oh no. This is a job for the tractor. Ground's hard here when it's this dry. Plus, *tractor*. Hello, fun. That was always my favorite part of visiting here."

"You've driven Tony's tractor?" I don't know if I'm surprised that she's driven it—she drove *nothing* on her TV show, not even a regular pickup truck—or that she's comfortable casually dropping *Oh yes, I used to visit here and liked it.*

Every now and again, when he was watching her show, Tony would talk about the times she visited as a kid, but I always got the impression he was willfully remembering it better than it had been.

Glad to see she grew up happy, even if she doesn't stop by as much anymore, he'd say when he'd stop himself midstory, getting a far-off look on his face like he didn't want to think about how long it had been since she was last here.

And damn if Maisey's expression doesn't go the exact same kind of wistful as she shields her eyes from the sun and squints up at me again. "Not since I was about Junie's age. Maybe a year older. Tony was that uncle everyone should have, and he was everything I needed when I was younger. Once I left for college . . . well. Anyway. If I'd known his time was short, which clearly, none of us did, but—the tractor. Right. I drove the whole thing into the creek the second time I tried it, and after he finished laughing, Uncle Tony took away the tractor license he made for me."

I grunt in what I hope is a normal ole *that's interesting* kind of way.

I *have* heard about her and the tractor.

Slipped my mind.

But if she can drive a tractor, she can take care of the cow herself. And maybe that's what she needs.

Maybe she needs to try this life, drive that tractor into the creek again, realize here isn't the fit she wants it to be, and then she'll leave.

And, yes, I'm well aware I'll be the one pulling the tractor out of the creek.

But if it makes her leave so she's not *one more thing* that I have to take care of this winter?

I will happily pull her out of the creek.

All of Hell's Bells knows this is a temporary thing for Maisey Spencer, until she gets over her divorce. There's actually a pool going about if she'll last through the winter.

Not because we don't like outsiders. We're a welcoming bunch.

But more because as far as any of us can tell, she has no plans, no clue, and we've all seen her show.

Maisey Spencer seems like a nice enough person. Never said a bad word about anyone on that show. I'll give her that.

But a Wyoming-winter person? A ranch person? A *competent* person?

I couldn't even begin to count the number of times she didn't shut off the electricity or the water on a project she was working on that required shutting off the electricity or the water, and how many times she got zapped or sprayed because of it.

She does *not* belong here, and I am *not* up for being the person who saves her ass every time she can't deal with a bear or a cow or her kid.

So maybe it's good that she's here. Once she realizes she's bitten off more than she can chew, she'll sell the ranch to the town, and everything can go back to normal.

"Looks like you got this cow under control, then." I tip my hat to her. "Welcome to ranching, Mrs. Spencer."

"Wait." Maisey shakes her head, and that TV-show smile slips off her lips as I turn Parsnip to leave. "Are there other cows we should worry about? If we're doing a funeral for one . . ."

Probably not. If Kory had more jailbreaks, someone would've found them by now. "No idea. You'd have to ask Kory next door. He took in all of Tony's cows. If anyone other than Gingersnap might've escaped, he'd be the one who knows."

"Gingersnap? You know this cow? By name?"

"You know the cow?" Junie—no, *June*, she said—pops up in the window behind us, pulling earbuds out of her ears. "This specific cow? That's really her name? You knew her?"

She's practically her mother's clone except for the dark-brown eyes and hair. Same round, white, freckled cheeks, same Cupid's bow mouth, same pointy chin. "Yeah. Tony—your great-uncle—told me she was born here before I met him. Spent a lot of time with Gingersnap over the years."

"So you could do her eulogy?" June asks.

Parsnip snorts. Probably because I jerk in my saddle at the request. If Maisey had asked, I'd be snorting right along with my horse.

But a teenage kid completely out of her element, without friends nearby, who woke up on her first day at her new home to *this*?

Fuck.

"Sure."

Chapter 3

Maisey

I'm not dressed for a funeral.

But then, I can't recall the last time I went to a funeral for an animal I didn't know under the baking-hot noon sun with a cranky teenager and a surly high school teacher–slash–ranch hand who's renting a building at the entrance to Uncle Tony's land.

"Can you at least show some respect and cover your shoulders?" Junie mutters to me as she, Flint, and I make our way to the burial site, which is a lovely patch of dirt that will be in the shade once the sun drops below the trees along the creek bank that borders the western edge of the ranch's property.

We're about a football field's length from the bunkhouse, which is as far as we can get from the rest of the buildings scattered about Uncle Tony's fifty acres without having to dig up ground that's as solid as concrete in order to get Gingersnap deep enough to prevent further investigation by the local wildlife.

"The cow's not wearing clothing at all, so I'm totally appropriate," I whisper back to Junie. "Also, shoulders are natural. Who's telling you it's your responsibility to cover them up? I need to have a talk with them."

Flint heaves a heavy sigh.

With the number of times I've heard that sound since he took over digging the hole and transporting the cow—*If we want this done before we all burn to a crisp, I'll do it, and then you can spend some time reeducating yourself on the operation of this tractor later*—I'm renaming him.

He's now Sir Sighs-a-Lot, which I won't be sharing with Junie because she seems to adore him.

Probably because he took the time to put a tarp over what was left of Gingersnap's body so as to pay some respect to the dead before transporting it over here in the tractor's bucket.

Also because he's a total stranger who's going to a cow funeral with us.

And that's after he rode back to the house to get a few knickknacks that Junie insisted the cow should be buried with but that she needed Flint's advice on picking out from among the eclectic collection of Uncle Tony's things that weren't sold at the estate sale or donated to charity by a few of the ladies in town who went through his clothing for me.

Lovely people here. I adore them already.

Mostly.

"If I die and you show up to my funeral with your shoulders bare, I'll haunt you forever," Junie tells me. "I just think it's respectful to wear something nicer than a sweaty tank top showing off your *screw you* divorce tattoo to a funeral."

My *screw you* divorce tattoo is a hummingbird. There's nothing offensive about it beyond the fact that Dean always said tattoos were crude and he thought I was dumb for liking hummingbirds.

Clearly, we know who the problem was here.

But I have an opportunity to make a point without arguing about my tattoo, so I smile at her with what I hope is a respectful enough smile. "If you died, I'd miss you. You're welcome to haunt me. I'd like that, actually."

Sir Sighs-a-Lot does it again.

Please note, he hasn't *once* sighed at a single thing Junie's said. Not when she asked him to show her what would mean the most to the cow, *since I never really knew my great-uncle or the cow, but I feel this connection to both, and I want to honor them right.* Not when she asked him if he'd please use the best tablecloth still left in the house as the tarp for the cow. And not when she asked him to do a eulogy for Gingersnap either.

"Did you at least put on sunscreen?" Junie asks.

"Of course I did."

I didn't.

Totally forgot when we got busy picking a burial plot and roping my uncle's *way younger than I thought he was* tenant and best friend into helping us put everything to rights.

And when I was trying to not ogle Flint's biceps. Or the way his jeans fit. And when I was trying to remind myself that I *very* much get the impression he's not happy I'm here.

Join the club, buddy. Nobody wanted us back in Cedar Rapids either.

A shiver slinks through my body as I realize there's a possibility he knows *everything*. The tabloids never picked up the other half of the story of why Junie and I had to move, but that doesn't mean someone who's determined couldn't figure it out.

Junie eyes me. No doubt she knows where my brain went.

All of it.

I catch myself before I sigh too.

I can still see the little girl who used to climb in my lap and ask me to help her with glitter crafts and tell her bedtime stories in this sullen teenager who's furious with me for uprooting her whole life.

And despite what she might think, I'm not doing this to make her miserable.

I'm doing it because we both need a fresh start.

It's not just the awkward situation with my mom. Or the way so many of my friends abandoned me because of what she did. Or how the rest of them took Dean's side.

And I even think Junie could've weathered the drama with the few loyal besties she had left in her old high school.

Probably.

Maybe.

Last year was *super* rough on her, and those loyal-friend numbers dwindled hardcore by June, which I should've realized so much sooner than I did.

But when Dean told me he didn't care if I took Junie and moved her a twelve-hour car ride away from home, it was the final slap in the face in our divorce and the final confirmation that we needed to leave Cedar Rapids.

I don't want you, and I don't want her either.

I watched my own father walk away when I was eleven. And he never came back.

He still sent child support. Sometimes. So we know nothing bad happened to him.

He just didn't want us anymore.

Leaving Mom, I get. She had her issues.

But me?

I needed my dad, and he just *left*.

I couldn't bear the thought of putting Junie through the pain of finding out her father doesn't love her, too, on top of everything else. Far better to let her think that I'm having a midlife crisis and set her up for success here with new friends, who hopefully won't care what her grandmother did or feel obligated to take sides like their parents did, than to let her think I'm all she has left in this world. Especially when I haven't been there for her the way I should've the past few years.

I want her to know she's strong enough to do hard things. But you have to do the hard things before you know you're strong enough.

Sucks, doesn't it?

But that's a problem for the coming weeks.

Right now, we have a cow to bury.

The three of us stop at the edge of the tablecloth tarp covering the cow, right next to the giant hole where Flint and I will be dumping the carcass as soon as Junie goes back to the house.

"Are we supposed to sing or something?" she asks. "I haven't been to that many funerals. Or, like, any."

Flint makes a noise.

I know what that one is. It's judgment.

Probably about missing Tony's funeral.

I'd told the local reverend I was coming. The attorney who handled Uncle Tony's estate. Probably Flint, too—I think I knew he was a tenant at the ranch at the time, and we'd been emailing.

But I hadn't seen what was coming, and I still have my own regrets about not being here for the funeral.

Those regrets are none of anyone's business.

So I ignore the jab, and I start singing.

I don't know *why* "Free Fallin'" is the first song that comes to mind, but it is. And everywhere Tom Petty would've said *girl*, I substitute *cow*.

And I improvise what the good cow loves, getting through *cheeses and her barley, too*, before Junie claps a hand over my mouth.

She used to love it when I made up lyrics.

Back when she was six.

"Can you please be respectful?" she says again, this time with so much sadness in her voice that it's not hard to bite my lip to keep myself from blurting that she never met this cow to try to take away some of her pain and remind her that she doesn't have to mourn everything.

She's right.

It's a tragedy, and if we'd gotten here sooner—like when Uncle Tony died, so we could've avoided everything that went down back home and this last season of Dean's show, which was *awful*—maybe we could've prevented it. And it sounds like this was Uncle Tony's favorite cow.

She *should* be mourned.

I squint up at the sun.

Prevented the cow's death? Uncle Tony's favorite?

I'm relatively certain all these thoughts mean I'm dehydrated.

Or possibly I need to get in touch with a therapist.

"Gingersnap was a good cow," Flint says, cutting me a look that says he, too, blames me for the cow being dead. Or at least that he agrees that I need to be more respectful. "She was the light of the pasture from the minute she was born, frolicking and bringing joy to everyone she met."

"She was?" Junie whispers. "And we killed her?"

"You didn't kill her." He scratches his copper-brown beard, shoots a look at me from under the brim of his trucker cap—please note, *he* didn't get chewed out for not being dressed appropriately—and then turns his focus completely onto Junie. "She was close to eighteen years old, which is pretty ancient in cow years. She loved to run. Wasn't so easy the past few years, but she loved to run. If you could've asked her how she'd pick to spend her last day on this earth, I'd bet you every ounce of dirt on this ranch that she would've said she'd go out running for the sunset."

Junie blinks quickly and tries to discreetly sniffle. "So she lived a good life?"

"Good, long life. Especially for a cow in these parts."

"Good."

I slip Junie a tissue.

"Once, Gingersnap got out of her pen and spent a whole night tipping other cows."

"*What?*"

Flint nods solemnly. "She was a real prankster."

Junie cracks up. "She did *not* go cow-tipping."

"You know what cow-tipping is?"

"Duh. I grew up in Iowa. Even us city folk know what cow-tipping is."

"So you know a cow's gone rogue when she tips her own."

My entire face flushes hot, and not from the heat.

Uncle Tony used to make the same joke.

Oh my God.

Did he tell me stories about this cow?

I think he did.

Was this the cow that got caught shopping inside the drugstore?

"What else did Gingersnap do? For real?"

Flint smiles at her.

My throat goes dry.

He is *not* the weather-beaten old man I thought I'd find here.

He's infinitely worse.

"She did bust out of the pen pretty regularly," he tells Junie. "Tony found her hip-deep in the creek, wailing and mooing because she was scared of the fish swimming around her."

"No."

"That one's God's honest truth. She was eyeballing those minnows swimming at her knees like they were gonna eat her. Tony took some video when it happened. Can probably find it for you back at the house later if you want to see."

"You knew my great-uncle?"

"Really well."

My daughter wrinkles her nose.

I can only imagine what she's thinking. Probably *I never even knew I had a great-uncle until Mom told me we were moving to this ranch that she inherited from him.*

I talked about him to her, didn't I? We'd email. Occasionally call. He was the funniest old guy, and I never knew if he was telling me true stories or if he was talking nonsense to make me laugh, but I always felt lighter after we talked.

Junie should've known him.

She would've loved him. And he would've loved her.

But instead, he was my crazy Uncle Tony. The black sheep of the family. The one with the *utter nonsense ideas about the world.* The one who got a wild hair to buy himself a hobby ranch in Wyoming when he hit the lottery thirty years ago.

Literally.

"I'm so glad Gingersnap lived a good life," I say. "All cows should."

"There was this other morning, she wouldn't quit mooing." Flint's smiling at Junie again. I need to find out what subject he teaches at the high school and decide if I want to make sure she does or doesn't have him.

If we even have a choice.

I was told the high school is pretty small when I called to ask how to enroll her the day after I decided we were moving here.

So I'll take solace in the fact that him not liking me doesn't automatically mean he'd be a bad teacher for her.

People are more complicated than that.

"Why was she mooing?" Junie asks.

"Only thing Tony could figure was that she didn't like how Helen Heifer was looking at her wrong. She'd quit mooing as soon as Helen Heifer looked away."

Junie cracks up.

I haven't heard her laugh in *weeks*, and here she is, laughing at a man telling us stories about a cow.

"And then there was the drunken-oats debacle." Flint shakes his head, eyes twinkling under the brim of his baseball cap. "Now, most of these cows get grass, but oats are good for them too. Until the oats get rained on and ferment, and Gingersnap gets into the feed truck and starts walking around like a tipsy old lady who's been cheating at cards. You ever hear a cow laugh?"

Junie shakes her head.

"Thing to behold. You get out and help feed 'em enough in the mornings, stick around for the milking, you might get to hear it too."

My cheek is twitching with the effort of keeping my appropriately moderated smile in place.

Junie finding something—*anything*—to like here is *good*. Connecting with someone who'll be there at the high school, possibly even as one of her teachers when school starts again next week, is *good*.

But watching an adult win her over in ten minutes with stories about a dead cow when she's so mad at me—she'll barely talk to me some days—is absolute torture.

"Do you take care of the cows every morning?" Junie asks him.

"Kory has all of Tony's old cows on his ranch next door. The Almosta Ranch. I peek in on them pretty regularly."

"But you won't now that we're here."

"Depends on if the cows need me."

"We don't know *anything* about cows, so they *definitely* need you."

Flint's lip curls just enough for me to know that he agrees, and he's not happy about it.

And I straighten. I've been in touch with Kory. He told me not to worry about the cows, that he had space for them, and he'd let me know if I owed him anything for vet bills or food. But on top of that, I've done my research. "I know a lot more about—"

"Mom. Reading kid books doesn't count. And that one episode you filmed at that farm in Ohio doesn't count either."

"I know the cows just go out in the pasture and graze all day, and Uncle Tony liked rescue cows, and he tended to treat them more like pets than like farm cattle, and it's harder to care for them in the winter, but Kory has the resources and has been watching out for them."

Junie looks pointedly at the tablecloth covering the dead cow.

I ignore it.

We weren't here. I'm not going to get mad at the person who took in orphan cows. "We'll make friends, and you can go help and learn from him until we decide if we'll have the capacity to take the cows back ourselves."

"I can take you up there," Flint says to Junie. "Kory's a good friend. You'll like him."

Junie perks up. "Does he have any teenagers?"

"Ah, no."

"Oh."

"He has a couple guard donkeys and chickens."

"Guard donkeys?"

"They're real asses."

Junie cracks up *again*.

Flint smiles at her.

My vagina launches into the macarena, because I'm that kind of cool, while my heart twists at watching my daughter smile like that at anyone who's not me.

She used to smile at me like that.

But that was before I foisted her off on grandparents and nannies while helping Dean chase his dream, thinking it was mine, too, because I was going to be better than my parents and I was going to support my spouse.

And it sounded fun at the time. Until about the fourth episode.

Of the first season.

I should've quit then. I truly should've quit then.

"Tell us more about Gingersnap," I say to Flint.

He flicks another dark glance at me like he was trying to forget I was here, lifts his cap, and scratches his thick dark-copper hair, then turns his attention back to Junie. "The thing you really need to know about Gingersnap is that she lived an amazing, long life, and there's not a person in this town who doesn't have a story about her. That cow did what all of us humans can only hope to do. She left a lasting impression, and the world's a better place because she was here."

Oh hell.

My vagina is asking if shorty can get low, my eyes are stinging, my heart is bleeding, and my pride has been sideswiped by a man who knows what to do in any situation—annoying, that—who clearly adored my uncle, dislikes me, and is charming my uncharmable daughter.

But this is okay.

This will all be okay.

Soon.

Hopefully.

Maybe.

I sigh.

If not, at least the views are pretty.

Chapter 4

Flint

I'm feeling the effects of getting tossed off Parsnip this morning as I head into town for a meal at Iron Moose Tavern a few hours after we get the cow buried. Tonight's a burger-and-a-beer night, then it's home for a hot shower, painkillers, and bed before my crack of dawn alarm goes off.

But pulling me out of my bad mood is an email from one of my former students.

Kid graduated from college a couple of months back and has been working his dream job in New York City. Couldn't be more excited for him. He was one of the first kids I took out to Tony's ranch when he was having a rough patch with family shit and looked like he was on the way to dropping out of school.

Seeing him happy and in a good spot is a win.

I'm smiling as I walk into Iron Moose, glad to be feeling more like myself after a shitty day, but my mood doesn't last long.

Why?

Because Maisey Spencer is holding court at my favorite table inside the converted log building.

If there's anything Hell's Bells loves more than fresh blood, it's fresh blood that comes with a story. And we get it so rarely that this is clearly a treat for everyone gathered in here today.

But the worst part?

You'd think the worst part is knowing that all my fellow Hell's Bells citizens have welcomed this woman like she didn't miss Tony's funeral when he was one of us. Like she's not a disaster waiting to happen out here. Like they want a brush with fame so badly—even low-budget, barely hanging-on fame—that they'll get excited over an inept home-improvement star.

If you can call her a *star*.

No, the worst part is that in those little milliseconds between hearing a throaty, sexy laugh when I walked in here and realizing who that laugh belonged to, every cell in my body lit up with undiluted, primal attraction.

And I can't make it stop.

"No, no, tell me more," she's saying to Kory, owner of Almosta Ranch next door to Wit's End and one of my best friends here in Hell's Bells, as they sit together by the window, under the antler chandelier with the one light bulb that's perpetually out.

Jesus.

First she moves into Tony's ranch. Then she has the nerve to laugh like that. And now she's at my table.

My table.

Leaning in and flirting with my best friend. "If there are tricks to being safe around the wildlife, Junie and I are all ears."

"The moose are super nice," Kory replies to a round of raucous laughter from the rest of the Hell's Bells patrons who are gathered around. "Definitely try to pet them."

He's a six-foot-four Black man who took over Almosta Ranch a few years before I came back to Hell's Bells. When he's not wrangling cows, who are pretty self-sufficient half the year, he's driving around Wyoming in his jacked up Ram to support his boyfriend, who's one of the top drag performers in the state.

So I shouldn't be bothered at all over the fact that she's flirting with him.

"Pet . . . the . . . moose . . . ," Maisey dictates as she prints something in an open notebook. It's a dot journal—several of my students use them every year—and I'd bet Tony's ranch that the cover has her face on it.

That seems on brand for what I saw of her on her show.

June snags the notebook and flops it shut.

Huh. I was wrong.

It's kid artwork.

"*Mom*, do *not* pet moose." June gives her a look. "He was *joking*."

Maisey beams at all of them. "I know," she stage-whispers back to her daughter. "But he's so funny, I want him to stay and keep telling us stories. Now. Kory. Tell us the best thing to do the next time we see a bear."

"You call Flint. Most of the bears love him. Used to train them in his spare time." He tips his chin at me, all broad smiles.

Like he hasn't been on the receiving end of all my muttering about how much she doesn't belong here and how I'll be saving her ass from trouble all too often, since we got the email that she was coming.

I scowl.

He covers his mouth, stroking his beard, but I've known him too long to believe he's doing anything but covering a chuckle.

"Too bad school's starting next week." Kory keeps grinning at them while he points to the open chair at the weathered plank table. "Always cuts into his bear-circus time."

I could leave.

Don't have to ruin my dinner by having it with Tony's niece and her sexy laugh and her *everything's fine* attitude.

But Iron Moose has the best bison burgers this side of the Rockies, and don't even try to tell me there are better onion rings anywhere in the world.

Nothing better to help a man heal after getting thrown off a horse.

Plus, Kory's usually pretty good company.

Usually.

I saunter across the room and take the open seat at my favorite table, which puts me between Kory and June. I'm facing the window that overlooks the bluffs west of town as the sun dips lower in the sky, but my view of the dazzling orange sunset is interrupted by my nemesis.

Why didn't *she* take the seat where she could see the view?

This is literally the best seat in the house.

Who *wouldn't* take this seat?

There's something wrong with this woman. Anyone who doesn't want to take the sunset-view seat at Iron Moose is broken.

"Order yet?" I ask Kory.

"Yep. You took too long. But lucky for you, Maisey here says she owes you dinner."

"And more." Maisey turns that smile on me.

Doesn't work.

Not for me.

Or her daughter, whose eyeballs are going round as she curls her lip. "*Mother*. Please don't ever say stuff like that in front of me again."

"Oh for goodness' sake," Maisey replies. "I was offering to sew him some curtains or take a look at his electrical box."

"I don't think that made it better," Kory mutters.

"Don't be inappropriate in front of kids," I mutter back.

"I'm not a baby," June's whispering to Maisey. "I know what innuendos are. Dad makes them in front of me all the time, and he's been letting me watch R-rated movies since I was seven."

Maisey's smile is turning brittle. "He shouldn't do that either. I'll have a talk with him."

"Like it matters. You're never going to let me see him again."

"*Junie*. I would never keep you—"

"You a senior this year?" Kory interrupts to ask June.

"Junior."

"Ever do drama?"

"I play soccer."

Fuck.

Kory's gaze slides to mine once more.

Everyone's gaze is landing on me.

Even the people in the tavern who are too far away to hear. They know a bomb just dropped.

"You any good?" Kory asks June.

She whips out her phone, and thirty seconds later, she's shoving a video at us. "That's me. Number forty-three. I have a kick that doesn't stop, and I've terrified goalies in six different states."

"As soon as we get Junie registered at the high school tomorrow, we're finding the soccer coach to ask about tryouts," Maisey says.

Kory looks at me.

I don't look back.

June looks down at my shirt.

Jersey, to be more specific.

I don't look at her either.

Or at Maisey.

Fuck again.

"Bison burger, Flint?" Regina Perez asks as she pauses at the edge of our table. Her family's been running Iron Moose since before Hell's Bells was big enough to be a dot on the map. Dated her once upon a time for about five minutes my senior year of high school, but that didn't work out.

She's married with three kids now, and she picks up shifts here to get out of the house.

"Yeah. Onion rings, too," I tell her.

"Oh, do you always get the same thing?" Maisey asks, either oblivious to the tension or willfully ignoring it. "We could've ordered for you if I'd known. I love little towns. And regulars. And everyone knowing everyone else."

"Nope," Regina answers for me. "He just gets this look when he wants a bison burger."

"I do not."

She lifts a dark, well-sculpted brow over her brown eyes.

Kory coughs.

I give them both a *shut up* look, and that simple motion pulls my lower back, because apparently, I don't handle getting tossed off a horse as well as I used to.

If fifty is the new thirty, and I'm in my actual thirties, shouldn't I feel like I'm about twenty-one?

"What are the Demons?" June asks.

"High school mascot, but in Flint's shirt's case, it's the soccer team," Regina answers. "He's the coach. Started practices this week, didn't you? Come straight from there?"

I clear my throat. "Yep."

"We missed tryouts?" June whispers.

All the color drains from Maisey's face. "Oh God, we missed try-outs?" Her gaze flickers to June, then to me, back to June, and finally lands on me. "But it's not too late to sign up to play on the team for new kids, is it?"

I hate being a dick.

Hate it.

Especially when it ruins a teenager's day. "Don't get kids moving to Hell's Bells very often. There'll be sign-ups for spring ball tryouts posted in March."

"But—" Maisey sputters. "But I told her she could play soccer. Can't she—can't she try out late?"

"Roster's full, and rules are rules. I add someone, I have to take someone else off. Not exactly fair to them, is it?"

"Got room for a cheerleader on the bench?" Kory asks me.

"Cheerleader?" June gapes at him, then points to the phone lying on the table between us. "I am *not* cheerleader material. I am *soccer* material."

"Junie—" Maisey starts.

"You told me I could play," she interrupts. "And now I can't play, and I don't have any friends, and we're surrounded by bears and dead cows, and the soccer team probably sucks anyway."

"It's coed, so there are *some* benefits." Regina winks at her.

June makes a noise that sounds more feral than Earl was this morning and shoves up from the table.

Maisey jumps to her feet too. "Junie—"

"I have my phone, and I want to be alone. Just—just leave me alone, okay?"

"I'll come with you."

"I want to be *alone*, Mom. That means *without you*."

Hurt flashes through Maisey's blue eyes, and it's hard to not feel for her.

For both of them, honestly.

"Okay," she says quietly. "Don't go far, and if you lose signal, come right back. I'll get you before it's dark. Don't do anything to make the bears think you're dinner. Do you have cash?"

June rolls her eyes and stomps out the door without answering.

"She'd be really good at drama," Kory says. "I'm heavily involved with the Hell's Bells Players. I could get her a tryout, even if it's late."

I give him a look.

"She's a good kid," Maisey says as she drops back to her seat. "She really is. The move is just . . ."

"I moved six times as a kid," Kory tells her. "Military brat. It sucks. Sucks worse when you're a teenager. I get it. Would be really nice if everyone did."

And now he's giving *me* a look.

"Oh no, I don't need you to bend the rules for us." Maisey reaches for the mason jar of water or Sprite or maybe straight vodka in front of her and fiddles with it, misinterpreting Kory's look. The one that meant *Tell her you get it, too, so you don't look like such an asshole.* "That wouldn't be fair to anyone who got cut. I understand. This is my problem to deal with, and we'll make sure she's signed up for tryouts in the spring."

"Can't bend the rules *at all*, Flint?" Kory says.

My cheek is twitching again.

I'd say I should've stayed home, but that would've just delayed this conversation until tomorrow. Maybe next week. "Team's set. League has roster limits. And the number one thing I need is team players."

"Junie's a team player."

I work overtime to keep my face from questioning that sentence.

June probably is a team player, despite her insistence that she's a star. I shouldn't judge a kid based on a bad first day in her new home.

"Why'd you move here?" I ask Maisey. I know what we assume.

But I don't actually *know.*

Kory coughs again as he reaches for his coffee cup. Dude drinks it like it's water. "Nothing like small talk, is there?"

"No, no, it's okay." Maisey's smile gets brittle as she keeps talking. "Like you said, people don't move here often. And I know I wasn't here much when my uncle was—was alive, so it's an understandable question. Why? Why now? Why not sooner?"

"That's none of our business," Kory says.

Of course he does. Doesn't really impact him beyond deciding how much he'll offer her for the land when she decides to sell.

She tries to beam at Kory, as if there's no tension at all at this table, but her smile is more brittle than glass. "If we're going to be friends, then of course it's your business. Why would you invest your time and energy in me if you thought Junie and I would bail at the first snowflake in December?"

"October," I correct.

She smiles even brighter at me, and *fuck.* Doesn't matter how hard or fake it is, I can't deny that she has the exact same smile as Tony did.

Genes must be strong in that family.

And I miss that old bastard.

"October! That's exciting. I love snow."

I grunt.

Kory chuckles. "You are truly adorable. Let's talk again in November."

Swear to God, she's gonna break her face if she smiles any bigger than what she's currently beaming at Kory. And I'm starting to think she's faking it in the hopes of actually feeling it.

There's something desperate about her.

What the *fuck* does she have to be desperate about?

Tabloids say she got a nice alimony settlement. She has the ranch. Her kid's pissed at her, but that'll pass if she's a decent mother.

If not, June's in a good place.

She has *that* going for her, even if she doesn't know it yet.

But my biggest problem with her desperation?

It draws me like a magnet.

I'm a damn sucker when it comes to playing hero to the desperate. Usually, helping out the kids in tough spots fills that need.

But Maisey Spencer is getting under my skin with those emotions flitting across her face, and I don't like it.

"I would love to talk *much* sooner than that," she's saying to Kory. "Junie wants to help with the animals. She really does. She's just having an off night. And I'd love to see her find new interests. Honestly, it would be lovely if Junie got involved with the theater, too, so we could see you all the time. But I can't pick what she loves for her."

"She'll find where she fits," Kory says.

Maisey sighs over her drink. "I should've had us here two weeks ago. No, I should've had us here two *months* ago. And we would've been here, but—well. How about I save the *woe is me* tale of our moving adventure until after we're good enough friends that you won't mind my occasional bitter rants?"

"Are you bitter?" Kory asks.

She frowns. "I don't think so."

"You don't know?"

"Have you ever been married?" she asks us both.

Kory chokes on his coffee.

"No," I answer for us.

44

"He means *hell, no,*" Kory offers, his voice raspy. "I'm in a committed relationship with a drama queen who'll probably never agree to marry me, no matter how much I bend over backward—and forward—and sideways—for him. As for this guy, you want your heart broke, date him. Hello, commitment issues."

I rear back. "What does that have to do with anything?"

He smirks.

I scowl.

I know that smirk.

That smirk says, *You're being an ass to a woman because it's your favorite defense mechanism.*

Any other woman, that might be true.

This woman?

This woman is a disaster waiting to happen on a ranch she has no business living on, much less *owning.*

She couldn't even handle a bear that had no interest in her this morning.

"Are we friends?" I ask him. "I thought we were friends."

"You tell her yet how much you take kids out there to the ranch to work out their frustrations?"

"Wait, what?" Maisey goes sheet white.

"Yeah. Tony used to let Flint take kids from the high school out to the ranch all the time to fix things, ride horses, drive cattle, use power tools . . ."

"But you don't do that anymore, do you?" Maisey asks me.

I glare at Kory.

"Of course he does," Kory replies. "What Tony always wanted."

"No," she says.

Kory lifts his eyes.

I settle a glare on her.

This.

This is *exactly* what I've been hoping to avoid. "It's what Tony wanted," I reiterate.

While I never wanted Wit's End for myself—not really, considering I know how much upkeep goes into the place—I've still spent the better part of the past year angry that Tony left it to her. The ranch should've gone to the town or the school. It's what he always said he planned to do with it.

Tony was a good dude. Funny. Unorthodox. Never judged and always opened his home and land to anyone or anything that needed it. He'd host annual barbecues. Let me bring kids out, like Kory said. He'd let youth groups have campouts under the stars.

And now that she's been here approximately twenty-four hours and already needed saving from Earl and help burying Gingersnap, she's confirming my fears that she's closing the place up and won't let the community use the land like Tony always did.

I hate change.

Hate it worse when it's bad.

And taking Wit's End from the Hell's Bells community?

This is bad.

"You *can't*." She lunges for her drink like it's vodka that can wash this conversation away. "I'm not insured to have kids working on the ranch. I'm barely insured enough to have *a renter* on the property. What if someone gets hurt? What if they sue me? What if what happened to the cow happens to one of the kids? Oh my God. No. *No.*"

And here we go. "Calm down—" I start, but I choke before I finish that last letter in the word.

Maisey Spencer, Avenging Ice Queen, levitates in her seat and turns a glare on me that could make even the most seasoned asshole shit his pants. "Do. *Not.* Tell. Me. To. Calm. Down."

"Yeah, probably don't tell *any* woman to calm down," Kory says out of the side of his mouth. "Even I know that one."

"No one's going to get hurt—" I start.

Maisey's not having it. "You can't know that."

"And if they do, we'll patch them up, and everything will be fine."

"You don't know that."

"Pretty sure I know how to do first aid."

"And how much other land is there that you can take your kids to? *Miles and miles* worth. I'm not having that liability at Wit's End. It needs to stop. *Now.*"

I lean back and cross my arms. "This is what Tony *wanted*. For the community to use his ranch. Hell, he always told us he'd leave it to the town. If he'd known how little time he had left, *you* wouldn't be here."

Her chest is heaving. Her eyes are on fire. "But we are, aren't we?"

Everyone in the entire tavern has gone silent and is staring at us, and she seems to finally realize it.

She abruptly stands up. "I'm so sorry, gentlemen. You've been lovely to welcome Junie and me, but she's clearly having a rough night, and I suddenly have a headache. Let me buy your dinner. Hopefully we can do this again soon. We're excited to meet neighbors and make new friends. Today's just been a long day."

Kory's silent as she gathers her things, including her journal, which—*fuck me.*

I know that journal.

It's the kind elementary school parents order for friends and family, featuring their kids' artwork.

That's June's artwork. With her name on it in what looks like kindergartener writing.

Not Maisey's own face or anything narcissistic.

Shit.

Shit.

I've been an ass.

But I'm not wrong. She doesn't belong here.

She drops two hundred-dollar bills on the table, smiles painfully again, and darts for the door.

Kory and I share a look.

"That got awkward," he finally says.

I rub my eyes. "And they say you don't know how to do understated."

"Scare another one off, Flint?" Regina asks as she stops at our table with a tray loaded down with three full dinners.

Not including my burger.

Dammit.

Maisey and June both left without dinner.

"My fault," Kory tells her.

She nods. "Stuck your foot in your mouth?"

"It's so delicious. Hey, you ever notice how often Tony'd leave the ranch and go visit his niece?"

Regina snorts. "Tony, leave the ranch? Never."

An unfamiliar and unwelcome heat crawls into my stomach.

I know where he's going.

Relationships work both ways.

Why am I holding one party responsible for making all the effort? And it's not like he was her father.

He was her uncle. Her eccentric, fun uncle who probably had more to offer a teenager than he did a grown woman with her own family and a career that, while she was fairly inept at it, still paid her bills and more.

I don't know why Tony never changed his will.

Won't ever know.

And I can keep fighting for what I wish he'd done, or I can accept it for what it is.

"I'll keep their dinners warm," Regina says to Kory. "You wanna go drop 'em off after you eat?"

"I'll do it."

They both look at me, clearly questioning my offer.

I sigh.

"Ink's hardly dry on her divorce papers, and her ex-husband just announced a new show with his mistress," Regina says.

"What the fuck does that have to do with anything?" Three hundred sixty-two days of the year, I'm the easiest-going son of a bitch you'll ever meet. I can handle teenage attitude. I can handle annoying school administrators. I can handle uptight parents.

But today's apparently one of the three days a year when I'm a bigger bear than Earl.

"You miss Tony," Kory says. "His niece is here and sad and single. Plus, she has something you want."

"I do *not* want—"

"You don't have to want the ranch for yourself to want what she has for a different purpose. And you don't have to like her to recognize that she's hot. This has *Flint Jackson Fucked-Up Relationship Special* written all over it."

I roll my eyes. "I am *not* interested in Maisey Spencer. And she is *not* interested in me. And I don't date students' parents."

"That's why we're warning you," Kory says.

Regina nods. "You always go for the unavailable ones that clearly won't work so you look like less of an ass when you bail after three sleepovers. And Kory's right—your head's in a bad place. Deciding to hate the woman who got Tony's ranch and finding out you either have to move or live down the driveway from her?" She tsks. "You're up shit creek, my friend. You want me to wrap your burger to go, too, or you gonna sit and eat here and let their dinner get cold?"

"You just said you'd keep it warm."

"Only so much a little ole server can do before that perfect crust on the bison pie starts to dry out."

One of them ordered the bison pie? *Dammit.* She's right.

That shouldn't go to waste.

Even if Maisey Spencer will have no idea how much she should appreciate it. June, either, but she's a teenager. She gets a pass.

"Fine," I mutter, fully aware that I'm once again doing Maisey Spencer a favor that she won't appreciate and shouldn't be my favor to do. "Mine to go too."

Kory points to the next table. The one *without* a spectacular view. "I'll move over there."

Worst part of all this?

They're right.

Unavailable women are my favorite kind, and one that knew and loved Tony?

Fuck.

Tony's gone.

Can't get him back.

But his great-niece is exactly the type of teenager I usually go above and beyond to help. She'll definitely be in one of my classes. Most likely on my soccer team in the spring.

Which means I probably need to make nice with Maisey.

Chapter 5

Maisey

I knew when I decided to move here that I'd be facing some uncomfortable situations.

I didn't expect them to all come at once, as an emotional-minefield sandwich with a side of angry-teenager coleslaw.

"Was this a terrible idea?" I ask my mom quietly over the phone as I sway on a swing at a small empty playground a couple of blocks from the tavern.

As if I had a choice.

We wouldn't be here at all if we had a single friend or family member back in Cedar Rapids that I could count on, but with the divorce, Mom's arrest, and her family imploding as a result, it was game over for Junie and me there.

We had to get somewhere without all that baggage hanging over our heads, and when I got an email from Flint a month ago with a note about an issue with the barn that he said would require something beyond his expertise, everything was crystal clear.

Uncle Tony's ranch wasn't a *responsibility*. It wasn't that thing in the background taking precious time that I didn't have to give to it in the midst of everything else.

It was a safe haven when everything else was falling down around us.

My daughter is hovering in the shadow of a building at the end of the main drag in Hell's Bells. She's crouched beside a cinder block wall that's been painted with a herd of elk in front of the river bluffs. Her back is to me, and her earbuds are definitely in, so I'm reasonably certain she doesn't realize I have an eye on her.

Dusk is falling quickly, but she's in a well-lit area—whereas I'm not, though there's enough ambient noise and light that I don't think we're at risk of an animal attack—so I don't think she'd notice even if she looked this way.

Pretty sure she wouldn't want to know her mom is watching out for her in case any random western wildlife wants to brave the noises and lights of town to grab a tasty teenage morsel. Or in case the teenage boys or girls around here smell fresh meat.

Much like driving, she hasn't shown interest in dating yet. When or if she ever does, I'm ready for whoever she might bring home to meet me. And if she never does, that's fine too.

So long as it's not because she's had such awful examples of what relationships are that she thinks it's not worth it.

Then I'll have mom guilt forever.

Correction: *more* mom guilt.

"Uprooting a city teenager and dropping her in the middle of Podunk nowhere to finish out high school might not have been your smartest move," Mom says. She's in her late sixties and recently faced a mandatory retirement from the real estate world after getting caught running shady, nonexistent homeowners' associations all over Cedar Rapids. She gets one phone call a week to us from her white-collar criminal prison facility, where she'll be residing for the next two years, and I almost missed this week's.

"Thanks." I lean my head against the chain, feeling even lower than I did when I realized I had to get both Junie and me out of Cedar Rapids for not just our relationship but our mental health too. If it wasn't friends siding with Dean in the divorce, it was friends who dumped me after they were scammed out of thousands of dollars by my mother's HOA-management company. More than a handful came after me, demanding I pay for her sins since *you're a rich reality TV star. You need to fix this. You owe us.*

While I was just as flabbergasted at what she'd done as they were, I still lost friends. I couldn't fix things. I didn't have enough to fix things. "Just what I needed to hear."

"Maisey, sweetie, there's no such thing as an easy answer when it comes to major life decisions. Something told you that you had to go. Maybe that something needs you to know that you would've been miserable there, too, so you can quit wondering and then come home."

I'll move anywhere else in the country with no history dragging us down before I'll go back home. Which isn't something I'll say to my mom. I know she did bad things. I know she hurt people. But she's still my mom, and I don't want to hurt her. "After the divorce, Cedar Rapids isn't home anymore."

"So *maybe* that something you're feeling is a need to stretch in ways you haven't stretched before so that you can find where you and Junie truly belong. Which is definitely not on some hellhole of a ranch in Montana."

"Wyoming."

"Same thing."

"It's not a hellhole. It's actually really pretty out here. Remember the sunset picture you had blown up for me after the last time I went to visit Uncle Tony? It's like that every day. And if you get hot in the sun, you can just step in the shade, and poof! All better. When you can find shade, I mean. I should probably just carry an umbrella. And you should come visit when you get out."

And move into the original cabin back behind the newer main house, where I can keep an eye on her.

This ranch has more buildings than I remember—gatehouse, cabin, bunkhouse, barn—but then, I didn't care about them when I was a teenager.

Now they're more to manage, which is actually a thrilling task to take on.

She harrumphs. "Come live on that ranch where that man abandoned the rest of us to?"

"He didn't *abandon* you."

"Did too."

Eventually, yes.

The ironic part?

Uncle Tony was the family member that Mom's relatives whispered about and never invited to anything, more so with every passing year. But he's the one who's provided Junie and me a safe haven, while my mother's the one in prison.

"I never understood why you quit talking to him," I say to her.

"*He* quit talking to *me*."

"Why?"

"I can't relay that information on recorded prison lines."

I sigh and shove my foot harder on the ground. The swing sways with a *squeeeak squeeeak squeeeak*, taking me back to childhood, when I used to escape the fighting inside my house by going to the park down the street.

At least, until my parents divorced and my father moved to Jersey, where he, too, has gotten himself into legal trouble.

Thank *God* Dean's show was small enough that the desire for gossip about us was fully satiated by made up details about our divorce.

Now that I'm out of the picture and there's constant *Are they or aren't they shagging?* speculation about him and his *new* costar, everyone's forgotten me.

"Did I hate you when I was a teenager?" I ask Mom, needing to find a safe subject where she might be helpful. And she *was* a good mom. It's been fascinating to realize that she can be both a good mom and a criminal. "I don't remember hating you as a teenager."

"No, you saved that all for your father. But you'll have it different with Junie. For one, she's half Dean. That puts you at a distinct disadvantage."

"Mom."

"It does. Your father was a piece of work himself, but Dean? He's a serious pill at a whole other level. Do you know he was in Cedar Rapids at the high school yesterday for some publicity stunt tied to supposedly updating the lights in the theater over the summer? While you and Junie were finally following that moving truck across the country, he was acting like a local hero, telling people you took his daughter from him and that he knows she'll come back and work for the family business when she turns eighteen and doesn't have to abide by the custody agreement anymore."

Three days ago, even with all the turmoil, I would've said my daughter would *never* pick her father over me.

Today?

Today, my stomach hurts.

"He can say what he wants," I tell her, as if Junie abandoning me when she turns eighteen isn't one of my biggest, most terrifying fears. "I don't have to justify my choices to him anymore."

"And he's a manipulative asshole," she says cheerfully. "But, baby, your father left us for that casino whore in Jersey."

"Mom. Can you please not?" While my first stepmother wasn't my favorite person, she was smart enough to divorce him as soon as she realized he was only trying to get his hands on her family money.

Mom huffs. "Yes, yes, we were both victims of his charms and should be soul sisters. You and your rose-colored glasses. But the bigger point here—you made Junie leave her father behind. You need to tell her he didn't want her."

"No, I don't."

"Maisey—"

"I know how that feels, Mom. I will *not* do it to my daughter. And—" Nope.

I cut myself off before I can say *She blames you too.*

Not helpful.

Mom fucked up. She fucked up *big time*. But running an illegal homeowners'-association ring didn't make her a bad mother.

Yes, it made her a bad role model in some areas. For sure.

But she *was* the parent who got me to doctor and dentist and orthodontist appointments. She was the parent my friends came to when they couldn't ask their own parents questions about puberty and periods and sometimes even sex. She was the parent who'd let my friends hang out at our house all weekend long, providing pizza and junk food and driving us to the mall to hang out whenever we asked.

Yes, she did something wrong, and she's in prison for it.

But that doesn't mean she's bad in every area of her life.

"Life hurts sometimes," she says quietly, still the voice of reason even when she's in an orange jumpsuit hundreds of miles away. "You can tell her the truth and support her through it, or you can be the asshole who makes her find out all on her own when she's thirty-six and divorced with a kid of her own."

I let that pass and change the subject. "How's the food this week?"

"About like you'd expect prison food to be."

"You're not losing weight again, are you?"

"We had *pudding* for dessert on Sunday. I ate all of it. I'm up a whole tenth of a pound."

And this is why we weren't here in time for Junie to do soccer tryouts.

Mom looked sick the last time I went to visit her, and since I feel partially like I'm abandoning her, too, on this *run away and find myself* journey, I had to stay long enough to make sure she was okay.

"Good. Eat more. And if you start to feel feverish—"

"Stop worrying about me and—"

The line clicks and goes dead abruptly, which means Mom heard her two-minute warning and didn't tell me.

Probably hoping the system would malfunction and we'd get to keep chatting.

She's an eternal optimist when it comes to breaking the rules.

I pocket my phone as a shadow falls across me, and I spin in the swing, ready to karate chop whatever animal is looming in the settling darkness.

But it's not an animal.

It's Flint Jackson.

Which might be worse.

I don't like it when people don't like me, though after my divorce, I'm getting better at telling myself that's their problem.

There's no question he's seen me at my worst today. And I probably didn't handle that bombshell about how he's been using Uncle Tony's ranch the best way.

But my biggest issue?

When he startled me, my head bumped the chain wrong, and now I can't move because my hair is stuck.

"Ow!" I yelp as I realize moving any farther will rip everything out by the roots.

And I just had my roots redone.

"What—" he starts. Then he does one of those sighs through his nose that makes his nostrils flare. Doesn't matter that the sun's dipping low and the light's dim. Pretty sure I'd see that nostril flare inside a pitch-black cave. "Are you stuck?"

"What? No. Not at all." I try to move my head away from the chain, and my hair threatens to rip out again. *Crap.* I am totally stuck. "Fancy meeting you here. Can I help you?"

He lifts two Styrofoam containers. "You left your dinner."

I grimace in the midst of trying to untangle my hair before I can stop myself. "Thank you. That's very kind."

"Tony would've wanted someone to watch out for you."

Right.

This isn't about me.

It's about a man who wants nothing to change from how his life has been. He has no idea how much I cannot afford the liability insurance that would be necessary for him to keep bringing kids out to the ranch.

He also has no idea how much more I do *not* need the publicity and scrutiny that a kid getting hurt on the ranch would bring.

Junie and I need to stay squeaky clean. Raise zero eyebrows. Cause zero problems.

I want her to have a true opportunity for a fresh start, not more drama dumped on our doorstep.

And there's only one way I know to get what I want.

I need to charm the hell out of *everyone* here.

Not because I want to play them for fools.

But because I want real friends. I want to fit in. I want to find a way to make things work so that we're a positive part of the community, and I am *clearly* off to a bad start here.

So I flash Flint an even more brilliant *Maisey Spencer, small-time home renovation TV star* smile that I don't feel and don't like either. "That's so kind of you."

His eyes narrow. "You know I see through teenage bullshit every single day."

"Guess I'm lucky I'm not a teenager."

"Not much different." He sets the cartons on the bench at the edge of the playground and approaches me, a looming mass in the dim light. "What did you do to your hair?"

"It's chain-chic. Latest trend."

He sighs. *Again.*

I do my best not to get snippy in response.

But then he does the very worst thing he could possibly do.

He slips a hand into his pocket, pulls out something flat and palm size, and then I hear the distinct sound of a pocketknife opening.

"Oh my God, no!" I shriek. I back up in the swing, some of my hairs getting pulled, and I work the knot around the chain faster. *"You are not cutting my hair!"*

"Mom?" Junie calls.

The light's fading fast, and I have no idea if there are streetlamps or park lamps or anything here, and I'm suddenly acutely aware of the fact that someone once told me mountain lions are most likely to pounce at dusk.

Are there mountain lions this far east in Wyoming?

I'm safe because I'm basically in a populated area . . . right?

Hello, sudden regrets. I should've offered to buy Junie an ice cream cone, packed her into the car, and driven back to the ranch.

It would've worked a few years ago.

But that was before I screwed everything up trying to save my marriage by making my husband happier than I made my daughter.

"I'm not giving you a *haircut*," Flint says. "I'm cutting six strands loose so you can go about your business."

"This is *way* more than six strands."

"It'll grow back."

"Cut my fingernails. Ruin my manicure. Rip my clothes. Steal my makeup. Throw a berry smoothie all over my best dress. Scuff my boots. I don't care. But *do not* touch my hair." It's the *one* thing I'm vain about. The one single thing I spend any time on in the morning and any significant money on for beauty-supply products.

Vanity and I aren't all that well acquainted—not really—but my hair?

I love my hair.

"It's already stuck in the chain and ruined," he says.

One lock comes free, but there's another clump still stuck. "Is this how you handle your students? *Let me take the nuclear option because you're being emotional, and I don't want to handle it now?*"

"I handle emotions just fine."

"Oh, I'm sure, Mr. *Calm Down*. Mr. *Couldn't Tell Me He's Been Putting Me at Liability for a Lawsuit since Uncle Tony Died*. Mr. *I Don't Like You, but I'm Not Actually Going to Tell You Why to Your Face*. I don't need *this* way of your handling *emotions*. Thank you for bringing my dinner. Now please excuse me. *Again*. I need to untangle myself and take my daughter home."

If the past year has taught me anything, it's how many facets there are to the diamond of life. I have friends—*good* friends—who picked Dean in the divorce because they thought I was what was wrong with my marriage.

And you know what?

I was part of it. Takes two, right?

But I wasn't all of it, and their thinking that he was totally innocent has been a blow.

Especially when he's already out promoting his upcoming new show with his mistress, who will forever be his mistress to me, no matter where their relationship goes. According to the private detective my divorce attorney recommended, Dean was already heavily involved with her before he filed the paperwork to make me his ex.

"I was going to talk to you about the kids and the ranch," Flint says quietly.

Like he's being the *reasonable* one.

I fucking—yes, *fucking*—hated it when Dean would *logic* me after he did something stupid that I had every right to be upset about, and I'll be *damned* if I'll let another man—even a man who's hotter than the Deep South in August—ever again make me feel *less than* because I have emotions.

Dammit.

"I'm sure you were," I reply as I work the knot in my hair. "And I'm sure you think I'm an absolute stick-in-the-mud for telling you no. But if my choice is between disappointing you or putting myself, and therefore my daughter, at risk, then it's pretty clear what I should choose, isn't it?"

If that's not another sigh coming out of his mouth, he really needs to have that loud breathing checked out by a doctor. "Can I please help you get out of there before Earl smells your dinner and comes to check it out?"

My heart leaps into my throat. Yes, I knew it was getting dark, but *why* didn't I think about the smell of our food?

Which *he* brought here and is clearly *happy* to blame me for. "I'm doing just fine."

"You're making it worse."

"Do *not* mansplain to me how to untangle hair, please."

"And how much experience do you have with hair in chains?"

"You'd be surprised."

"Shit. Right. You did it all the time on your show."

"You watched my show?"

"*Tony* watched your show. He talked about you all the time. Whenever I'd swing by, he'd make me watch it too."

A wave of grief for a man I talked to not nearly enough in my adult life stabs me in the chest.

He finally had a tie-severing falling-out with most of Mom's family several years ago, and I talked to him less and less after that.

Knowing what I know now, I wish I'd made more of an effort to stay in touch beyond the occasional email or phone call. He always had a way of making me feel so happy anytime we'd communicate.

While we've been talking, Flint's approached me like I'm a wounded mountain lion.

I hold a hand in front of myself. "Do *not* cut my hair."

"Hold the light," he replies gruffly, handing me his phone, the pocketknife nowhere in sight. "You can't see to untangle it from that angle."

I take his phone. Our fingers brush, and I smell salt and lime. The man smells like a margarita without the tequila burn. Ironic, considering all he does is burn me.

"Shine it on your hair," he orders.

"I *am*."

As well as I can, anyway. When he tugs gently to untangle the strands, I feel it on my scalp, and my scalp is a freaking traitor.

I used to love it when Dean would play with my hair, but that was eons ago.

"Hold still," Flint says.

I grit my teeth and try to hold still. I could do this myself, but that time I got my hair caught in the chain on Dean's show?

When it aired, the editing made it look like I spent the entire job trying to get it untangled.

Much like every bit of the rest of the show, it wasn't an accurate representation of what I did on that job—we shot and worked that house for a full week, and I was *not* stuck to that swing for very long—but it still took three of us a good fifteen minutes to accomplish the task.

Help is good.

I know this.

But I still distract myself while he works the knot—which *is* coming free—by staring at his phone.

And then I get mad all over again because while I'm twisting the phone to try to keep the light aimed correctly, I catch sight of the picture on his phone's home screen.

It's his Demons soccer team that he won't let Junie try out for.

"Mom?" Junie says again. She's close now. I can tell by her voice.

"Got my hair tangled," I tell her. "I'm fine. I'll be fine."

And now my daughter is sighing just like the man whose fingers keep brushing mine, making sparks shoot up my arm and my vagina flip inside out.

You are getting nowhere near this man, I remind her.

His breath on my ear makes her flip again.

Clearly, I have a type.

I like the guys who don't like me.

"How did you get it this knotted?" Flint asks.

"I asked myself, *Self, what's the very worst way we could tie our hair up around this chain and make for a super-uncomfortable situation for everyone tonight?* and then I did that, but worse."

Yep, I am *totally* at my best today.

"Back up," Junie says to Flint. "*You're* making it worse. Mom, stay. I've got this."

"Junie—"

"Remember last Fourth of July parade? And the lamp chain on your float?"

I wave Flint's phone at him, gesturing for him to take it back. "She's right. We've got this. Thank you so much for thinking of us and bringing our dinner. That was very kind."

"I'm half done," he says.

"Half done isn't all—"

A howl cuts her off midsentence.

A not-soft howl. A not-distant howl.

It's answered by three more howls.

Chills race across my body. The hairs on the back of my neck stand straight up. My stomach flips, and my shoulders hunch in on themselves.

That's an *I'm on the hunt, and I can smell you* howl.

"And we're done," Flint says.

I've barely registered the click of his pocketknife snapping open before I'm free.

"Where's your car?" he asks.

"*Oh my God, my hair*," I gasp.

"*Mom.*" Junie grabs my hand. "The truck. *Where's the truck?*"

Flint grabs me by the shoulders, turns me toward the main drag, where streetlamps are flickering on just a bit away, and shoves. "Turn on your flashlights, and be as big as you can be."

"Are wolves going to eat us?" Junie asks.

"Probably not. *Be big*, Maisey."

My hair.

My hair.

And also—"I'll offer myself first, baby," I tell Junie while I stumble in the darkness, one hand grasping for hers, the other testing the spiky hair on the side of my head while I tell myself the lie that if the wolves eat me today, Junie will know to put me in a good wig for my viewing.

Won't she? Crap. I need to tell her. But probably not before I've patched up our relationship a little more.

Are those wolves?

Or coyotes?

And does it matter? "When they attack me, you run, and know that I love you."

Flint snorts.

Junie sighs.

And then we're back in civilization, which wasn't that far away, with raucous laughter spilling out from Iron Moose just down the street.

"There's my truck," I blurt. I have to get in my truck. Get Junie safe from the wolves. And then I'm taking us both home, where I can park in the garage and shut the door before we get out and then find out what my hair looks like.

And then also deal with the mess that I left all over the house as I was cleaning out the last of Uncle Tony's belongings from the room that the estate sale people left them in before our moving truck arrives tomorrow.

I am so ridiculous.

And this was a terrible idea.

All of it.

Dinner. The park.

Moving Junie somewhere with predators who like to eat women *who have done their research* and can theoretically but not actually handle wildlife.

"Thank you for our dinner," Junie says stiffly to Flint.

He grunts out a "welcome," and then I'm hustling my daughter to safety.

We get buckled in, her holding our dinners in her lap, and when I'm sure the windows are rolled up, I turn to face her. "I'm so sorry I was too late in getting us here for you to try out for soccer. I'll make this up to you."

She snorts.

"I mean it, Junie. I'll get you a private coach or find another league somewhere in the state for you to play in, no matter how far we have to drive, and—"

"Mom. It's okay."

Seven thousand pounds lift off my shoulders even though I don't entirely believe her.

"I don't think it is." I squeeze her hand. "I know this is hard, and I keep disappointing you."

"I don't want to play soccer if he's the coach."

"Junie—"

"Stop, Mom. I get it. You have to do this life-adventure thing and figure out who you are now that you're not Dad's second fiddle and everyone hates you for what Grandma did. And I'm stuck in the middle, the semikid, semiadult who has to finish high school because that's what society says I have to do, even though I could take care of myself *just fine* if I faked an ID and a diploma and got a job and an apartment."

I ignore the amount of thought she's clearly put into this. Junie's conversations only show you the tip of the iceberg when it comes to what she's researched.

Teenagers are smart, and they have *entirely* too much information at their fingertips.

"You forgot the part where you have to learn to drive," I say.

"I'm also going to get a sugar daddy who comes with a chauffeur."

Hand me a paper bag. I need to hyperventilate. But I stuff it all down inside to peer at her in the growing darkness. "You're not mad anymore?"

She snorts again, but this one is decidedly less funny. "Right now. Right now, I'm just glad to still be alive."

Right now.

I'll take it.

Chapter 6

Maisey

Getting to know a new stylist wasn't supposed to be the first thing on my to-do list this morning—our stuff is being delivered in a few short hours, and I still need to finish clearing out the last of Uncle Tony's things from the room Junie picked as her own, plus formally register her for school—but here we are, with my hair taking priority over turning my inherited house into our new home.

"Oh, you did a number on this, didn't you?" Opal of Opal's Cut 'n Curl says as she studies the crazy clump of hair sticking out sideways over my ear.

No amount of washing, combing, styling, or hiding it with my longer hair worked to pin it down.

My options were spending the next year in a bandanna or moving a haircut to today's top priority.

When I called Opal this morning and said I was new in town with an emergency, she knew exactly who I was and told me to come on in.

I'm having regrets.

Don't get me wrong—the salon is charming, and I adore it. The bright-white walls are tastefully covered with artistic silhouettes of chic women having good hair days. There are two massive windows on either side of the glass door, letting in a ton of natural light. Translucent globe lamps hang at various lengths through the space, supplemented with recessed lighting. The waiting room chairs are bright and fun, in yellows and pinks and purples, and the end tables have piles of recent celebrity-gossip and women's magazines.

Please don't ask how I know they're recent.

All I'm saying is, in the six years that I played the comic, inept supporting role in *Dean's Fixer Upper*, it never got popular enough to warrant pictures of us on the covers of celebrity magazines. We were a D-list show that the network kept renewing because we weren't controversial and Dean was a smooth talker. The tabloids never even picked up on my mom's trial.

But my regret in being here isn't even about being confronted with my ex-husband and his new girlfriend on the cover of a second-rate gossip rag, since he's apparently at least B-list now that he's dumped me and moved on with a new show in a more prime-time slot.

My second thoughts are all courtesy of how packed this place is.

I swear half of Hell's Bells is crowded into this building. The salon has eight chairs, seven of them currently in use, and nearly all the chairs in the waiting area are occupied.

It's a Wednesday.

Don't people have nine-to-five jobs?

Or are work hours that flexible here?

I want to make friends. I do.

But I'm mildly intimidated and nervous that I'll make the same mistakes with everyone else here that I somehow did with Flint yesterday.

"I didn't do this," I tell Opal quickly, trying hard to keep my tone light and amused. "Someone with a pocketknife and a death wish did this."

"He was trying to save us from being eaten by wolves, so I guess he gets, like, two points for that. But he could've cut closer to the chain instead of trying to take your ear off." Junie's seated in a bright-pink egg chair along the wall opposite my salon chair, her eyes glued to her phone, which she occasionally lifts higher like she's trying to get a better signal.

"Oh, are you the reason there was a clump of human hair in the park this morning?" Opal asks. She's a white woman in her mid- to late fifties with her hair shaved on one side and the longer part flipped over her head dyed bright blue. Her smock loudly proclaims *Don't fork with me*, and she's wearing it over skinny jeans, high-top Converse sneakers, and a crisp white blouse. "There was a whole hullabaloo on the Facebooks about it."

Junie snorts softly.

I try to catch her eye in the mirror to give her the *Do not mock people* eyeball, but I catch Opal's eyeball instead.

And that eyeball is dancing merrily, like she's waiting to see if either of us will call her out on *hullabaloo* or *the Facebooks*.

"I had a small mishap on the swing last night," I tell Opal. "My hair had a larger mishap."

"I'd say. Who's this *he* who saved you?"

"A total basic snood," Junie mutters.

"Ooh, a story," Opal says before I can ask Junie what a *snood* is. "Do tell."

"A local teacher from the high school found us outside in the park at dusk and startled us," I tell her.

"Which teacher?" one of the other ladies calls.

"Mr. You Can't Join the Soccer Team Because We Already Had Tryouts," Junie answers before I can speak up.

There's a collective gasp, and then everyone turns to stare at me.

No, not *me*.

Opal.

They're staring at Opal.

Her lips quirk. "Mr. Jackson?" she asks Junie in the mirror.

Junie rolls her eyes. "Whatever his name is. He helped us bury a cow and made me think he was a decent human being and then dashed all of my dreams for an easy transition to a new high school."

"That's Opal's nephew," someone whispers.

I almost come out of my chair, but she plants her hands on my shoulders and keeps me down. "I'm a much better hairstylist than he is," she says dryly.

I eyeball her half-shaved blue head. Am I that brave?

Am I?

Could I go drastic?

No, you're a chicken, I answer for myself. *You didn't even participate in tattoo day in high school when all your friends turned eighteen. Also, Junie will be mortified and quit talking to you forever if she thinks you're trying to be young and hip.*

"Not the first time she'll have fixed his attempts at a haircut," someone says with a chuckle.

"He's such a stickler for rules," someone else adds, which, for the record, I do *not* snort at.

"And a heartbreaker," the woman in the seat next to mine mutters.

Half the women in the room twitch.

I swear they do.

Opal ignores the murmurs. "I'm thinking we'll give you a pixie cut."

Junie gasps.

"Oh no, I can't do short hair." I cringe to myself—*Who's the stick-in-the-mud?*—but I keep pushing anyway. "I have to be able to pull it back in a ponytail so it doesn't get in my way when I'm working."

"It's called a headband and hair clips," she deadpans. She runs her fingers through my hair, swishing it this way and that. "You'll get used to it. And you don't have a lot of options with this short clump here."

"My hair—"

"New life, new hair," Opal interrupts. "You can't get out of a rut if you don't make changes, and your hair's a good change. Ponytail says *I'm a mom who can't fully get my life under control and is happy to let someone else take credit for my work.* Pixie cut says *Watch out, world, Maisey Spencer is sassy, ready, and fabulous for whatever you think you're gonna dish out.*"

"*Hey,*" the olive-skinned woman in the chair next to me says. She points to her own long hair. "Rude."

Opal rolls her eyes, but she also looks amused. "On Maisey, not on everyone," she corrects. "You make that ponytail look badass, Charlotte."

"Thank you," Charlotte says.

Opal ruffles my hair again. "Definitely a pixie cut. And if you truly hate it, it'll grow back in another three or four years. What's three or four years of learning to love your hair again in the grand scheme of things?"

"You don't pull punches, do you?"

"Not when it comes to helping ladies step into the next fabulous version of themselves."

"Can you talk to Coach Jackson and convince him that my fabulous version of myself involves being on the soccer team?" Junie asks.

Opal smiles at her. "You want on the team, you go talk to him."

Junie meets my eyes in the mirror, then goes back to her phone. "His loss."

"I love teenagers," Opal murmurs. "They're so very intelligent, and also so very belligerent. Sort of like newly divorced mothers who think moving across the country and into a random ranch they inherited from a free-spirited old guy will solve all of their problems."

This could go really, really wrong. "You knew my uncle Tony?"

She arches a brow.

"Right. Small town. And Flint rents his gatehouse. Of course you did."

"There's not a person in town who doesn't have a story about Tony."

"Or Gingersnap?" Junie asks.

"Oh, that cow." Opal chuckles. So do half the other people in the building. "She broke in my back door and got into my hair dye one night a few years back."

"She broke into my law office *while I was meeting with the governor* and made a snack of his toupee," Charlotte adds.

Something clicks in my brain, and I jerk my head to look at her. "Oh my gosh! You're Charlotte. You did Uncle Tony's will."

She nods and gets her head grabbed by her stylist, much like Opal's grabbing my head and turning me to face forward again too. "He updated it about ten years ago."

My heart suddenly hurts. Junie was six, and Uncle Tony invited us out so she could ride horses.

Dean didn't want to go.

He insisted we take her to Disney World instead.

It was fun, if overwhelming, but I wish we'd come here.

Junie never met Uncle Tony. Not in person.

"Bunch of people thought it was interesting he left the ranch to someone most of us have never met," Opal says.

I don't sense judgment.

Mostly curiosity.

"He was the black sheep of my mom's family," I say.

Junie makes a noise that needs no interpretation. *How much worse was he than Grandma if she's in jail and he was the black sheep?*

I shoot her a look, but she's fully hiding behind a magazine now.

One with a front-page picture of Dean and his girlfriend.

Best of luck to her.

The girlfriend, I mean.

"Now how was Tony Coleman the black sheep of *any* family?" Charlotte demands. "He was a little . . . eccentric . . . but he was always lovely."

"He was apparently pretty wild in his younger years." I smile at some of the stories I've heard. Mostly low-key things like marijuana, parking lot racing, and one incident involving cherry bombs in a sewer that I've been sworn upon pain of death to never, ever, ever repeat. "When I was *really* little, I was told he had the mark of the devil on him and that he was an immoral lost soul bound for hell. But then we changed churches, he won the lottery and bought this place, my parents got divorced, and suddenly he was good enough to babysit me out here for a week or two every summer."

"*Mom*," Junie says. "You never told me any of that."

"I know. I'm sorry, ba—Junie. I'll tell you more stories now. Promise."

"Was he wild out here?" Junie asks Opal, who's shaking out a smock and getting me prepped for my haircut.

"He never met a soul in need he wasn't willing to help," she tells my daughter. "Animals. Human. Once, he adopted a cactus that fell off someone's car as they were heading out of town."

That sounds like Uncle Tony. I blink back the slight sting that's basically perpetually threatened my eyes since we got here. "We should've come visit more."

"You talk to him much?" Opal asks.

"He'd call every once in a while. Email more often. But he and my mom had a big fight a few years ago—"

"Mm. Yes."

I study Opal in the mirror. "I never got a straight answer on why," I say slowly.

"Something about a new business venture she wanted him to invest in," Charlotte pipes up. "Your mom doesn't steal babies and sell them on the black market, does she?"

"Oh my God, *no*."

Junie slinks lower in her seat, the magazine so close to her face she can't possibly read the words.

"Why—why would you ask that?" I ask Charlotte.

"Never saw Tony so angry," she replies. "All he'd say was *Stupid family, stupid ideas—that's not me.*"

"That's . . . all he said?"

"To any of us," Opal says.

"Huh."

Out of the corner of my eye, I catch sight of Charlotte smothering a grin. "I figured it was one of those multilevel-marketing schemes. Only other time I ever saw him that hot was when he took in a guy passing through who got stuck here with car troubles for a couple of days. Two of them were at Iron Moose, having their BLTs and bison roast one minute, and the next, Tony had that table turned upside down and was yelling at the guy to get out of here with his slimy snake oil sales pitch."

"The man probably shouldn't have led with the vitamin for impotence problems," Opal murmurs to me.

If Junie heard that one, she doesn't react.

I do, though.

And the story gives me the first honest laugh I've had since I got here.

"I would've thought he'd have been all in with the herbal supplements," Charlotte says. "He fit the profile in most other ways. But this is why we don't stereotype, now isn't it?"

I slide another glance at her while Opal picks up the scissors.

Is she making a subtle inquiry about the things people here have assumed about me?

"I don't mean you," she says quickly. "Tony never said a bad thing about you. Actually, when he came in to redo his will ten years ago, he told me you were in a bad relationship, didn't know it, and one day, you'd need a place to go. He said he wanted to make sure you had it whether he was still here or not."

Chills race down my spine, followed by a warmth that feels like a hug.

"You'll hear people say he planned to leave the place to the town, and honestly, he'd make noise about it every now and again," Charlotte continues, getting her head pointed straight again by her stylist as she talks. "But anytime I'd ask him if he wanted to update his will, he'd say *Not until I know my niece doesn't need a backup plan anymore.*"

I will not cry. I will not cry. I will not—

"We got your back, hon," Opal murmurs. "*All* of us, even if *some* of us might have acted like assholes yesterday."

Crap.

My eyes are getting too hot to handle.

Yep.

I'm gonna cry.

Opal squeezes my shoulder. "Is this your natural part here? Or do you want to part your hair on the other side once it's short?"

I nod quickly and try to surreptitiously wipe my eyes while pretending I'm brushing a lock of hair out of them.

And I fool absolutely no one.

"We know what Tony wanted, Maisey," Charlotte says. "We don't know why you're finally here or what you plan on doing with the ranch, but Opal's right. We've got you. Especially if you join the PTA."

Everyone cracks up.

Even me.

"You gonna do a reality show about the ranch?" someone calls.

I shudder and make myself think about the future. "I *never* want to see another camera again in my life. But I *am* going to fix up whatever needs it around the ranch. And I woke up this morning thinking about a couple girlfriends I know online who are going through divorces. They don't have an uncle Tony with a home in waiting when they need it. How many people do? And I was just thinking, wouldn't it be lovely to add a couple modest houses to the land? *Not* develop it. Not develop it. Just a couple more places to take in wayward souls."

"Like Tony used to," Opal murmurs.

I nod. "In the meantime, I'll probably renovate the bunkhouse—how fun would that be for an artists' retreat?—and tear down the barn—"

The stylist at the chair on my other side drops her scissors. Three women and the one guy in the salon this morning gasp.

Junie lifts her gaze from her magazine and gives me the raised brows of *What just happened?*

"Does Flint know?" the lone guy asks.

"He's going to lose his shit."

I flinch.

Right.

Mr. Rule Follower for Soccer has been using Uncle Tony's ranch for wayward kids while I didn't have the insurance to cover accidents. "I need to take a closer look, but from the outside, it doesn't appear structurally sound, and I don't need the liability if it collapses while someone's in it."

"Reasonable," Opal says.

"I'm not saying I won't rebuild a barn, but I've started a priority list for the ranch, and—"

"And safety comes first," Charlotte finishes.

"*Yes.*"

She gives me a look that says she suspects there's way more to my story.

But it's not the same suspicion that Flint aimed my way yesterday.

This feels like genuine curiosity coming from someone who appreciated my uncle enough to give me a chance.

"When's the last time you were here?" she asks. And I don't think it's judgment. I think it's curiosity.

I glance at Junie and do quick math. "Maybe eighteen years ago. I didn't come back after I left for college."

"So you and Flint wouldn't have been here at the same time," she muses.

Hello, story that I don't think I want to hear. "I have very little recollection of anyone here from back then other than Uncle Tony."

"Suppose you should know that Flint's used the ranch for years to help struggling teenagers who needed an outlet."

I sigh.

I get it. I do.

I'm the outsider with land that was used for good before I was here, and now things are changing, and that's hard. "I'm not saying that's out of the question," I say slowly. "But I need to get liability insurance first, and that's going to involve the ranch being inspected, and that's going to take time."

Opal sucks one of her cheeks in. And I don't know if that's a good or a bad sign. Is she amused?

Or does she think I'm some big-city person who loves lawsuits?

"I know things are different in small towns," I say quietly. "Believe me, I've been in a lot of them the past six or seven years. But this is the home I need for Junie right now, and I *cannot* do anything to risk her stability."

"We'd all do anything for our children," Opal replies, equally quietly.

"You have kids?"

"Just Flint. He moved in with me right before his junior year of high school."

Junie peeks over the magazine.

I open my mouth to ask what happened, but Opal cuts me off.

"Are we fixing this mess or not?" she asks me.

"My hair, or the mess your nephew thinks I'm making of the ranch?" I ask dryly.

She ruffles my hair. "Keep talking. I'm gonna start cutting."

"I didn't actually mean I agree with this plan to cut so—"

"Get the pixie cut, Mom," Junie says. "You'll be so adorable I'll have to screen all of your gentlemen callers, which will be so gross that I'll be glad to go to school. And then if Mr. Jackson gets too annoying living there at the gatehouse and not letting me on the soccer team, we can move in with one of your sugar daddies. That's way preferable to let *you* have a sugar daddy who'll hire me a driver. Win win win win win, right?"

I squeeze my eyes shut. "Okay. Okay. Pixie cut it is."

"And no more swings," Junie says.

"Or hanging out around men with pocketknives."

"Unless they're handsome," Opal says.

I peek out of one eye. "Not funny."

"You don't want to date?" she asks.

"Moving here is about reconnecting with Junie—"

"Because there's literally nothing else to do, so she's *making* me spend time with her," Junie interjects.

"Clearly," I agree dryly. "Almost being eaten by a bear and burying a cow and almost setting the oven on fire making breakfast this morning, since I didn't know it was broken, and going shopping for cowboy boots and out to dinner yesterday and making new adult friends and then cutting me loose from a swing yesterday was *so boring*."

She rolls her eyes.

I roll mine back even bigger just to prove that I can.

Opal visibly stifles a laugh.

"And moving here is about finding myself again, and I don't mean *finding myself with a new man*."

"Girl power," Charlotte says. "Welcome to the awesome divorcée club of Hell's Bells. We meet a couple of times a week for book club. And by *book club*, I mean wine and whine club."

"I am *so* in."

She lifts an imaginary glass. I clink with my own imaginary glass, and look at that.

I think I have a new friend.

Opal grabs my head and turns me back to stare at myself while she snips a gigantic chunk of my hair off.

It takes a herculean effort not to whimper, but I manage it. Moving here is about embracing change. I can do that with my hair too.

"So your daughter plays soccer," she says softly while she snips more of my hair.

"Lives for it."

"And she missed tryouts."

"There was an issue with my—with some family stuff and then another issue with the movers and—yes. Yes, I was late, and I failed to call the school early and ask the questions I should've asked, and—"

"Late cherry crop this year," she muses. "Did you know cherry crisp is one of the very best things about Wyoming?"

"I didn't. What else—"

"Very best thing," she interrupts. Strongly. With emphasis.

Someone behind us snorts softly.

Someone else coughs.

Charlotte makes a strangled noise.

And I realize exactly what's going on.

Opal's telling me how to push Flint's buttons to get Junie on the soccer team.

Either that, or she's completely sabotaging me.

"Are you seriously telling me bribes work around here?" I whisper.

"Bribes? You're not the type of woman to *bribe*. You're the type of woman who'd go above and beyond the call of duty to get to know your child's teachers, since you're doing this solo for the first time in your life and you know how important it is to be involved."

She is.

She is *totally* telling me how to bribe Flint to get Junie on the team.

Well then.

Not like I have a lot to lose on that front at least.

I beam at Opal. "Meeting you is making me so glad I had a hair mishap."

She smiles back at me. "Let's hope you still feel that way after your haircut and cherry crisp."

Chapter 7

Flint

My first day back in the school building to prep for a new year after having the summer off is always one of my favorite days.

The hallways are empty except for my fellow teachers and the small administrative staff. Everything smells like fresh paint. No one's smoked anything in the bathrooms yet, and there's an air of possibility permeating my classroom.

My new posters are hung. My *ask a question* prize jar is full. I'm lounging in my chair, feet up on my desk, scrolling through my rosters on my laptop, when someone walks past my door.

I glance up, expecting to see one of my fellow teachers, but instead, it's a woman I've never seen before. She's in a soft-blue sundress with short, sun-kissed hair, a long neck, straight posture, a round ass, and strappy-heeled sandals.

I sit straighter.

Is that someone new from the district?

Why wasn't she at this morning's staff meeting?

I crane my neck, twisting to look closer, but she's gone, sashaying down the hallway and around the corner.

Probably just as well. I'm not opposed to having some fun—and I do like *fun*, even if I refuse full-on relationships—but work is one place I make an effort to not find fun.

Learned that lesson the hard way.

Left my last school district to move back here because of it.

I grunt to myself and go back to scrolling the roster. Looks like I have Juniper Spencer in my second period. Trigonometry. So she's advanced. *If* they stay, I'll have her in calculus class next year.

I grunt again. It's a small class every year, maybe five students, which means we get tight.

Crap.

This isn't a mistake, is it?

It's for June's own good, I tell myself. Hell's Bells High was where I finished high school, too, and I wish someone would've told Mr. Simmerton to go easy on me in English Lit until I found my bearings, which I never really did. This is me looking out for a new kid in the school in ways that some of my fellow teachers might not consider.

Especially the teachers who have lived in Hell's Bells more or less their entire lives.

Which is basically most of the rest of them. And same for the students.

Not a lot of turnover in Hell's Bells, and the high school is small. Little over a hundred kids total most years. Some oil magnate donated the building to the town decades ago. If they hadn't, our kids would be busing to a county school about twenty miles away every day. We make it work, doing our best to balance our limits with meeting each of the kids where they are.

And it looks like June will be in regular junior-level courses for the rest of her schedule.

Which means now I'm wondering if Maisey pulled her back a level in everything else to ease with the transition and she should've been advanced everywhere. Or if advanced math is wrong. Or why I'm getting involved in this at all when June Spencer will *not* be one of the kids coming to me for help if she struggles with anything.

Not if I won't let her on the soccer team.

I'm scrubbing my face to cover a sigh of frustration when I catch another hint of motion in my doorway.

She's back.

The blue-dress woman is back, and this time, she's not walking away.

This time, she's stopped right there in my doorway, smiling brightly at me.

"There you are! I completely misheard Mrs. Vincent in the office and thought she said to look *left* at the end of the hallway, not *right*. Is this your classroom? I *adore* that poster of Einstein. Not that that should dissuade you from leaving it up. I'm sure the teenagers will love it too. Who doesn't love a genius sticking his tongue out?"

My jaw has gone slack, and I cannot find the muscles to pick it up off the ground.

This is not Maisey Spencer.

It's not.

It *can't* be.

For one, she's in a dress.

Showing the tiniest hint of cleavage.

And curvy, shapely legs.

Jesus.

Who knew she was hiding knockout calves and adorable knees under those jeans?

And her hair.

Her hair.

For the love of all that's holy, someone please tell me she didn't give herself an entire makeover that's left her as a total bombshell.

She has small diamond studs in her earlobes, pink lipstick decorating her Cupid's bow lips, and she's done something with her eyes to make them pop.

Suspicious?

No.

I'm about seven levels past that.

Worse, though?

I have never, in my entire life, been the kind of guy to let loose a hubba-hubba, but that is exactly what my dick's saying right now.

Maisey Spencer is *hot*, and I am not immune to noticing, no matter how much it pisses me off.

She lifts delicate, newly shaped eyebrows at me. "Flint? Everything okay?"

"You're a girl."

Motherfucking fucker, I did not just say that.

I drop my feet to the ground, scrambling to cover the fact that those words actually left my mouth, and in the process I drop my laptop onto the school-grade tile floor.

"Are you all right?" She steps smartly into my classroom, heels clicking like a ticking time bomb coming to set off my libido, while I bend to pick up the device that damn well better not be broken, which puts me in exactly the right—*wrong*—spot to notice her dress swishing just above her knees.

Her *adorable* knees.

What the *fuck*?

Who thinks *knees* are adorable?

And why am I frozen, staring at the tiniest peek of the bottoms of her thigh muscles, which should *not* be what I'm noticing about this woman, and should *definitely not* be what I want to see more of?

Who wants to see a woman's *thigh muscles* when there's that hint of cleavage and that slender neck and those plump kiss-me lips painted pink?

No.

No, I am not all right.

I jerk back to my feet and set the laptop safely on my desk. "No food in the classroom," I grunt.

I'm a damn caveman.

Her lips purse, but her eyes—her *eyes*.

They're dancing with amusement.

"My apologies," she says with entirely too much cheekiness. "I was making the rounds, introducing myself and handing out cherry crisps to all of the staff, but if you don't want yours, I'm sure—"

I growl.

It's feral.

And I should be ashamed, but *cherry crisp*.

Oh, fuck.

The hair. The cherry crisp. "You met my aunt."

"Opal?" She slides the aluminum foil pan onto my desk, then follows it by sliding her ass onto my plain wood desk, too, making the dress ride up enough for me to see even more of those firm, thick thighs. And then she swings her legs.

I'm going to have a very visible problem very, very soon.

"She's *so* talented." Maisey swishes her hair. "I owe you a debt of thanks for cutting me out of that swing. Never in a million years did I think I'd ever cut my hair this short, but *oh my God*, I *love* it. I feel like a new woman. So thank you."

Mental note: become a hermit. While living at the gatehouse on her ranch. Which she'll drive by probably eighteen times a day.

Hell, I saw her drive by at least six times every day since that moving truck showed up a few days ago, and I'm only home about four waking hours a day right now.

Fuck.

"My pleasure," I manage to choke out.

I did this.

I did this to myself, and now I will pay for it.

Dearly.

"I saw you have Junie for Trigonometry. If we were still in Cedar Rapids, I'd ask you to not go easy on her. She has this habit of saying she can't do it so she can get out of it. I'm pretty sure she's afraid of failing, so she'd rather not try at all. But with all the changes she's had to go through—"

"I can handle teenagers just fine."

It is annoying as hell when she beams at me like that.

More annoying?

It doesn't feel fake today. Not forced. Not manipulative.

She just looks like she's having the best damn day of her life.

"That's what I've heard," she says. "Everyone says you're the absolute best with the kids."

"Are you buttering me up?" I wave a hand in the general direction of her entire person, realizing I'm standing way too close to her, and take a giant step back. "Is that what this is? Did you get all dolled up and put on a dress and pouty lips and bake me my favorite dessert so you can get your kid on my soccer team?"

She rears back. "Are you serious right now?"

I wave a hand at her again. "This—this is—you're *seducing* me."

That lush mouth sets in a grim line, and fuck me if it isn't even hotter than her smiling.

And when she slides off the edge of my desk, squares her shoulders, and glares at me straight in the eye?

Yeah.

Seriously.

She's *glaring* at me straight in the eye.

And I *like* it.

"Mr. Jackson, has it ever occurred to you that when a woman dresses up, she's doing it to feel good about *herself*, and your opinion matters for less than zero? I just divorced a man who had no respect for me *or* his daughter. What in the actual hell makes you think I'd try to seduce *you*? What makes *you* worthy? This?"

She waves a hand at me exactly as I was waving a hand at her a moment ago.

And I shrink.

I *shrink*.

She doesn't notice, or if she does, she clearly thinks it's not enough. "This? You? You come in a very nice package. Ooh, *muscles*. And floppy bedhead hair. And a beard and tattoos and a glower. So irresistible. Let me be frank, Mr. Jackson. While it was incredibly kind of you to help us with the bear and the cow and my hair, you *clearly* don't like me. I'm working very hard on having enough respect for myself to only have people in my life who are willing to appreciate me too. I'm here meeting teachers and handing out cherry crisps for *Junie*. And that's *it*."

If you'd told me over that dead cow last week that Maisey Spencer would *ever* reduce me to the size of a flea, I would've laughed you all the way out of Wyoming.

But that's exactly what's happening now.

Worse?

Watching her stick up for herself is triggering a primal instinct deep inside of me that wants to throw her over my shoulder, march her across the state, and tell her to repeat herself so my mother can hear what a woman who respects herself sounds like, despite the fact that I haven't talked to my mother in years.

And it makes me want her.

Maisey.

Not the woman who raised me until I couldn't take living in that house with her and my father for one more minute.

I shake my head, and my temper roars to life.

I do *not* want Maisey Spencer.

Correction: I don't want to want Maisey Spencer.

My body is very clear on the fact that it doesn't much care what my brain thinks on this matter. "You're not leaving until I tell you June can be on the soccer team, are you?"

If I thought she was prickly before, I was sorely mistaken.

"Have you even asked the kids on your team how they'd feel about rotating in an extra player every once in a while, since she was too late for tryouts? I haven't been the best mother the past few years. I'll own that. But if there's one thing I'm learning—and quickly, at that—it's that teenagers have an innate sense of right, wrong, and fair. But if you don't even want to ask, *fine*. Thank you for your bluntness, Mr. Jackson. I'll make sure the next time I stop by the school to see if there's anything any of you need, I won't bother with coming in here."

She turns, giving me a view of that ass and the blue fabric sliding across the muscle, and stalks out of my classroom without so much as a wobble on her heels.

Maisey Spencer, the woman who once spent an entire episode of her TV show in the hospital after she tripped over her own two boots, stalks out of my classroom like she was born on a runway.

And if that wasn't enough, when she reaches the doorway, she turns and meets my gaze with hard, unwavering, but shiny blue eyes. "And I hope you think of me when you eat that cherry crisp. It's the *last* thing of mine you'll *ever* eat."

Every ounce of blood drains from my head to my cock at the images that flood my vision.

I'm hallucinating about eating Maisey Spencer.

And I don't think it'll ever stop.

Chapter 8

Maisey

It's getting dark, so I need to get back to the main house and heat up dinner for my recluse—I mean, my daughter—but there's something so cathartic about beating the crap out of the half walls between the horse stalls in the barn with a sledgehammer.

"How's that feel?" I ask the very bad chalk drawing of Dean's face after I put the sledgehammer through it.

It doesn't answer.

Obviously.

So I move on to the next chalk drawing, this one of a copper-haired, math-teaching, soccer-coaching cowboy that looks more like a snail wearing a donut on its head.

I let the sledgehammer swing, feeling the burn in my arms and shoulders and lower back at lifting the heavy tool once again. When it lands with a satisfying thwack right between that cowboy snail's eyeballs, I feel another jolt of satisfaction that's quickly followed by regret.

"I really want to hate you," I whisper to the splintered wall. "You break the rules and use the ranch without making sure the liability insurance is there, but you won't break the rules for my kid and let her on the soccer team. How is that fair?"

"Guy I used to know liked to say nothing's ever fair," a deep voice says behind me.

My shoulders bunch, my entire face twitches, and my freaking backstabbing vagina swoons.

I could act surprised and jerk around and *accidentally* swing my sledgehammer at him, but I don't need *that* lawsuit either.

So I put the sledgehammer down and turn to face Flint. I'm nearly done taking out the stalls in the rickety barn that won't collapse today but definitely should *not* be used frequently. The load-bearing walls and support beams seem to be in so-so shape. Definitely need to be replaced. Or the whole barn needs to be rebuilt. There's splintered wood all over the floor and a cobweb in the doorway lit by the setting sun. If it weren't for the man blocking the view, I'm pretty sure I'd be gasping in awe at the colors lighting the sky over the bluff in the distance, beyond the trees.

It is *so pretty* here. And I feel like I have too much to do to stop and breathe and just enjoy it.

"Can I help you?" I ask him.

If ever a man was born with a more natural mulish expression, I don't want to meet him either.

I would! my vagina squeals.

And now my face is twitching again.

Flint lifts a quilted bag. "Peace offering," he grunts.

"Cyanide and local poison berries?"

"Homemade meatloaf, scalloped potatoes, and green beans."

He cooks!

I give up on discussing with my vagina how *This is not happening* and also *He probably got takeout and then put it in a bag to make it look like he cooked* and let her do whatever it is she's going to do.

"Is *that* poisoned?" I ask.

"Tony was . . . a lot more relaxed than you about certain . . . *rules* about having kids out on his property."

If he makes my face twitch one more time, I might be the person who makes all those old wives' tales come true when it gets stuck. That last one hurt. Who knew a cheek muscle could cramp like that?

I turn around and pick up the sledgehammer again. I'm so over people who like the rules only when they're convenient. "Thank you for dinner. Junie will appreciate it."

"It's for you too."

"Thank you. Not hungry."

"Maisey—"

"I get it. You can't let Junie on the soccer team. I can't let you have kids out here until I get the right liability insurance. We don't like each other. You're trying to be nice because you still rent Uncle Tony's gatehouse, and you're going to be one of my kid's teachers, and we'll have to see each other regularly. Trust me, I can nice your ass off. Got a *lot* of experience being pleasant around people I don't like. You won't even know if I paint your face on a wall that I take out with a sledgehammer again, okay?"

"We can find some middle ground here."

"Can we? Are you capable of that? Because so far, the only message I've gotten from you is that I'm a huge inconvenience ruining your life, and you know what? I have enough of that from my teenager. I don't need it from a grown-ass man too."

All my frustration fuels my next swing into the stable wall.

"Okay, okay, I'll talk to the kids on the soccer team about June trying out to rotate in every once in a while," Flint says.

"I'm not—*ungh*—threatening—*oof*—or bribing—*ermph*—you to get my daughter—*aarrrrggghhh*—on the damn soccer—*umph*—team." I drop the sledgehammer and hunch over, looking for my breath as I swing a quick glance around the dilapidated barn, wondering how this must look to Flint.

First seven stalls weren't this hard to take out.

But swinging a sledgehammer for an hour will take it out of a girl. Especially after hauling out all the random other crap that needed to go into a dumpster.

Might be time for a real break.

"You have water out here?" Flint asks.

The irritated edge is gone from his voice, replaced with something I'd call concern if he were anyone else in town.

I wave to my empty water bottle. "I'm fine."

Little black dots choose that moment to dance in my vision.

Crap.

I am *not* fine.

The dots pass after one more deep breath, but Flint Jackson is once again frowning at me. He grabs a three-legged stool from a pile of broken boards and barn scrap that I haven't gotten to the dumpster yet, flips it so he can sit on it, and digs into his quilted bag.

Quilted.

What bachelor has a quilted bag? And it's not bold, masculine colors. Those quilt squares are soft pinks and blues and yellows, with flowery patterns.

At least, I think they are.

The light isn't the best in here, even before the dots in my vision.

He rises and crosses half the barn to stand next to me, a can of sparkling water in his hand. "Drink."

"Thank you."

I'm so tired of being mad at myself.

Drink more, Maisey. Between the elevation and the lack of humidity out here, you know you need it. You've studied how to handle wildlife, so put it into action and quit freaking out every time you see even a chipmunk move. Don't go wandering outside at dusk. See previous reminder about wildlife.

It's what I repeat to myself over and over every day.

Yet here I am, halfway across the property from the house at dusk, dehydrated and standing next to a wild animal that I *should* know how to handle, but who's not acting at all like I expect him to.

And if he could *please* quit rubbing his hands down his thighs and highlighting just how solid they are, I'd appreciate that greatly.

The last thing I want is to have to ask him if he has another can of water because his body makes my mouth go drier than the Wyoming summer.

"I always thought you didn't come because you thought you were too good for Tony," he mutters.

It's a really good thing I'm not holding that sledgehammer *now*. "That's a lovely thing to think about someone you've never met."

He shakes his head. "I miss him. He was—if I could've picked my own father, I would've picked Tony. And you showing up now is bringing up old memories that are good but that hurt, too, because they remind me that he's not here anymore."

I watch him, not sure what to say.

This almost sounds like an apology, and *I'm sorry I thought you were old* isn't an appropriate response.

"When I moved back here to Hell's Bells six years ago, Tony took me in like one of his other strays. I was in a rough spot. Bad breakup. Lost my job over it. But Tony set me up in the gatehouse and would have me up to his place for a beer after school to shoot the shit and watch the sun set. It was . . . nice to have a friend without expectations."

"I'm sure he enjoyed that."

I don't mean to sound sad.

But he's right.

Uncle Tony was a good person, and I didn't see him nearly enough in his last years. I took him for granted.

And I miss him too.

"He was really proud of you and that stupid show," Flint says.

I hide my face's reaction by taking another drink. I don't think I've actually grieved him. I've been too busy. Or maybe I feel like I don't have the right.

Not the way everyone here does.

He was part of this community.

And I'm just the lucky person who hung out a few weeks for a couple of summers twenty years ago, inherited his ranch, let it sit for a year, and is now changing everything up.

"He never told you?" he asks.

I slide a look at him out of the corner of my eye. "Are you treating me like one of your students?"

"I'm trying to treat you like a human being who's doing the best you can, just like the rest of us are."

"Why?"

"Because, like you said, I rent your gatehouse. I'm one of June's teachers. We'll see each other regularly. I'm the closest thing you have when you hit the wrong wall and take down the barn, and—"

That's it.

I straighten and glare at him. "Let's get one thing *crystal* clear. You know *nothing* about who I am and what I'm capable of if you're judging me on what you saw on that television show. Understood?"

He blinks fast and takes a half step back. "I—"

"You think I'm a worthless airhead who doesn't know the difference between an impact driver and a roof shingle."

He visibly gulps, then casts a covert glance at my sledgehammer.

"Yes, I *do* know what that's technically called, too," I inform him, "but I call it the hand of justice, and I can swing it like a mofo."

If he takes one more step back, he'll fall into the hay trough, and you know what?

I'm freaking here for it.

"Did you—" He stops and clears his throat. "Did you just say *mofo?*"

"She knows words. Hallelujah. She *also* knows how to screw your front door shut, rewire your truck engine, and poke holes in just the right spot in your roof to make you want to move out."

He licks his lips, goes one more half step back, and catches himself before he topples.

Dammit.

More dammit?

I think his pupils are dilating. And—oh, fuck me.

There is *definite* movement under the fly of his jeans.

Yay! my vagina cheers. *He likes us feisty!*

She is *so* in time-out.

I *hate* being cranky like this. But he just brings it out—no.

Wait.

You know what?

He pushed me to this.

Screw all this *I need to be nice* stuff.

I was *nice* to Dean, and where did that get me?

Here.

It got me here. So Flint can *freaking deal with it.*

"Maybe we start over," he says. "I may have made some assumptions I shouldn't have made. Would be a lot easier if we can clear the air and get along."

"Because you want to butter *me* up to let you use the ranch as an escape for wayward teenagers."

He sighs and scrubs his hand over his beard.

Yep.

Nailed it.

I hate being cynical almost as much as I hate that I'm nixing the use of the ranch—*for now*—for kids who need an outlet.

But—"Why can't you use Kory's ranch?"

"Liability," he mutters.

I lift my brows at him.

He sighs again.

I take another drink.

"I can get waivers signed," he says.

"I'm gonna go out on a limb and guess the kids you'd bring out here aren't the kids who'd feel like they could ask their parents to sign a waiver."

"You're very cynical about this."

"I'm reasonably certain Junie's been forging my signature on field trip forms for the past three years. Which is my bad. *Completely* my bad. I'm doing better now."

I feel his heavy gaze on me, and despite my irritation with him, I don't have the nerve to meet it.

Do I feel judged around teachers?

Yep.

Do I deserve it?

Also yep.

"Teaching gives your life purpose, I suppose," I say quietly.

It's a long moment before he answers. "It does."

"I don't *have* a purpose. I'm well aware I was the court jester on Dean's show, and I accepted that for years because *It's all for show, babe. We both know you do the work.*"

Flint makes a noise that I've heard in my own head in response to that statement more times than I care to admit.

"I'm not taking that kind of crap from anyone anymore," I tell him. "I let him bruise my self-esteem and take top billing when I was the one pulling so much together on every single job when the cameras weren't rolling. I told myself I was okay with not getting credit because I still got the paycheck—which was *not* what people think it was, for the record—but all the while I was letting my mother and Dean's parents and sometimes strangers raise my kid, and also setting an example for her that it was her job to play second fiddle to the men in her life, regardless of if he was worthy or not."

He makes a noise.

I ignore it. "I am *not* that strong, independent woman the world says I'm supposed to be. I'm battered and bruised and tired. I need to find where I fit in my own life. My own purpose. And maybe I'm completely misguided in thinking it's here, in patching this ranch to make it something beautiful and good where I fit first before I use it in any way that resembles how Uncle Tony did it, but I have to try. For the first time in my life, I'm going after something that feels *good*. And *right*.

Without tearing myself down and without having to rely on anyone who doesn't believe in me. And *I can't put that in danger*. Not while I'm trying to make everything up to Junie and be the mom I haven't been for the past six years."

I don't look at him.

I can't.

But I feel the heavy heat of his gaze anyway.

God, I hate being vulnerable.

But I'd rather put all my cards on the table in the hopes that he's willing to help Junie than hold back for the sake of my own pride.

He's quiet for a long time.

I don't offer any more.

I've put enough of myself out there to satisfy even the most grizzled Maisey-hater.

"Okay," he finally says.

I slide a look at him over another sip of sparkling water.

He lifts his hands. "Okay," he repeats. "If we can get the school's liability insurance to cover things out here, would you reconsider?"

"Yes."

He studies me a minute longer. Then his gaze dips to my lips. My neck. And back up again. "Thank you."

"For what?" Junie asks from the doorway. She looks between us, and it does not take an expert in teenager to know what's going through her brain.

Why is the enemy in here with my mom?

She doesn't overtly call him the enemy, but I know she's pissed at both of us for the soccer situation. And she told me she gets it—multiple times—but she can both get it and still be pissed.

"Suggesting that I ask the team if they'd be up for you trying out to fill in on days when we have someone out for whatever reason," Flint answers. "No limit on equipment managers, and you could practice with us. Good solution to a clear problem."

I might have missed too much of the last six years of my daughter's life, but I do *not* miss the suspicion darkening her brown eyes. "What's really going on?"

"I was being loud with the sledgehammer, and Mr. Jackson came to investigate—" I start the same time Flint speaks too.

He lifts the quilted bag. "Delivering dinner for you two. Moving sucks, and the last time I was at the house, the oven was acting up. Figured you'd like a home-cooked meal. *And* it gave us a chance to negotiate the soccer situation."

The utter disbelief rolling off her is brutal. "My mom is *not* interested in dating right now."

"*Junie.*"

"You just got divorced. You're vulnerable. And I don't like how he's looking at you."

"*Juniper Louisa Spencer.*"

She doesn't flinch. Instead, she rolls her eyes, flicks one last dismissive glance at Flint, then looks back at me. "It's getting dark. I got worried and didn't want you walking home alone in the dark."

Crap.

My eyes go hot again. "Thank you, sweet—Junie. I'm coming. I'll finish this tomorrow. Or next week. Let me close the barn door, okay?"

"I'll walk you both back," Flint says.

I cut Junie off with a look before she can sass him again. "Thank you."

"Earl gets hungry this time of night."

He's joking.

I think he's joking.

Probably.

Maybe.

But the point stands. We should get back to the house. I test my legs as I shove off from the wall, waiting a moment to see if the black dots will come back into my vision. "How do ranchers keep their cows alive with all the animals that want to eat them out here?"

"Guard donkeys."

I swear he's smirking, so I make a mental note to hit Google as soon as I'm back at the house to find out how many farm and ranch animals die from wild-animal attacks every year in Wyoming.

If it was *that* dangerous, and not overblown, induced anxiety on my part, would people really live out here all the time?

Doubt it.

Plus, we're on the east side of Wyoming. I'm pretty sure there are fewer predators here.

Pretty sure.

Kind of.

He hands Junie the bag of food. "Not poisoned. I promise. That'd be more trouble than it's worth."

"My mom is *not dating*," she repeats.

"I don't date students' parents."

She studies him in the gathering darkness. I shoo them both, and when I go to shut the barn doors, Flint helps.

Good thing.

My arms are starting to feel like limp rubber bands.

And I swear he notices when the doorframe shifts. At least, that's what I assume his sigh means. *She's right. This is a liability hazard.*

If he doesn't pick up on that, though, I *seriously* need him not bringing kids out here.

"C'mon," he says.

We follow him.

And I leave a good twenty feet between us too.

And I'm ogling his ass the entire way.

I have problems.

So many, many problems.

Chapter 9

Flint

The first few weeks of school pass pretty quickly, with everything settling into a normal routine.

The days, anyway.

There are classes with my kids figuring out how far they can push their limits. Soccer practice with June Spencer as our equipment manager, slowly finding where she fits and making friends. Convincing Kory to let me bring a couple of teenagers out to help with the calving to distract them on particularly rough days while I keep working on my principal to get approval for liability insurance so I can take kids back to Wit's End, where I know there are more fences down and where I can take Parsnip anytime. Grading. Parent-teacher conferences.

Everything I need to keep me happy and busy at work.

And then there are the calls from other friends around town to help replace a microwave or stop in to check on their dogs while they're out of town filling up what's left of my free time.

But my nights?

Every time I climb into bed and close my eyes, I see Maisey Spencer swinging a sledgehammer. Sashaying into my classroom in that blue dress. Setting her jaw and talking about finding a purpose. Her eyes lighting up when she smiles at a new friend when she drops June off.

The way she run-trots when she's dashing across the parking lot to drop off the water bottle June forgot at home, then dashes right back to her car before any of the kids notice her.

How she comes to every game to support June in her role as our equipment manager. How she sits on her hands at every game like she's afraid if she makes any noise at all, she'll mortify her daughter.

We've nodded or said hi in passing—which happens more than I want it to, but I rent the house at the end of her driveway, and she's now the PTA president's right-hand woman at the school. It can't be helped.

There's been no more mention of what she's doing with the ranch.

Not from her, anyway.

Aunt Opal loves the idea of her putting a couple of small homes out there for wayward souls once she gets the rest of the ranch updated and renovated.

So do half my coworkers at the school.

Brad at the hardware store.

Johnny, the local painter.

Annabelle, the local electrician.

Kory, who's excited at the idea of supplying more beef to the hobby ranch turned practically unused land next door.

Everyone.

Everyone.

I'm still holding out to see what winter brings before I get excited about the possibility of *more* newcomers.

Turns out I have some curmudgeon in me.

Never thought I did until I met Maisey Spencer.

If I could get her out of my head, maybe I'd be happy about what she's planning too.

But I can't.

And tonight, it appears I can't avoid her in person.

"Your mom's not answering?" I ask June for the seventh time.

We're hanging out at the soccer field after an evening home game on a Wednesday night. June's the only student left. Her mother, who's never missed a game before, is nowhere in sight.

"I need a car," she grumbles.

"You have your license?"

She shoots me a look that could mean *My mom won't let me get it,* or it could mean *I'm secretly afraid to drive, and I don't want to tell you, so I'm going to let you think this look means that my mom won't let me get it.*

See the latter option more often than you might think. Good 10 percent of any given junior and senior class these days voluntarily don't have their licenses.

She lifts her phone to her ear one more time, and this time, I shake my head. "I'm going where you're going. C'mon. I'll give you a lift."

She squints at me, her lips pursing exactly like her mother's. "I'm not supposed to get in a car with a grown man all by myself. I shouldn't even be here with you right now all by myself."

I stare at her.

She stares right back.

And that's how I end up driving June home with my aunt riding shotgun.

"How's school, Junie?" Opal asks. She's changed her hair again, and now it's purple. Sometimes I think my students go easy on me because they think I have such a cool aunt.

"Fine. And it's *June.* Please."

"June. Got it. Parents are the worst at keeping nicknames too long, aren't they? I still—"

"No, you don't," I interrupt.

"—call Flint *Snuggybottoms.*"

She smiles at me.

June snickers.

I shake my head, but I'm not pissed.

While Opal did indeed call me *Snuggybottoms* one time after I moved in with her when I was in high school, she only brings it up when she's around kids who need to know I'm not scary and they can count on me.

"My mom named me *Juniper*," June says. "I told her if she keeps calling me *Junie*, I'm telling my friends I want them to call me Nip. It's so much better than *Per*, you know?"

"That would be something," Opal says. "But not original. Flint, what year was it that you had that girl named Virginia in your class? The one who wanted everyone to call her *Vag*?"

June's eyes bug out.

"Two years ago," I reply mildly.

"And then the boy who wanted everyone to call him *Peenie*?"

Now she's making shit up. "I'm not allowed to discuss that."

Opal turns to look at June. "Sorry, sweetheart. The school put a hard limit on nicknames after that. But I hear kids these days are changing their names to whatever they want so long as it's not a word that seems likely to make someone uncomfortable. What would you name yourself if you weren't a Juniper?"

June's mouth opens, then shuts. She frowns before turning to stare out the window at the scraggly landscape around us.

One good thing about taking June home?

We'll get there about the time the sun sets over the bluffs, and there are clouds on the horizon tonight.

Should be gorgeous.

And while I have a decent view at the gatehouse, the view from Tony's old house is unbeatable.

"You're making friends, June?" Opal asks.

She shrugs.

Kid finally got her chance to fill in tonight after weeks of playing equipment manager without much hope this day would come, and she kicked the game-winning goal. Got smothered in the middle of a team hug for it, but I know that doesn't mean she feels like she fits.

I see her every time she hands a water bottle to someone beating themselves up at halftime over a missed kick or a lost ball. She doesn't just hand over the water bottle. She squats next to them, says something—I'm starting to pick up on what—and then claps them on the shoulder or squeezes their arm or fist bumps them before going on to the next player.

But I don't know if she's doing it because it makes her feel like she fits or because she's doing her best despite knowing she should be on the field instead of the sidelines.

I looked up her old high school and her old team, and it gave me a minute of feeling like an impostor.

Hell's Bells isn't state bound. We don't play top-tier teams, never mind *beat* them regularly. I don't know soccer so much as I was the guy standing there when they needed a soccer coach, and everyone knows if you want something done, you ask me.

Once I moved back here, I realized it was up to me to find a way to fit in. Never quite made it in high school.

Hard to when everyone knows you're *that runaway*. The kids who wanted to hang out with me *because* I ran away from home aren't the kids I wanted to hang with. And the kids I did want to hang with thought I was a bad influence.

So maybe I overcompensate now.

Wonder if June's doing the same with how much she's not complaining about being our equipment manager. And how much effort she's putting into building up every kid on the team regardless of their skill or gender or orientation.

Does she look at them like they're her competition to get on the team in the spring, and she's worried they'll hate her if she's not nice to them now?

Or is she one of those people naturally gifted at building up everyone around her, no matter the potential cost to herself?

Does she play because she loves it, or does she play because she wants to be the next Mia Hamm or Megan Rapinoe? I don't know if she feels like part of the team or if she feels like everyone else is taking pity on the new girl.

But I know if I, a grown adult, sometimes feel like I can't do enough to fit in, it's a million times worse for kids.

Teenage years are complicated, and if I were her, I'd be wondering.

And if she's like half the kids in my classes and cares more about what her mom thinks than she lets on, then she's probably not okay.

Her mom missed the game and isn't reachable.

And from everything I was told and everything I've seen with my own two eyes this past month, Maisey should've been there.

Shit.

I should've called Kory and sent him over to check on her.

"Are you excited about your mom's plans for the ranch?" Opal asks June.

Another shrug. And she's still staring out the window.

"Ah. So you're still a captive in your own life?"

I shoot my aunt a look.

"Can't solve things if you don't face them, Snuggybottoms."

"Can we get to the ranch and make sure Maisey didn't fall through the floor of the bunkhouse or something before we ask June to go through all the reasons she hates her mother right now?" I mutter.

But not quietly enough.

June shoots straight up in her seat. "You think my mom hurt herself?"

"Oh, sweetie, no," Opal says as I turn into the long driveway to the house. I pass my comfortable gatehouse and give the truck a little more gas. "I'm sure she got tied up with something completely safe and lost track of time."

"But the bear—" June cuts herself off with a gasp as Earl himself races across the driveway in front of us.

And I do mean *races*.

Haven't seen him move that fast since a truck of berries turned over a little way up the road and he heard a crew was on the way to clean it up.

Not that I think Earl can understand English, but I'm telling you, that's how it happened.

I press my foot heavier onto the pedal and navigate the bumps in the dirt driveway like I still come up the drive every day, and within moments, the stone-front, high-gabled ranch house with its covered porch and rejuvenated flower beds comes into view.

She planted wildflowers.

Tony used to get so pissed at his own black thumb, but Maisey has a thriving wildflower garden.

"Oh my God, *Mom*," June gasps.

I slam on the brakes, barely getting my truck stopped before she lunges for her door and tumbles out of the back of the extended cab.

And then I almost forget to set the brake before I leap out myself.

A mud-coated, Maisey-shaped figure is limping out from behind a thicket of scrub brush.

"Mom? *Mom!*"

June's sprinting like she didn't already run an entire soccer game. I'm not far behind.

"Oh my God, *that bear*," Maisey says as June tackles her in a massive hug, mud and all. "Where did it go? Is it okay?"

"Is the *bear* okay?" June gasps.

"It's a *bear*," I agree. Why is my heart in my throat, and why do I want to grab her and hug her too and make sure she's okay?

Because we're friends, I answer myself.

My dick snorts in utter amusement at the bald-faced lie.

"What the hell happened to *you*?" I ask her.

"And her hair," Opal murmurs as she catches up to us. "That's gonna take one hell of a shampoo. Oh, honey. Come in tomorrow. I'll squeeze you in again."

Maisey hugs June back. "I'm fine. I'm fine. It's fine. I—" She stops, looks at me, then at my aunt, then to the west. And then she's hugging her daughter all over again. "Oh, Junie. Oh, baby, I missed your game.

I'm so sorry. I should've been—you smell like sweat. *Oh my God.* You played. You played, didn't you? And I missed it."

I want to be mad, but there is clearly a story here.

Also?

Now that I know she's safe, Maisey Spencer covered in mud is giving me terrible, awful, filthy ideas.

Fucking haircut.

Fucking dress.

Fucking *competence.* Who knew I had a thing for women who could swing a sledgehammer and win a battle with a mud puddle?

And it's not just the sledgehammer.

I know she's been all over town helping patch roofs and tackle a plumbing job here and there and painting rooms and repairing that damn light fixture over my favorite table at Iron Moose.

She's right.

She played the fool on that show, but she knows what she's doing.

More importantly at the moment, though—where the hell did *mud* come from?

It hasn't rained here in at least ten days, and that last rain barely counted as rain.

"Are you covered in literal shit?" June lets her go but still hovers close, like she's afraid something worse than a normally lazy, nonconfrontational bear and some form of dirt are about to happen to her mother. Her nose quivers, and she lifts her own arm to sniff the mud. "Did that bear *shit on you?*"

"No, no, honey. I'm fine. It's fine. How was your game? Tell me all about your game. Did you play?"

"Yeah, but it's not like you knew I would," June mutters.

"I had an alarm set so I wouldn't miss it. I did. I—oh, crap." Maisey's patting her hips near about where her pockets should be. "My phone. I lost my phone."

"Why are you covered in shit?" June asks.

"It's mud! It's mud, honey. It's just really stinky mud. I think. I hope. I was nowhere *near* the septic tank, but—" She cuts herself off, waving a hand. "Come inside. I'll get cleaned up, and you can tell me about your game, and I'll make you dinner. And maybe we can use your phone to find mine."

"I thought you *died*," June whispers.

Maisey blinks at her daughter. "Oh, baby, no. Shh. No, sweetie, I wouldn't give your father the satisfaction."

I don't realize my own heart is in my throat until that exact moment, when I realize Maisey Spencer is 100 percent okay, and 100 percent on my shit list now.

I don't know if I should yell at her for doing all this by herself, or if I should hug her and tell her I'm glad she's okay and ask if she needs help cleaning up.

The ideas a filthy, dirty Maisey Spencer is giving me . . .

I settle for scowling at her.

It's the safest option.

"I thought you *died*," June repeats, this time through a sob.

"Oh, baby." Maisey reaches for her.

June rears back. "You moved me here and I hate it and then you missed the *only* game I've gotten to play in and you didn't answer my calls and I thought a bear ate you and I'd be all alone because I know Dad doesn't want me, and now you're all *Oh, no, this is fine*, and it is *not fine*, and *stop looking at me*. Just stop looking at me."

She turns around, stares in horror at me and Opal like she forgot we were here, and then takes off at another dead run, this time straight to the house.

Maisey gets three steps before Opal intercepts her.

"Sweetie," Opal says, reaching out like she wants to pat Maisey on the shoulder but also doesn't want to get dirty, "why don't you go find a garden hose? I have a little experience with teenagers who hate you because you've made them live here. I've got her."

I don't call Opal on the lie.

I loved living here with her, even if I never found where I fit in at school and avoided coming back out of fear that she'd taken me in out of obligation.

But the reassurance from my aunt has Maisey's entire body deflating.

She's like an empty sack formerly known as a human, coated in mud and the weight of the world.

"Thank you." The only thing worse than her dull voice is the shine starting in her eyes.

Dammit.

Not the tears.

And the utter defeat.

And the knowledge that my aunt is leaving me here to hose off a woman that I'm currently having unwelcome fantasies about that involve naked mud wrestling.

She's newly divorced with a teenager who needs all her attention. She's the mother of one of my students. She has her hands full on this ranch—even if she *can* handle more than I initially gave her credit for—and I don't have time or patience for any more drama in my life.

Already spend my days with teenagers, and while I love it, I have my limits.

She is *not* next-fling material.

No matter what my dick thinks.

"C'mon." I jerk my head toward the house, knowing my voice is gruff and hoping it's gruff enough to telegraph *Stay away* rather than *I'm seriously looking forward to this.* "I'll hose you off, and then we can talk about the people you can hire around town to be out here with you while you're working so you don't do something dumb, like dropping a log on yourself and turning into wolf food, which *anyone* can sometimes do no matter how much experience they have."

Those wounded baby blues study me long enough to make my stomach churn.

Can she see right through me?

Does she know I'd love to have my hands all over her right now?

"You're seriously going to enjoy this, aren't you?" she mutters.

"Good chance."

"Hoping the water's cold?"

"Like ice."

I'm lying.

I don't want to spray her with ice-cold water out of a garden hose.

I want to strip her naked and take her into a steaming-hot shower and kiss her out of sheer relief that she's okay.

Worse?

I think she knows it.

Somewhere between me riding over to check out what was going on at Tony's house that morning that she scared Parsnip into throwing me with mountain lion sounds and right now, this very minute, in my head, we've become something like friends.

Even if I've been avoiding her like the plague.

But no one else in town has appealed to me in the past couple of years the way she has.

Is it just that she's new?

Is it that she knew and loved Tony?

Is it that I know all too well what it's like to move to Hell's Bells to get away from a bad relationship?

Twice?

This isn't just complicated.

It's way past that.

She holds my gaze for a long moment before she sighs and trudges past me. "Then let's get it over with so you can go home and I can clean up everything I've fucked up all over again with my teenager."

Speaking of ice water.

There it is, splashing down on all my fantasies.

I don't fool around with my kids' parents. Not my students' parents and not my players' parents.

No way in hell I'm letting anyone say I'm playing favorites because I'm boinking someone's mother.

Again.

No matter how serious or not serious it is.

So I'll hose her off.

I'll keep my dick in my pants.

Then I'll go home and make myself a frozen pot pie, watch a true-crime documentary, jerk off in the shower, go to bed, and do it all over again tomorrow.

At least, that's what I *should* do.

We're about to find out if it's what I *actually* do.

Chapter 10

Maisey

You know it's been a day when facing freezing-cold water from a garden hose isn't the worst of it.

But having Flint Jackson being the man about to spray me down is pretty damn close.

Much as I want to dislike him, I can't. And not disliking him makes me like him in ways I have no business liking him. I need to find *me*, not the first available man who doesn't hate me.

Anymore.

"How was the soccer game?" I ask Flint while he screws the hose onto the faucet on the side of my house.

We're standing between an empty flower bed and a dead boxwood. Legit didn't know you could kill those things, but I guess Uncle Tony had to have *some* weaknesses. I'm covered in drying mud. I have once again ruined my teenager's life—but at least I know she doesn't want me to die—and I'd like nothing more than to pretend Flint *is* that old man I always thought he was on the occasions Uncle Tony would mention him.

Flint shoots me a look that I like to call his *What the hell is wrong with you?* look. Dean would regularly ask me what the hell was wrong with me. Once I realized the biggest thing wrong with me was that I was married to a man who thought there was something wrong with me, it was damn easy to figure out what I needed to do to solve my problem, even if executing that plan was one of the hardest things I've done in my life.

So if I lump Flint Jackson into the category of men who will never be satisfied with who I am, it's much easier to tolerate this unwelcome attraction.

One of my friends who's a therapist says it's self-protection.

I say I really don't want to look deeper than that until I know who I am and am safely on the path to working for what I want.

"We won," Flint says abruptly. "What happened to *you*?"

"It's not important. Did Junie score?"

There's that *You are not right* look again. "Game-winning goal."

"Dammit."

He sighs.

"I don't mean dammit that she did well. I'm *thrilled* that she did well. I'm disappointed that I wasn't there for her. *Especially* for this game. That's all that meant."

"I know."

"You know?" Translation: *you've noticed me and think there are parts of me that are worthy? Squee!*

Damn right he did. We're hot, my vagina reminds me.

He finishes attaching the hose and cranks the handle. "Haven't missed any other games, have you?"

Stop being a ball of hormones, I order myself when I want to squeal in my head that he has noticed I've been there, as if I haven't made an effort to at least say hi and compliment him on his coaching every single game. *Concentrate on Junie.* "I worry about her. I know moving during high school is hard. And I missed too many games the past three years, so—*aaaaaaahhh!*"

The wave of cold water shoots out of the end of the hose and smacks me square in the nipple.

He jerks the hose away from my body. "Shouldn't have come out that fast," he mutters.

"Seems to be a theme around this place," I say around gasps for breath.

I get another look.

This one clearly says *Keep talking*.

Right.

People who arrive at your house when you're covered in mud and who saw the bear running away will have some questions.

"It's really not an interesting story," I tell him.

"Earl doesn't run."

"Do you call all of the bears around here Earl, or is there something about him that you recognize? Does he have some special marking that I should pay attention to?"

"Only bear around here. What happened?"

"But how do you *know* he's the only bear around here?"

"Because I do. And so does the local wildlife expert. Earl's a fluke. Runt as a baby. Shouldn't have made it. Did, and wandered over our way. Don't usually have many bears around here. Better habitats for them a little west. *What. Happened?*"

"Are you going to spray me again if I don't answer?"

He growls.

And then, yes, he turns the hose back on me. But this time, he grabs me by the shoulder, aims down my back, and crimps the hose enough to minimize the blast of pressure.

I stifle a squeal.

It's cold, but it's honestly not the coldest I've faced today.

"The bear, Maisey. What happened to him, and is he hurt?"

I pretend the water coming out of the hose and getting swished down my back is a warm natural spring, ignore the heat coming off Flint's hand as he brushes mud clumps off my arm, and concentrate on Earl. "We were having a showdown. I was being big, you know, like this—"

I lift my arms wide and go up on my tiptoes, and I get a shot of water in the armpit. *"Hey!"*

"If you'd *quit moving*—"

I spin to glare at him. Yes, he's helping me. Yes, my mother would tell me I should be nice to the handsome man who brought my daughter home.

But he's pushing my buttons. And then every time I look at him, a primal part of me swoons like I don't freaking know better, and then I get cranky all over again.

But Flint Jackson is all wet.

His Hell's Bells Soccer Demons jersey is plastered to his broad chest and puckered nipples, highlighting his wide collarbone and the muscles straining his arms too.

Those tattoos on each of his biceps are peeking out from beneath his sleeves, and I'm positive one's a wolf and the other's some kind of geometric design.

And his jeans?

Also soaking wet.

Plastered to his trim hips.

His solid thighs.

The bulge behind his fly.

No.

Nope nope nope.

I didn't see that. It doesn't mean he's hard or semihard or just packed under there. He's probably wearing a cup.

Yep.

A cup.

To protect himself from errant soccer balls to the groin while he's standing there on the sidelines doing his coaching thing.

Men wear cups with jeans all the time.

All the time.

I am *so* bad at lying to myself.

"Do you want help or not?" he spits out.

Pippa Grant

Is he irritated with me?

Or is he irritated that I noticed that he might not be irritated at all?

I gulp.

Then I point to my other arm. "It's starting to dry here."

He grips me by the elbow, shoots a stream of hose water down my biceps, and I feel like his touch has just branded me for life.

I swallow hard again and try to go back to normal. "So I was trying to be big and intimidating, and the bear—Earl—was standing up on his back feet and staring at me. I knew I needed to find something to make me even bigger, but I didn't want to break eye contact, and then the universe stepped in, or maybe it was Uncle Tony, I don't know, but one minute, I was thinking I was going to die, and the next minute, this geyser shot up out of the ground right underneath him and scared the living hell out of him."

"Geyser?"

"There's a ridiculous amount of pressure coming out of the well here, which *should not be a thing*, because *physics*, and I thought I solved it, but apparently there was something I overlooked, and there was too much pressure on a soft spot in a pipe. Don't worry. I shut that valve off. We won't waste the whole county's groundwater supply with a flood here."

He mutters something that I sincerely hope he never mutters in the classroom.

"I know. *Replace all the piping to the house and the cabin and the bunkhouse* wasn't on my bingo card, but then, so few things have been out here. I'll roll with it. Kinda have to. Hey, how's the water in the gatehouse? Do I need to tackle that too? Actually, I haven't asked if you need anything fixed there at all. I should've. Everything running smoothly?"

He sighs again while he twists me to tackle my back.

I stifle a yelp when the water hits my spine. And then I stifle another yelp when he swipes his other hand down my back.

It's merely been too long since I've been touched by a man, and this one is hotter than the sun. He's like a flaming ball of gas that just doesn't stop, but replace *gas* with *testosterone*, and that's Flint Jackson. He's the testosterone sun.

And I clearly need a very large bottle of water with a margarita chaser and about three days of sleep if that's how I'm thinking of him.

"How'd you get so muddy?" he asks as his hand approaches the danger zone—a.k.a. my ass—four times over.

I swallow again. "I noticed standing water by the wellhead out at the bunkhouse, so I was a little wet and muddy by the time I figured out what was wrong and got it fixed, but once the leak was taken care of, the showers exploded at the pressure and the shutoff valve was broken, so I had to shut it off at the well, but my fix had blown, so it was an entire mud puddle that I was swimming in by then to get everything shut off."

"I told Tony he needed that inspected," he mutters as he grips my elbow and makes me turn so he can spray my front.

"I'm pretty sure Uncle Tony's favorite phrase was *It's fine.*"

Flint's grip tightens.

So do his eyes.

But for the first time, I don't think it's bitterness toward me for not being here more often when Uncle Tony was alive.

I think it's grief.

"Thank you for being a good friend to him," I whisper. "He was a good man. I'm glad he had friends here. Especially after the rest of the family cut him off."

His eyes lift and meet mine before settling back to his task, which now involves cleaning my boobs. "We were a good fit."

"Everyone needs a friend like that."

He grunts, swipes mud water off my chest, and pretends he doesn't notice that my breath is getting shallow and my nipples could cut glass.

"I was on the phone with a well company in Laramie when Earl showed up," I blurt. Anything for normalcy. "I know when I'm in over my head, and I'm pretty sure we're going to have to dig a new well here, and that is definitely over my head."

He grunts and aims the hose lower, and *oh my God*, I haven't had a man shower me *there* since I was a newlywed.

I'm in jeans too.

I shouldn't be having a reaction to a cold stream of water aimed at my pubic bone over thick denim.

But I very much am, and no small part of me wants to spread my legs and ask him to get up between my thighs.

"I set an alarm on my phone so I wouldn't miss Junie's game," I blurt to cover my discomfort, which might not be discomfort at all. "I don't know why I didn't hear it. But it has to be somewhere back in the mud. I was on the phone when Earl showed up, so I must not have dropped it down the well. And I must've set the alarm wrong. I didn't realize how late it was getting. That happens when I'm hip-deep in a project, which is why I set the alarm. Unless I forgot to set the alarm. Or maybe I set it for a.m. instead of p.m., and I'll be getting a rude awakening about three thirty tomorrow. And—"

"Maisey."

"Yes?" Oh God, he's getting my thighs. He's spraying and stroking my thighs. My quads. My hamstrings. Inside my thighs above my knees. That ticklish spot on the outside of my thighs.

Breathe breathe breathe, Maisey. Breathe.

I've threaded my hands through his hair, and I'm hanging on for dear life and pulling his face to my crotch.

"You're not the first woman I've hosed down. Cool your jets. You're fine."

I unclench my fingers and leap back from him. "I should go check on Junie."

"You're dripping wet, and your ass is still covered in mud."

"I'll strip in the laundry room."

Our eyes connect, and oh. My. Holy. Smolder.

Flint Jackson *wants* me.

Because he's a horndog and wants anything with breasts and an ass? Or because he wants *me*?

He clears his throat and leaps to his feet. "Here. Almost done. Finish yourself. I'm late. For—something."

He shoves the hose at me and leaves me standing there on the side of my house, gaping at the new mud hole that we've made while trying to clean me off.

My teeth chatter.

Goose bumps pebble across my soaked skin.

Flint's truck roars to life, and a moment later, I hear tires spinning out on gravel.

Like he can't get away from me fast enough.

There's a screech and the sound of tires sliding over gravel at the exact moment that I remember his aunt is inside with my daughter.

"Opal!" His voice echoes across the ranch. "Time to go! I'm late."

I squeeze my eyes shut, sigh, and head for the back door and the laundry room.

I knew coming here would be hard. I knew there would be wrenches thrown in the works and hiccups I never saw coming.

But even in my wildest doom predicting, it never crossed my mind that I'd be hurting over being rejected by Junie's cranky math teacher.

Chapter 11

Flint

She's doing it again.

Maisey Spencer is making my life hell.

After a very long weekend of soccer games, working on clearing out the last of the dying vegetables at my own little garden at the Wit's End gatehouse, ignoring the hints from Opal that if I'm attracted to a woman, I should see where it goes, and helping Kory with a couple of calves, I'm back at school Monday morning expecting the usual stuff.

And I get some of it.

One of my first-period kids catches me before I walk in the building and asks for an extension on the homework they were supposed to turn in this morning.

One of my fifth-period kids stops me in the doorway of the old brick building to ask for a college-application recommendation letter.

One of my third-period kids gets to me before I've made it halfway down the hallway to ask when they can go back out to ride horses at the ranch.

June Spencer is tagging along with two of my soccer players, and all three of them clam up and walk past me as they head toward the cafeteria, which is where most kids hang out before classes.

All normal.

Until *Maisey*.

She's taken over the teachers' lounge, casually sitting on the counter next to the sink, and she's charming the pants off my colleagues.

"I was so busy working the past few years, I didn't even realize how much Junie loved to bake," she's telling Libby Twigg, the social studies teacher, as she waves a hand at the other half of the counter, which is covered in plates and platters of baked goods.

I know the plates and platters.

They've been in storage in Tony's house for years. He'd use them whenever he'd pretend he baked the cookies he bought from the bakery to bring to cookouts and socials, and they were among the things no one wanted during the estate sale Maisey contracted out before she got here.

"We spent all afternoon yesterday with her showing me how much she's learned about baking over the years," Maisey continues. "Have you tried that oatmeal-cranberry-walnut cookie? It only has honey in it for sweetener, so it's healthy breakfast food. Dip it in milk and you've hit all the food groups."

My brain *needs* to go to a place where I turn around, walk out of the teachers' lounge, and head to my classroom to get ready for the day.

Instead, it continues the nonstop assault it's been making on me since I found myself hosing mud off her Wednesday night and conjures images of her soaking wet, fresh out of the shower, barely wrapped in a black silk robe, feeding me oatmeal-cranberry-walnut cookies freshly drizzled with honey.

I wasn't this horny back in high school.

Or maybe I was, and I was less sophisticated about it.

"Oh my God, Flint, try this muffin," Libby says, turning to me and shoving a treat at my face. "I never understood why you loved banana-nut muffins before, but this—this is utter heaven."

I grab the muffin just to get her hand out of my face, then take another cautionary step back.

As if that's enough to stop the barrage of suggestions my hormones have for what to do with the muffin now in my hand.

"Isn't it amazing?" Maisey says to her. "I had no idea Junie had this level of talent. And I still have half a trunk full of what she made yesterday, so I should head off to the hospital and drop those off too. Don't want to make you all late for class."

She's dressed in jeans, a faded T-shirt, and work boots again today. No dress. No jewelry. No makeup. Her short hair is clipped back at the sides with barrettes decorated with tiny butterflies.

And she's fucking gorgeous.

My brain is conjuring images of her soaking wet, her nipples straining her T-shirt, those jeans stuck to her curvy legs and hips, all that mud—

Nope.

Nope nope nope. Shut it off, brain. Shut it off *now*.

She smiles at Libby again as she slides off the counter. "Don't make a big deal in front of Junie in class today, okay? She's already mortified that I'm bringing these in, but it's you or Earl, and I'm pretty sure I've fed Earl enough lately."

"Flint," Libby repeats. "Try the muffin."

"Forgot to plan my lesson," I stutter as Maisey's gaze lands on me.

And like a total chickenshit, I hightail it out of the lounge before Libby can force-feed me the muffin in my own hand.

Which she would absolutely do.

But instead of heading to my classroom, I wait just around the corner.

I don't know if I have a headache or if I'm having an allergic reaction to being attracted to Maisey.

Whatever it is, I have to fix it.

And there's exactly one way to do that.

More students are arriving as it gets closer to the bell, and while I know June *should* be in the cafeteria, *should be* and *is* aren't always the same.

So when Maisey strolls past, I grab her by the elbow, ignore her startled gasp, and haul her into the janitor's closet during a moment of empty hallway.

"We need to talk," I say when I have her alone.

She squeaks again.

"What are you doing here?" I ask.

"Dropping off Junie's treats."

"Why *here*?"

"Because we had a ton leftover after stopping at the fire station and the sheriff's outpost and the senior center, and school is where you take baked goods."

I need to let her go. I need to block her permanently from my brain, walk away, and replace all images of her in my head with something terrible and awful, like Earl. Every time I think of Maisey, I need to force myself to picture Earl in a bathrobe or Earl in nothing but an apron or Earl licking my dick, and see if that solves anything.

"I don't date my students' parents," I blurt.

"So you assured Junie," she replies.

"But you keep showing up—"

"I'm not here for *you*, and *you* were very kind to drop Junie off on Wednesday, but as we've established, that was a parenting fail and *not an attempt to seduce you*. Oh my God."

"There's a serious appearance of favoritism—"

"There is *not*. Junie says you give kids rides home all the time."

"If I date you."

"I'm not dating anyone, least of all you."

"I saw how you were looking at me on Wednesday—"

Her nostrils flare.

Her eyes go dark.

She visibly swallows.

And I am so hard my dick could hammer a hole in my jeans right now.

She slowly licks her lips. "And you also saw that *I didn't act on it.* Junie's number one. I'm number two. Fixing the ranch is number three. And there is *no* room for a number four in my life, and even if there was, it wouldn't be you."

I rear back and bang my head on a shelf of bleach. "*Ow.* It wouldn't be me? Why not? What the hell's wrong with me?"

I should not have asked.

As I rub my head and her gaze smolders into mine, she ticks off her fingers, her voice almost completely steady. "One, you took an instant dislike to me, probably because I made you get thrown off a horse, for which I am *very sorry.* Two, even if you didn't dislike me, I am *well* aware that you're still sneaking kids out to work on the ranch when you think I'm not there. Three, you very clearly assumed that I'm nothing more than the personality painted by a TV show run by my ex-husband, whose very mission in life was to squash me so that he could look better. Four, *you're Junie's teacher and coach.* She's number one. Making her uncomfortable is the *last* thing I would do, and me dating you would make her very uncomfortable. And five, I don't think you're worth taking my clothes off for."

Five makes me choke on my own shock. "I am—"

"Arrogant, condescending, *trapping me in a broom closet* because you think you need to tell me to keep my hormones to myself instead of telling yourself that, and *ugly.*"

I rear back again, my jaw hanging. "I am *not* ugly."

Her nose wrinkles. "Must be your personality coloring my opinion. Don't be a dick to my daughter, and let me out of this closet before I show you what I can do with a mop bucket."

Jesus.

What the hell is wrong with me?

And I don't mean that in the same sense I just asked Maisey what was wrong with me.

I mean that in a *What the hell am I doing?* way.

I don't trap women in broom closets.

This isn't me at all.

I lift my hands. "Sorry. Sorry. I didn't—shit. Sorry."

I don't wait for her to say anything else, and instead, I retreat out the door, leaving it open for her to exit at her leisure.

I stride down the hall, ignoring curious looks from a few more students, and fling myself out the side door to the two picnic benches that the staff sometimes use in nicer weather, and I keep walking toward the football field and beyond, to the stables, where anyone who rides their horse to school can keep it for the day. When I'm sure I'm alone, I grab my phone and dial Kory.

"Late for class?" he drawls when he answers.

I work with teenagers all day long, but I rarely act like one.

Until today, apparently. "Why do I have a stupid crush on Maisey Spencer, and why am I losing my fucking mind over it?"

"Because she's hot, you thought she was moderately evil for bringing *change* to your life, you found out she's not unreasonable, and also that she's emotionally unavailable, and that despite your idiotic assumption that since she looks like an airhead on television, she's competent with power tools, and that's hot, even to me, and all of that together basically makes her the first fresh blood in town that's completely your type in about three years?"

I close my eyes, suck in a big breath through my nose, and tell myself not to hang up on my best friend.

That doesn't end well for me.

Don't ask how I know.

"And let's not forget the part where she's the closest thing you'll ever have to Tony again," Kory adds softer. "You're fucked up, my friend."

"This has nothing to do with her being Tony's niece."

"You sure? Because I'm pretty sure if any other woman had moved into any other ranch that you'd been using for giving some of your kids an outlet and, let's be real here, finding an outlet of your own, you wouldn't have been such an ass. I think you're afraid she's too much like Tony and that you'd get hurt if you let yourself be nice to her."

I grit my teeth.

Kory keeps talking. "And if you think you're extra immune to women who know they haven't been doing their best by their kid but are doing everything in their power to make up for it now, before it's too late, you're fooling yourself. After the way you grew up? Dude. You are *fucked*. Maisey Spencer is your catnip."

"She is not."

He snorts. "So you don't find it admirable and attractive at all that she knows why her kid's unhappy, and she's working to make things as comfortable as she can for June? And where's June's daddy? Running off with some other woman and telling people his ex-wife stole his kid from him. But is he fighting to get her back? Is *he* dropping by out here? You ever hear June ask anyone to send him pictures of her playing? You ever see Maisey calling him to tell him about what June's done on those rare instances when she gets to play? Nope."

"What's your point?"

"I repeat, my friend, *she's your catnip*. And she's off-limits. For real. Not in the *she's off-limits, so I'm going to try harder to score with her* kind of way. Get over yourself. Leave Maisey alone. And call me next time you need a reminder."

"Way to kick a guy when he's down," I mutter.

"If you're down, you did it to yourself. Won't get better until you expect better from yourself. You can be better, Flint. Quit being a grumpy asshole who assumes nobody would love you if they saw your flaws and insecurities, and get out there and let people in. Sure, some of 'em will hurt you. But more will surprise you."

"I let people in."

"You spend your days building up kids that you *know* are going to turn around and leave. You *like* knowing you don't have to get attached. And then you spend your nights alone, or hanging with me and my love-muffin, or making excuses to go see Opal instead of taking a chance that you could find a woman who's legitimately available and who'd love you in spite of yourself. We both know you don't want to be a grumpy, *lonely* asshole, but you're too afraid of your baggage to let yourself actually try to find someone who would make you happy. That's on you, my friend. I still love you, but that's on you."

The bell rings in the building behind me.

I'm late for class.

Late for class and completely fucked in the head today.

I owe Maisey an apology.

And probably more.

Chapter 12

Maisey

The one thing I promised Junie that I'd never do again was lie to her.

Yet here we are, three days after the closet incident with Flint, on our way home from a crushing defeat at a high school an hour from Hell's Bells, where she didn't get to play at all, which I know was killing her, and I'm lying to her.

I train my eyes firmly on the road so I don't have to look at her while I do it. "What do you mean, I was acting weird? I wasn't acting weird."

"You went out of your way to avoid Coach Jackson when the game was over."

Deflect. Deflect! Don't let your face tell any story that contradicts your mouth! "He made some very poor decisions in the first half, in my opinion, but he's the coach, and I am not, so I respect that he did what he felt he had to do. I just didn't want to get close enough for my mouth to accidentally say that for me. What did you say to Vivian out there when she got pulled in the second half? Have I told you how proud I am of you for making the most of this situation I got you into?"

"*Mom.*"

I've never once wanted to be a criminal like my own mother has become in her later years, but I wouldn't mind if I could tell little white lies easier. *"What?"*

"I can't even say his *name* without you making a face and trying to change the subject. And it's not the face you make when you talk about Dad. It's like—it's like—*ugh*. This is so disgusting."

"What's disgusting?"

"It's like you *like* him."

Dammit.

I hit the brakes and pop on my turn signal, then pull my truck to the side of the road.

I handled the puberty discussion like a champ. The sex discussion too. Though I probably shouldn't have left five minutes later—after each of them—to board a flight to another taping location.

I didn't flinch when I had to tell Junie that Grandma was going to prison, and I was straightforward and matter of fact when I told her that her father and I were getting a divorce.

But I do not want to have this conversation with my daughter.

"Junie, I'm about to say things that are going to make you cringe, and I apologize for that. Please pretend I'm not your mother for the next five minutes."

"Oh my God, Mom."

"Also, please remember you were very recently glad that I wasn't dead."

"This isn't getting better."

I reach into the cooler behind me and come up with a juice box, a cheese stick, and a lunch-size packet of chocolate chip cookies. "Let's have a snack. Low blood sugar will only make this worse."

Congratulations to me.

I have now earned the ultimate *teenage disdain* look.

Gonna have to add that one to my mom badges when I get home.

"I stood on the sidelines for an hour," she says. "My blood sugar is *fine*."

"Can you just humor me and have a snack just in case? The cheese stick might not help, but it definitely won't hurt."

She rolls her eyes.

I take a deep breath, shove the food into her lap, and open my mouth, not at all sure what's about to come out, because that's what Flint Jackson does.

He addles my brain.

"Coach Jackson is an objectively attractive man—"

Junie's face telegraphs an intense desire to fling open her car door and throw up.

"—but I have no interest in dating *anyone*, least of all an adult in *your* life, and *especially* your coach."

The dubiousness hangs thick between us.

I don't know which of us believes me less.

"He was really mean when he hosed me off the other day. And not nice about it at all when I took your muffins and cookies into school on Monday."

She rips open the string cheese and takes a bite right off the end.

There was a time in my life I would've acted horrified and called her a savage for eating string cheese wrong, but she hasn't wanted to joke around with me much lately. I give half a thought to trying, but she snorts softly while she chews, like she's preemptively rejecting the joke, and I go back to the matter at hand.

"I don't want to trash-talk your father, but I wouldn't be doing my job as your mother if I didn't tell you that the relationship left me unful-filled, and all of us—*all of us*—should walk away from relationships that suck our souls dry. Whatever that relationship is and whoever it's with. I don't know how it got to that point, but I know that I can't be a good partner to anyone if I don't know what I want and what I'm willing to offer. So you can rest assured that no matter how objectively attractive *any* man might be, I won't be dating until I'm satisfied with myself and where I am in my own journey of loving myself."

Her chewing has slowed, and she stares at me like I'm an alien.

Not just an alien, but an alien sitting in the middle of the couch, shoving popcorn up my nose, and using my feet to flip through all the channels like an anxious man on crack.

I sigh and turn back to the road.

Still have half an hour to go, and it's getting dark.

Last thing I need is to add *making roadkill of an antelope on a dark Wyoming road* to my list of accomplishments today.

"That was really deep, Mom," Junie says quietly. "I didn't know you had that much self-awareness."

Leave it to a teenager to think they have the market covered on self-awareness.

I stifle my smile and let only a small one curve my lips. "Thank you."

"But do you mean it, or are you just saying that?"

"Coach Jackson would need a personality implant before I'd consider dating him."

She takes a long suck off the juice box while I pull the car back onto the highway, and then she falls silent for a few miles.

And when she finally says something again, it's not good. "He's a really good coach. I know there are the weird things with him being pissed that he can't use the ranch the way Uncle Tony let him, and I don't like the way he looks at you—it makes me want to throw up in my mouth and kick him in the balls—but he's never treated me any differently because of any of that."

My biggest issue?

I agree.

Maybe not about the *kicking him in the balls* part—not so keen on my teenager doing that unprovoked—but definitely about him not treating her any differently than he treats the other kids. "People are complicated. They can be good coaches and teachers and want things in conflict with what we want and also be attractively unattractive to the parents of the kids they coach and teach."

"Vivian told me that Coach Jackson dated her aunt a few years ago and left her a total disaster. Like, she had to move to *Rhode Island* to get away from him. And then Abigail was like, *Oh my God, my neighbor too.* And apparently he was a total ass when he was in Mr. Simmerton's class back in the Stone Age when he was in high school, but I don't think anyone should be judged on who they were in high school."

I smile at her. "So you wouldn't judge me on who I was in high school?"

And there's another eye roll. "I would. Partly. But not all the way. Some people are still finding themselves in high school, and they're hurting and hormonal, and they don't understand the damage they're causing. But if they get therapy and do the work and overcome their traumas, I think they can be good people too. But only if they do the work, you know?"

These are the times when I think teenagers could do a better job of running the world than we adults do. And also when what they learn on the internet scares the crap out of me.

I can't imagine using the phrase *overcome their traumas* back when I was in high school.

"Normal isn't real," I say. "We all have things we need to work through."

"Like being raised and trained by embezzlers?"

Don't twitch, Maisey. Do. Not. Twitch. "Grandma was a good mom in all the ways that count. People can be good at relationships but bad at following the law. Or they can be good at following the law but bad at relationships. Case in point? My marriage. Though for all that my marriage to your father ended poorly, I'll always be grateful that I met him and went into business with him young enough that he could correct my misperceptions about how books, billing, and payroll are handled."

Yeah.

There were signs young that Mom wasn't the best role model in business.

And she gets a gold medal, I can hear my therapist friend saying.

But Junie snorts. "If that's the best you got out of your relationship with Dad—"

"I got you. *You're* the best part."

"Ew, sappy."

"Ew, teenagers being uncomfortable with truth."

"Would you jump Coach Jackson's bones if you didn't get off on the wrong foot with him after you got him thrown off his horse, and if he wasn't my teacher and coach?"

"Can you *please* save some of these questions for when I'm not paranoid that an elk or an antelope or a wolf is about to cross the road in front of us? And there *are* other cars on the road that I shouldn't swerve into."

Nope. She can't. "Even I know it's really dumb to put yourself at risk of a lawsuit by having kids working on fixing fences and playing in a falling-down barn on your property. I don't get why he's being such an ass about it."

"It's complicated, Junie." I don't tell her not to say *ass*, because if cussing is the worst of her rebellious ways, I'm totally fine with that.

"Mom, I know that means *I'm going to pretend it's complicated because I don't want to talk about it right now, but you actually nailed it, and you're right, Coach Jackson is being an ass about that.*"

Time to deflect. "You want to have a driving lesson this weekend? If you don't want to drive the truck, I think I can afford a slightly used sedan with really great airbags for you."

Doesn't work. She grunts. "I'm counting the times Dad says he's going to come visit. He's said it like seventeen times already. But do you know what he hasn't said? He hasn't said *When's your next soccer game, hon? I'll fly out for the afternoon and heckle your coach until he lets you play.* And you know he could. He just signed a contract for like five million dollars for his new show."

"Juniper Louisa Spencer, *I love you.* And I don't know if I can love you enough for both of the parents who are supposed to be here for you and all of the grandparents you never got to know or who got themselves sent to prison, but *I love you.* And I will put you first until the day you leave my house as an adult, and for the record, I don't mean the day you become a legal adult and leave. I mean the day you *feel* like enough of an adult to spread your wings and fly on your own."

She doesn't answer.

I slide a peek at her and find her watching me, straw from the juice box in her mouth, but she's clearly not sucking on it.

"You're a big dork," she finally says.

I'll take it. Especially since she's not making a fuss about me feeding her *toddler food*, or insisting that we talk more about if I want to date her coach, or about any of the rest of our family.

"It's hereditary," I tell her. "You'll be a big dork one day too."

Don't have to look to know she's rolling her eyes again.

"Deer," she says suddenly. "Deer. *Deer. Horse!*"

I hit the brakes once more as I process why she's shrieking about deer-horses.

Her cookie pack goes flying and hits the windshield.

We both jolt in our seat belts.

I mentally berate myself for giving her more *driving trauma* that'll keep her from wanting her own license for another several months.

And a massive elk steps into the road about ten feet in front of us.

"Oh my God, it's huge," Junie says.

Two more follow.

And then three more, plus a little one.

"A *baby*," she squeals. "Are baby deer supposed to be that big?"

"It's an elk," I tell her. "You can tell by the big white butt."

"In Europe, this is a deer. Only moose are called elk over there."

I glance at her.

She's not being snotty.

She's enthralled.

"Mom, there are three thousand of them," she whispers.

Maybe fifty.

They're on one side of the road amid the straggly, drying grass, the herd slowly following the leader across in front of our car, some noshing on whatever they can find on the ground, one with smallish antlers trying to mount another, and way more than just one baby.

"Aren't they pretty?" I whisper back.

"They're gorgeous."

Her eyes are wide as she leans forward in her seat. "Put your blinkers on. Don't be a sitting target on the highway. And flash your lights so the cars coming the other direction aren't stupid either."

"Aww, look at you with all the driver's-ed smarts. Does this mean you're ready to try it behind the wheel again? We *do* have a lot of flat acres you could practice on."

"Don't be sarcastic in the presence of elk. They'll eat you."

I watch the herd cross the road for a bit, but mostly, I watch Junie.

The sheer awe on her face—she wouldn't have gotten this if we'd stayed in Iowa.

Maybe this move didn't ruin her life after all.

Chapter 13

Flint

I suck at apologizing.

It's been mostly intentional through my adult life, mainly because I try to live my life in a way that doesn't lend itself to regrets or the necessity of an apology.

Or to getting attached enough to anyone to have to apologize to them.

When I do screw up, I'll apologize to Opal. I'll apologize to my colleagues.

But I've made a point to not apologize to a woman. Especially a woman who might think we have a future.

The one time I did—don't want to talk about it.

Much as I'm certain Maisey Spencer doesn't think we have a future—even a very short-lived quickie kind of future—it's still hard to make myself knock on her door early Sunday morning. I know June's at a sleepover with half the soccer team, which means this is my only chance to catch Maisey alone.

I knock three times before she answers, and when she finally swings the door open, I have instant regrets.

She's wearing bright-pink pajama pants decorated with squirrels, a Half-Cocked Heroes concert T-shirt, and there's an eye mask shoved up onto her forehead, making her bedhead stick out even worse.

Her feet are bare. The dark smudges under her eyes are pronounced against her pale cheeks, and there's no question in my mind that she's braless.

I don't want to apologize to Maisey Spencer.

I want to lift her off her feet, shove her against a wall, and devour her.

"Tony has a secret root cellar that should be cleaned out soon," I blurt, and it sounds pretty much exactly like my brain at 3:00 a.m., when I bolted awake suddenly remembering that I'd willfully forgotten about it and that June should *not* be the person who finds it.

Or even Maisey.

Maisey should definitely not find it until I clean it out.

Also?

Never mind my practiced *I'm sorry I was an ass, here's a coffee. Let me tell you about some of the quirks of the property, beyond the aging well.*

Nope.

The sight of those sleepy baby blues and that short blonde bedhead has rendered me stupid, and it's all I can do to hang on to the one ounce of reason remaining in my brain to spit out my purpose in being here.

She rubs one eye and stares at me like it's too early in the morning for my words to compute.

Probably is.

Shit.

It's not even seven o'clock.

On a Sunday.

"What about the—" She pauses, her jaw stretching wide as she yawns so big, I can see her tonsils. When she's done yawning, she smacks her lips three times, swipes away the tears glistening in her eyes—*Jesus*, that was a yawn—and slouches in the doorway. "What about the root cellar?"

I wince. "I'm gonna take care of it. I just wanted you to know there's a root cellar, and I'll be down in it today, taking care of cleaning it out. So you don't have to. And so June doesn't . . . know."

Apparently, *I'm gonna clean out your root cellar* is code for *You need to wake up immediately because there is way more to this story than I'm telling you*, because Maisey visibly jolts awake like her brain has been snapped with a rubber band.

"What's in the root cellar?" she asks.

"Mold." The word flies out of my mouth with all the force a normal person would use to say *hazardous waste with a side of serial killers.*

Her lips purse, and her eyes telegraph a very clear *I don't believe you.* "What's in the root cellar?" she repeats in a voice that has my dick twitching and my brain conjuring dirty librarian fantasies.

"Look, I know you have no reason to like me or trust me right now, but you should trust me on this."

"When's the last time you were in the root cellar?"

To the best of my knowledge, she doesn't know where the entrance is.

But also to the best of my knowledge, teenagers have a way of figuring this shit out, and the first time June has a sleepover here and offers to show her friends around, they'll notice.

Anytime I bring kids out here to work, we stay far away from the house. *Respect for the owner,* I always told them.

And they were good kids, so they listened.

"You're gonna have to trust me on this," I repeat, trying my own teacher voice on her.

She folds her arms over her chest.

No watch.

No jewelry.

Just toned arms covering her lovely—erm, her chest.

It's just a chest.

And they're just arms.

I am not attracted to them in the least.

Especially not in ways that I shouldn't be.

"The last time I trusted you, I ended up trapped in a janitor's closet with a crazy person. So please excuse me if I'd like a little further information on what, exactly, is going on in my uncle's root cellar."

"I'm sorry." I don't sound sorry. I sound desperate and irritated, and I know it. See, again, I don't apologize well. So I take a deep breath, and I try again.

"I'm sorry," I repeat, and this time, I almost believe myself. "That was not my best behavior. You didn't deserve that. I'm sorry. And I'd like to make it up to you by taking care of a mess before June and her friends find it."

She studies me with those plump lips still pursed, her eyes far more alert than they were a minute ago, faint lines marring her forehead. "I told Junie that you'd have to be a completely different person before I'd ever consider dating you."

And now my balls are sweating. "I don't want to date you. I just want to do something nice for Tony's family. And Tony. This is really more for Tony than it is for you."

"You don't want to date me."

"I'm a serial heartbreaker."

Not the single brow lift.

Jesus.

Not the single brow lift.

Such a small gesture to say so much. *You really think anyone could care enough about you for you to break their heart? You're not that attractive, Flint Jackson. And you're an ass to boot.*

Or maybe it says, *I'm well aware there's more to that story, and if you think I'm going to take you at face value, you are sadly mistaken.*

I deserve that.

"Leaves a lasting impression to watch one of your parents tear down the other in the name of *love* for most of your childhood." The words taste like stale whiskey. And for the record, I hate whiskey about as much as I hate telling *anyone* why I am the way I am. But I've been an ass to her. She deserves to know why. And this is why I hate apologizing. "So I don't do relationships. But it's fucking hard to watch you do for June what I always wanted my own mother to do for me and not have some kind of reaction to it."

Maisey doesn't answer.

She stays right where she's at, leaning in the doorway, one brow arched at me, arms still crossed over her chest.

I know this trick.

I use this trick daily in my classroom.

And hell if it isn't working on me despite knowing not to fall for it and despite all the ways I'm telling her that's as much of my story as she gets. Fucking guilt. "Love sucks, okay? It sucks you dry and leaves you a husk of a human being without the will to get out of bed in the morning to take care of the kid you thought would solve all of your relationship problems and instead made it all worse, until your kid's the one taking care of you when he's supposed to be being a kid, until he can't do it anymore and he breaks too. So I don't date. I fuck. I have my kids at the school. I have a brother in Kory. I have my aunt Opal. I had Tony. I have all of Hell's Bells acting like cousins I never had. I don't need anything else. I don't *want* anything else. So don't count on anything else."

Coming here to apologize was an awful idea.

My chest aches. My veins are buzzing.

I said too much.

I never say that much.

I said too much.

And she's watching me with wide blue eyes that tell me she did *not* sign up for my level of fucked up.

She blinks once and pushes herself upright. "Give me ten minutes to throw on clothes and make coffee, and I'll go with you."

I crack one of my knuckles, my chest still aching, all my senses on full alert for whatever she's about to throw at me. "No."

"Make me skip my coffee, and I'll follow you to wherever this root cellar is, lock you inside, call the sheriff, and have you removed forcibly from my property, then call Opal, and then also call a few of Junie's friends' mothers and my new book club friends, and we'll see how long it takes for everyone in this town to know about whatever it is you're hiding in that root cellar."

Jesus. "It's not mine."

"You clearly loved Tony more recently than I did, so it'll clearly hurt you more than it'll hurt me for the entire town to find out what's in there."

I'm not supposed to sweat like this at 7:00 a.m. on a beautiful fall morning. "It's his porn collection."

Her nose wrinkles, but otherwise, she doesn't seem surprised.

Also?

Getting back to Tony's porn—which isn't really standard-issue porn but is definitely not something I want June discovering here—and Maisey's normal sass is easing the ache in my chest.

Fuck.

Of course it is.

She doesn't care where I came from or why I'm fucked up. She wants to go back to the way we've been so she can forget this happened too.

"So help me," she says quietly, so very *Maisey* that I'm able to take a real full breath, "if you're lying to me and it's worse than simple porn, I will erect a building right in front of your front porch so you never see the sunset from my gatehouse again."

The depth of her knowledge about me and my habits is startling.

Especially given that I don't have time for sunset gazing in the fall and winter months.

Fuck me.

Opal.

She's in book club with Opal.

The traitor.

Maisey smirks, and I don't know if it's at my visible surprise or if it's sheer evil joy at knowing how to get under my skin.

Either way, this feels *normal* for us.

And not a forced normal.

Just regular ole normal.

"It might be a little different than a normal porn collection," I mutter.

"Like *Bring in a truck of dirt and bury it all before Junie gets home* worse? Or like *Don't drop a match in because it'll cause a massive explosion* worse?"

Neither. Exactly. "Both."

Her forehead wrinkles again. "Theoretically, if everything was removed from this root cellar, would it be salvageable as an actual storage unit?"

"I don't know."

"Ten minutes. Coffee. And then we're going to find out."

"Maisey—"

"In case you were unaware, which would probably be willful negligence on your part by now, I've spent close to the last two decades of my life letting a man tell me what to do for his benefit. I'm uninterested in continuing my life that way. Ten minutes. Coffee. And then we're going to find out. Understood?"

Hell if bossy, evil Maisey isn't more attractive than sleepy, yawning Maisey, which is even more attractive than *cherry crisp delivering in a dress* Maisey.

Apologizing was a bad idea.

Telling her why I don't date was a bad idea.

But both were also completely and totally necessary.

Tony did a lot of good for a lot of people while never asking for much for himself.

Pretty sure he would've wanted me to take care of this.

Chapter 14

Maisey

There is no amount of coffee, sleep, or sanity in the world that could have prepared me for Uncle Tony's root cellar.

And I'm irrationally angry at the level of trust that I don't have in Flint that made it necessary for me to come down here with him, and equally angry that hearing just a tiny bit more of his life story makes me want to wrap him in a hug and fix everything for him.

I keep telling Junie that people can be really great at one thing and bad at another.

Flint is good at being a teacher, but he's terrible at being—well, whatever it is that he feels like he needs to be to me.

But the very, very, *very* worst part?

If I'm reading between the lines right and piecing together the puzzle of him with even the slightest bit of accuracy, his parents broke him to the point that he had to move in with Opal when he was roughly Junie's age.

The thought of my own daughter feeling so desperate and unloved that she needs to live with someone else makes my heart crack in two.

Poker face, Maisey. Poker face.

Which, for the record, is *not* easy given what's awaiting us in the root cellar. I use my coffee tumbler to gesture to a poster hanging to one side of the ancient television with the built-in VCR player. "I hope you appreciate how much I'm pretending I have no idea what all of this means and how much I'm assuming you have no idea either."

Flint's been quiet and reserved in a far more unusual way since I got my coffee and we headed back behind the original log cabin, deep in the backyard of the more modern house that Junie and I live in, like he's regretting the little bits that he shared and wants to take them back, lest I use them against him.

His hooded eyes shift in my direction for a fraction of a second before he goes back to clearing one of the shelves that should have been used for things like canned green beans and bags of potatoes, but which Uncle Tony had other uses for.

I don't press him for more conversation. Instead, I start to sit in the green floral easy chair positioned in front of the television, take stock of the video collection and the slipper collection beneath it, briefly ponder when he ran electrical lines down here to the root cellar that's far enough from the house that he *definitely* had to intentionally run electricity to it, and decide I don't actually want anything near that chair unless I was already planning on burning it.

I loved Uncle Tony.

I did.

And I know he had his own wants and needs and hobbies. God knows I've found some interesting things while I've been cleaning out the house to turn it into a home for Junie and me.

Nothing too out of the ordinary. Thirty-year-old canned goods and a collection of herbal remedies for various ailments, from high blood pressure to impotence, in one of the kitchen cabinets in the bunkhouse, which, yes, was a weird place to find them. Stacks of muscle car magazines, which is the most anti–Uncle Tony thing I've ever seen, tucked in among the various leftover items that didn't sell during the estate sale and that I asked to be saved for me to look through in case I found something I wanted to keep for sentimental reasons.

A horseshoe collection in the barn, which I am 100 percent regarding in a new light right now.

Seashells, even small seashells, that he filled with candle wax in another missed cabinet in one of the bathrooms.

A stained glass portrait of what I think was a bear and a llama in a compromising position behind a door in the original cabin.

We all live our lives and have various interests, right?

But I'm not so certain I needed to know that Uncle Tony had a foot fetish.

"Did you two hang out here a lot?" I ask Flint.

"No."

"Occasionally, then?"

"No."

"When one knows this exists and shows up on a person's doorstep demanding solo access to clean out the previous owner's belongings before seven a.m. on a Sunday morning, the current occupant is entitled to ask questions."

"Found it by accident. One-time thing. Gingersnap's fault, actually. Stopped by to drop off pastries for Tony one morning, found the cow mooing like she lost her best friend right outside the door that I'd never noticed before, knocked, let myself in, found . . . this, and I never came back. Never told Tony I found it. Forgot it existed until I caught a kid with something that sparked a memory yesterday."

I believe him.

His skin turned the color of a beet about the moment he realized he wasn't getting access to this root cellar without me, and it hasn't wavered since.

If he were any other man, I'd say it was adorable.

But with this man, I am totally keeping my guard up.

Especially with how much I still want to give him a hug.

I take a sip of coffee and do a slow turn again, taking in the foot posters, the abstract foot art, the foot sculptures, mostly in the box at

Flint's feet now, and the labels on the videos—*beach feet, boot feet, bed feet*—once more.

And while it's mostly feet, that's not *all* it is.

"Did he ever date?" I ask.

Flint gives me a hard look.

Utter sadness floods me. Grief for a man whose family cut him out and who clearly felt like he had to hide who he was despite living in such a welcoming community like Hell's Bells.

I haven't met a single person who hasn't had a story about Uncle Tony and the times he did something nice for them.

Uncle Tony was exactly the kind of man you'd want to win the lottery. He did so much good with his winnings over the years. He left his house to me on the hunch that I'd need a safe escape and specified in his will that, while I got Wit's End and all physical possessions in and on it, every last dime in his bank account was to be split among his favorite various charities around the country.

"Do you think he ever wanted to date?" My throat's starting to clog, and I can barely get the words out.

"Hard to believe in love when it's used as a weapon," Flint mutters in response.

God.

No wonder they were tight.

Mom always told me Uncle Tony was the black sheep of the family because he was a carefree hippie who didn't put in the hard work. That if a man's crowning achievement was winning the lottery, he wasn't the best role model.

I'm slowly realizing just how lucky I was that she was willing to send me out here for a few weeks those summers I was in high school, because I'm *certain* my grandparents shunned him for entirely different reasons.

I know he grew up in different times, my grandparents, too, but that doesn't make me any less sad for him. If anything, it makes me more sad.

I clear my throat and gesture around us, desperate to not wallow in how much being thrown out of his family must've hurt my uncle. "This reminds me of a secret room I wasn't supposed to find when we took down the wrong wall in a house in Indianapolis during season two. The husband regularly hosted swinger parties when his wife was out of town."

Flint's lips part, and he shifts a glance at me that suggests he thinks I'm making it up.

"You wouldn't have seen that episode. It never aired. Even if the producers hadn't nixed it on the spot for the fact that we were a family-friendly show, the husband had a total shit fit, like it was *our* fault he was keeping a secret from his wife, and threatened to sue us if we didn't get off his property immediately. No idea if they ever finished that reno, but I know she got the kid in their divorce."

He stares at me.

I shrug. "I've seen things. Also, the best part of being considered the ditzy, airheaded, stupid comic relief on a dumb reality TV show is that no one ever suspects it was you who secretly paid for her private investigator who got the pictures of the *other* things he was into that were *not* okay. Secret sex room? Whatever. Have your fetishes. Digging up the hundred-thousand-dollar gambling debt he'd racked up in questionable crowds so that she'd have cause to *get* the kid in the divorce? You hear that? That's the sound of justice, and I fucking *love* it."

He gapes at me for another second. Then he cracks a grin, and *oh my God*, is he adorable.

No, Maisey. No. He's a pompous ass who thinks he's the hottest thing since a forest fire and who also thinks he knows everything. He is not adorable.

"You ever tell Tony that?" he asks.

"I have never spoken those words aloud. Congratulations. You caught me in a caffeine deficit and now know my biggest secret. Tell anyone and I'll go justice on *your* ass too. Don't test me. *I will find all the things.*"

He shakes his head, still grinning, and lifts a particularly colorful butt plug. "Like this?"

"Like that. Which would be an absolute piece of art if I didn't know exactly what it was."

He chuckles. "About five years ago, he caused a massive fuss in town. Gertie at the general store got a load of these. Thought they were lamp pulls missing their chains. Tony bought the whole box, and not five minutes after he departed with the lot of them, someone told Gertie what they actually were. Spread like *wildfire* that Tony bought the whole box. About the time they started debating if anybody was gonna tell him, I noped out of the whole conversation."

"They thought he was an innocent old man who had never heard of sex before and didn't want to tell him?" I feel like Junie, rolling my eyes now.

"Town was split. Half of 'em thought he was going to use them as lamp pulls or, like you said, art. Other half thought he was sparing Gertie the embarrassment of having these on her shelves for anyone passing through town to find."

"Could've been both," I murmur.

"Everyone kept angling to get an invitation to his house for dinner so they could see if he'd hung them on his lamps."

"That's a warning, right? Buy my sex toys online in discreet packaging?"

"Jesus Christ," he mutters.

"I'm not used to small-town life. I need to know these things."

He turns his back to me, but his neck has gone even redder than it was before. "Cece Jones used to wait tables at the diner. Not long after Tony bought his box of, ah, lamp pulls, Cece got caught sleeping with a married minister two towns over, and everyone forgot about Tony."

I wince.

"She wiped her social media accounts, quit her job, and hightailed it out of the county. Everyone got more tied up in guessing where she went than with worrying over Tony's lamps." He shakes his head and tosses the blown glass butt plug into his box. "This town's great in so many ways. You need someone to come clear out your root cellar, all you have to do is put out a call on one of the town's social pages. But you want to keep a secret . . ."

I shiver.

Can't help it. I know it's only a matter of time before someone finds out my mom's in prison and why. Junie and I are both finally feeling like we might fit in here. Not quite all the way to fitting entirely, but close enough to see that it's a possibility. I can't drop into Iron Moose, the diner, the sandwich shop, the bakery, Opal's, you name it in downtown, without getting greetings from people that I'm starting to think of as friends.

And yes, I know I'm overcompensating by volunteering for everything under the sun, from taking a look at a running toilet to switching out faulty outlets to offering to help paint someone's nursery, but I have those skill sets, my alimony is enough to pay my bills, and right now, I need to feel like a contributing member of the community more than I need to feel like people like me merely because I was famous at exactly one level above *I had five minutes of fame for going viral on social media.*

But the biggest point is that we're almost there. We very nearly belong. I don't want to know if the people here would shun us if they found out what Mom did.

I just want to live in my happy bubble where I feel like I'm finding my place and Junie's talking to me again and I feel optimistic about the future.

It's lovely to be here in this mental and emotional space again.

But stronger than I was when I was with Dean.

Knowing that if I can walk away from my marriage and start over again with Junie here, I can handle anything.

"You have secrets?" Flint asks me, clearly curious about my silence.

If he thinks he's getting another secret out of me, he is *so* wrong.

"Do you *honestly* think taking me down into a root cellar and showing me my uncle's foot-fetish collection earns you the right to any more of my secrets?" I deadpan.

He stares right back for a split second, and then the craziest thing happens.

He laughs.

And not just any old laugh.

No, this is a full-on, doubled-over, *wheezing so hard he probably has tears in his eyes* kind of laugh.

An *I've been trying to hold it together and be stoic all morning, and you have finally broken me* kind of laugh.

I back up and sink to the steps in the small stairwell under the door and watch him completely lose his shit in the best possible way.

This man has a past. He has relationship damage. He definitely has trust issues. He's probably every bit as lonely as I've felt more times than I care to admit in the past few years.

But even with all his own issues, he's taking care of Junie at school, and he did the best he could to make room for her on the soccer team.

"What are you going to do with all of this?" I ask him once he's quit laughing. "Because I am one hundred percent on the *This is Flint's Problem* train, for the record."

He looks down at the box, then flashes me the most mischievous grin I have ever seen in my entire life. "EBay or Etsy."

"Oh my God."

"Athletic department budget got cut last year. I know a guy who'll put it up for us, won't ask questions, and funnel the profits back to the school. Might even be enough to get that liability-insurance package the principal won't approve. Those are some hot feet there. They'll fetch a pretty penny."

"Oh my God."

He grins broader.

Every ounce of me freaking *swoons.*

Trouble?

No.

It's way worse than that.

Chapter 15

Flint

The worst part of small-town living is that you can't avoid anyone.

Ever.

Avoidance isn't usually my thing—I prefer to face a problem head-on—but my problem is that I want to bang Maisey Spencer, and I can't.

Seeing her when she picks June up from practice or comes to the team's games doesn't make it better. Seeing her drive past the gatehouse a few mornings and evenings a week doesn't make it better. Running into her having dinner with new friends at Iron Moose or walking into Opal's house on book club night and accidentally overhearing her commiserating with friends over feeling like she'll never be a good enough mother doesn't make it better.

Not seeing her doesn't make it better. Not when every morning, I wake up, peer up the driveway, and squint to see if I can catch any motion at the house.

Which I can't see from the gatehouse.

Never been able to. Won't ever be able to.

Reality—and geography—doesn't work that way.

But I still look.

And I *hear* her. I hear saws. I hear hammering. I hear boards being tossed on one another.

Telling myself that she's just as unavailable emotionally as I am doesn't help.

Teaching and coaching her daughter every day doesn't make it better.

Trying to work up being mad that she missed Tony's funeral doesn't help. Watching her put all the effort into being a good mom, hearing stories about times she was happy here with him as a teenager, and knowing that Tony was cut out by most of the rest of her family has made me acutely aware that there's always more to a story than anyone thinks there is.

And watching Maisey putting everything in place to fix all the things that he never got around to because he didn't think any of them were important on an *old hobby ranch*?

Getting quotes on lumber to reinforce the barn. Fixing the well. I know she started rewiring the original cabin on the land that was converted—poorly—into a guesthouse. Replacing the oven in the main house. Sealing the windows. Replacing the door and locks on the bunkhouse once she realized how easy it would be for Earl to break in.

Fucking hot.

And here I am again, once more thinking I'm in the clear as I dash back to the school at the start of soccer practice to grab the colored jerseys that I left in the locker room, when I hear her voice ringing through the air in the outdoor staff alcove near the back entrance.

"I don't know, Mom. Ask your guard," she's saying quietly right around the corner from me.

I slow and stop short when I should pivot and go around the long way to get into the school building.

Ask your guard?

That's not a normal thing to say to normal moms.

"I checked the tracking. It was delivered last week. I don't know why they haven't gotten it to you—*Mom*. You realize the more jokes you make about me putting shivs in your packages, the less likely you are to make parole early? *I am not helping you with this.* Stop it. Junie and I have a new life, and she doesn't need more drama."

Oh, fuck.

This isn't real, is it?

She didn't just say that.

There's no way she just said that.

I angle closer to this wall, out of sight of the alcove, and hit my phone while I keep listening. Maisey Spencer mom prison, I type.

"Yes, I want you to come here. There's an adorable cabin a little ways from the house that I'm fixing up just for you, and you know Junie—"

She cuts herself off with a sigh while my phone brings up absolutely nothing relevant.

Maybe I misunderstood.

"You're right. You don't have to let me take care of you. But I have a little bit of land. I have a small home for you. I have an opportunity for you to start over—*yes*, even at your age, don't get lippy with me, Ms. Forever Twenty-Nine—and if you're going to refuse it because it was Uncle Tony's, and you didn't like it when he quit talking to you over the exact same activities that landed you exactly where you are now, then that's on you."

I try again.

Maisey Spencer Dean's Fixer Upper Mother Mom
Jail Prison.

"Stop it. This is *not* charity. And there's nothing weird about Uncle Tony's—erm—house."

I stifle a grin and barely stop myself from chuckling in amusement.

Pretty sure there's still weird stuff somewhere in Tony's house. I never looked in his attic, and to the best of my knowledge, the company she hired for the estate sale didn't either. Wonder if Maisey has.

Also?

Still nothing popping up on my search on my phone about Maisey's mom.

"I'm going to pretend you didn't say that. Look, you don't have to come. You don't. But Junie would love to have you here. I'd love to have you close enough to keep an eye on you. If this wasn't Uncle Tony's place, you'd love it. And don't tell me there's not some small part of you that would take joy in living basically at his expense when you're still mad at him for not participating in your scheme."

Happy feelings gone.

Doesn't even matter that I can hear the disgust in her voice, like she's making herself say it to manipulate her mom and doesn't like it either.

"Mom? Mom, are you—*dammit.*" Maisey sighs.

I shove away from the building, intending to circle around to the front before she catches me, but a sharp inhalation stops me.

She's come around the corner holding her cell phone up like she's looking for a better signal. And I'm busted.

"How much of that did you hear?" she asks.

"How much of what?"

Her nose wrinkles as she gives me the wariest of wary glances while her pale cheeks go pink, and this is why I need to avoid Maisey Spencer.

I can *feel* her insecurities. Her vulnerabilities. There's something about her body language that says *Today has been hard, and I absolutely cannot take any more.*

I've been faking my way through book club and PTA events and soccer games and life.

I'm alone and worn down and tired of putting on this brave face for the world.

If you're going to be one more hurdle to me making a new life for Junie and me, I will destroy you, but I need a nap first.

And all the while, my brain is feeding me stories I do *not* need to hear.

She's thinking about you too. She's avoiding you too. She wants to jump your bones but can't contemplate it until her kid graduates from high school, which will give both of us time to get our shit together. Call a therapist, and you might have a chance then.

It's wrong.

She's probably thinking that I know a secret worse than that her uncle had a foot-fetish and adult-entertainment collection, which isn't a bad secret.

Not compared to her mother being in prison.

Her mother's in fucking prison.

"You have friends back in Iowa?" The question pops out before I can think better of it.

Her mouth sets in a grim line. "Lovely seeing you, Flint. Don't let me keep you. I'm sure you have better places to be."

"You don't."

She turns around like she's headed back into the school.

And here I go, opening my mouth again. "What's she in jail for?"

She swings back to face me. "Please, *please*, for Junie's sake, forget you heard any of that."

"Yes, my first order of business in my classroom tomorrow will be announcing that June Spencer's grandmother is a jailbird. Can't wait. Ties in so well with geometry and precalc."

Her eyes go shiny, and she blinks twice quickly before turning her back on me again. "At least it'll sort out who's worthy of being Junie's friend before she gets any more invested in anyone who's not."

"Hey." I snag Maisey by the elbow. "Of course I'm not telling."

"Sure. Whatever." She shakes her arm loose.

"Maisey. Nobody here's gonna judge, and I'd bet you every last donut at the bakery that half of June's friends already know anyway."

"Unless you're about to tell me your deepest, darkest secret, I would very much appreciate if you would leave me alone and let me go on living my life believing this conversation never happened."

"I hate mushrooms."

She rolls her eyes.

"Like I'm actually afraid of them."

"You're afraid of mushrooms."

"Ask Opal." I'm almost thirty-five years old, telling a woman to ask my aunt about my fear of mushrooms. "I don't talk about it because teenagers are assholes and I'd end up with piles of mushrooms on my desk every year if I did."

Shit.

I'm thinking about piles of mushrooms on my desk, and I'm sweating.

She studies me like she's trying to decide if I'm the type of asshole to make up a dumb fear to mock her gullibility, too, or if I'm serious.

"I got sick off a wild mushroom when I was a kid, didn't get to the hospital when I should've, got way sicker than I should've, and I've been terrified of all of them ever since. Even when I know they're safe. Can't even see the word without getting the shakes."

Her suspicion doesn't waver, which is a kick to the gut after I told her more than I usually tell anyone about my childhood.

Probably didn't register for her what a fucking big deal that was for me to say so much out loud.

She says everything. She doesn't hold back.

Why *would* she understand how hard that was for me?

I scrub a hand over my hair, equal parts frustrated that she doesn't believe me and frustrated that I care.

If you'd told me six months ago that I'd be worried what Tony's niece thought of me, I'd have laughed you out of town.

But she's not the villain I thought she was.

Don't get me wrong. I still think she's in over her head with managing this much land in Wyoming, and I still think she'll need more help than she expects come winter, and I still want to find a way to get my troubled kids back out to the ranch to work off their frustrations.

But she's not the bad guy. She's done too much good around town to be the bad guy.

If anything, she's the lost guy.

Girl.

Woman.

She's a lady in need of being rescued.

No, she's a lady trying to rescue herself.

I don't know a single person who has never felt lost. Some recognize it. Some don't. Some blame other people. Some try to get help. Some try to fix it themselves. Some try to fix the world around them. Some pretend there's nothing broken and push through.

I've felt all that and more at one point or another.

All I know about Maisey and how she views her situation is that I haven't once heard her say it's someone else's fault.

She gets a lot of credit from me for that.

"Tony would've been super pissed at me if I hurt you," I say. "And if I didn't help you where I could."

She's not getting any less suspicious.

I shove my fists in my pockets, trying not to let my frustration show. It's my own fault she's suspicious of me. So I need to own this the way she's owning her problems too. "In case you haven't figured it out yet, nobody here will care what your mom did to land in prison. They care that you're doing shit like showing up for your kid and dropping off baked goods all over town and hiring local contractors who are often hard up for work, while you're also all over town helping anyone who needs your skills but can't afford to pay for it. You might not be taking in strays, but you're living up to what people expect of Tony's family."

"I ruined Junie's favorite shirt in the wash and didn't know it until she went to put it on this morning. My coffeepot broke. A raccoon somehow got into my garage and was eating Junie's leftover lunch inside my car. Junie saw Dean on a morning talk show telling the host that he misses her so much, but he hasn't called her *once* in the past ten days. I finally got all the mud cleaned out of all the crevices on my phone after that incident with Earl, and then I dropped it and cracked the screen when I got to the deli to take myself out for lunch, and the minute I walked into the deli, I saw a picture of Uncle Tony hanging on the wall, and I was in the photo, too, and I remember that day because it's the day I fell off a horse and he thought he killed me, but really, it was the funniest thing ever, and he spent the rest of the day taking me all over town buying me anything I wanted, and *I miss him.*"

Her voice cracks, and a single tear slides down her cheek.

She swipes it away like she's hoping I won't notice, but the truth is, I miss the old bastard too.

"I don't miss him because he bought me things," she whispers. "I miss him because he paid attention and he took the time to do things with me and he treated me like I was his favorite guest ever when I was a kid, and now it's too late to ever tell him how much it meant to me, and I took him for granted when I should've been a better niece and been here, and instead everything is crap, and *I don't know how to do all the things I'm trying to do.*"

I don't know who moves first.

Probably me, which I don't want to think about or read into or analyze.

All that matters is I'm suddenly hugging her tightly with her head tucked under my chin and her ear pressed against my chest, the two of us tucked into the alcove where the staff hides from the kids at lunchtime when the weather's nice, out of view of the fields where the soccer and football teams are practicing.

Shit.

Soccer practice.

I need to get back to it.

A shudder escapes her as she wraps her arms around my waist.

I am 100 percent on board with staying here, though.

"I miss him," she whispers again. "I miss my mom. I miss feeling like I knew what I was doing. I miss Junie telling me everything, like she used to when she was seven. I miss not knowing everything that was wrong, and I miss the parts of life that used to be easy, even if they were wrong. I just want something to be *easy*. Just for a minute. So I can catch up and breathe."

I stroke her hair and tell my dick she's one of my students so it'll get itself under control. Not the time. Really not the time. "You're okay."

"I am *not* okay."

"Okay, yeah, you're not, but you will be."

She laughs, but it doesn't sound amused.

It sounds desperate.

And that is *not* what I associate with Maisey Spencer.

She's optimistic. She's fearless. She's capable. She's determined.

She's often a pain in my ass.

Definitely costing me sleep.

And right now, in this moment, I want to be the one holding her world together.

Chapter 16

Maisey

Oh God, this feels good.

I can't remember the last time I was wrapped in such a solid, warm, comforting bear hug.

Which officially needs to be renamed something else so I don't picture Earl trying to wrap his arms around me, because that's actually terrifying.

Ah.

It's a *Flint* hug.

And—oh, no.

No no no.

He's stroking my hair.

I'm having a significant emotional event because I feel like I'm trying too hard to fit in and I've had a string of little annoyances—okay, and some *big* drama—and this man who's supposed to be completely off-limits is stroking my hair and telling me I'll be all right while his heart drums beneath my ear.

I can't *I'm not dating* my way out of the reaction my body's having to his tender care.

I can't *He hates you* my way out of it either.

I don't think he hates me.

I don't think he hates me at all.

If he's feeling anything like what I've felt since the first full day Junie and I were here, I imagine he *wants* to dislike me, because it's easier than giving in to the temptation to like this man that I need to stay away from so as to not complicate my life or my daughter's life.

But being hugged by someone in this world who clearly cared for my uncle, who cares about the land, who cares about his students and his players, but who understands that relationships are more complicated than *You're wrong because I say you are* is more like finally having someone who *gets it*.

More—it's like forgiveness.

It's forgiveness for not making more of an effort to spend time with Uncle Tony.

Forgiveness for making his horse throw him. Forgiveness for me being such a pain about not wanting kids on the ranch. Forgiveness for having a mother who did bad things and for putting my husband's dreams ahead of my child in an attempt to make my marriage better.

"Mom was arrested two days before Uncle Tony's funeral," I whisper.

His body goes stiff, and then a breath whooshes out over me.

"She was—she did bad things. I had to choose between Uncle Tony's funeral, when she hadn't talked to him in years and was frankly irritated with me that I still emailed him occasionally, or being there to help her find a lawyer and put together bail money and figure out what was going on."

"What did she do?"

The question is gruff, but he's tightening the hug, and I don't care if he's judging me.

I just know this feels good.

So good.

"Bad things," I whisper. "She stole from people. She stole from a lot of people. Her friends. My friends. Junie's friends' parents. A lot of people."

"You didn't know?"

"I didn't even have time to keep up with my own *daughter*, much less my mother." Yep. Truth still hurts. "I don't have anyone left in Cedar Rapids. Junie doesn't have any friends left in Cedar Rapids. I didn't want anyone here to know because she deserves the same safe space I had when I was her age and I'd come out here. I don't care if anyone knows for *me*. I care that they don't know for *her*."

"That's why you don't want kids on the ranch."

"I *cannot* take any risks. I can't put my daughter's security and comfort and safety in jeopardy." I shudder at all the doomsday scenarios that have played through my head over the past year or so. "I need to be dependable for her. I don't ever want her to feel the way I did when I saw my mom put in handcuffs. She's been through enough already."

He strokes my back and presses a kiss to my head. "Okay. Okay. We'll take care of June."

We'll take care of June.

That's everything I need.

I need to know that my daughter will be okay.

"Thank you," I whisper.

"People here won't judge you on what your mother did," he says gruffly. "They know Tony thought the world of you. Up to you to make them think less."

"By getting them thrown off a horse, being a pain in the ass about liability, and trying to convince them to let Junie on the soccer team with a cherry-crisp bribe?" I whisper.

His chuckle rumbles through his chest, passing into me, and there's no more denying it.

I'm in trouble.

I like this man.

"So you admit it was a bribe."

"But I took one to *everyone*. And I even gave Mr. Simmerton an apple crisp because I heard he liked those better."

"We definitely judge parents who bring us treats. You're our least favorite. Treats are awful."

He's gripping me tight with one solid arm and teasing his fingers over my back with his free hand. His lips are hot. His breath is hot. Every nerve ending in my body is igniting in ways I haven't felt in *years*.

And his sarcasm is making me hornier.

I want to kiss him.

I want to remember what it feels like to be kissed by someone who wants to kiss me back.

Flint definitely wants to kiss me back.

There was no mistaking the hunger in his eyes when he rinsed me down after the Earl incident. The way he watches me every time I'm around the school or within sight of the gatehouse. The bulge I can feel *right now* against my belly.

"Tell me you're this nice to everyone," I say.

"Everyone but you."

"You're being nice to me now."

"I'm a sucker for damaged goods."

I should be offended, but I'm enjoying being this close to his body too much to put the energy into it. "Why?"

"I have issues."

"What kind of issues?"

"We're talking about you."

"Thank God. I hate it when men are emotionally healthy and open to sharing their own struggles. That's so much harder to resist."

Suddenly, my back is against the wall, and Flint is staring directly into my eyes. How did I not notice before that his are brown? They're a light brown. Flecked with gold. I thought they were hazel. Do they change in the light? I'll have to watch and see.

"This isn't happening," he says, low and tight.

"I'm aware."

"No matter how much I can't get you out of my head."

I haven't had a man-induced orgasm in at least three years. At least. But I just felt a quake of *something* in my clit. "We shouldn't see each other."

"Stop coming to the school."

"I'm making up for six years of *not* doing the things I should've done."

He growls.

Growls.

And there's that tiny earthquake in my clit again, prompting some action in my vagina too.

"I wish you'd been a crotchety old man who yelled at everyone to get off his lawn."

"I wish you'd been a selfish opportunist wanting to subdivide the ranch and put crappy houses on it."

"We can't do this."

At least, that's what my mouth *says.*

What my mouth *does*, though, is a different story.

Because when Flint crashes his lips on mine, I am ready, willing, and 100 percent on board.

My eyes drift closed, and I hook a leg around the back of his thigh. He tilts his hips harder against my stomach, letting me feel every inch of his erection while he destroys me with a deep, hard, unrelenting kiss.

And I love it.

I love matching every stroke of his tongue.

I love the desperate grunts in the back of his throat.

I love the feel of his thick, rough beard against my skin.

I love the way his hair is long enough for me to grip it in my hands, and I love the way I feel *wanted.*

Needed.

Desired.

As a woman. As a *human.*

This is no simple kiss. It's filling every wish I've had for someone to *want me* for longer than I care to admit.

And I didn't earn this kiss by sacrificing who I am. What I want. By putting someone else's dreams ahead of mine.

I *earned* it by being a pain in his ass. By being *me*. By refusing to back down from what I believe in and what matters to *me*.

I whimper as he grips my hair, too, lifting my leg higher around his and angling to feel him against my clit.

This.

God, I want this.

"Coach?" someone calls.

He jerks away as I gasp and jerk back myself, banging my head into the brick wall of the school building.

The school building.

Oh my God.

Anyone could've seen this.

A student. A teacher. A parent.

Anyone.

And any one of them could tell Junie.

I'm at my daughter's school, kissing one of her teachers, and I *cannot.*

I can't.

I pat my pockets like I'm looking for my phone, the sting in my eyes suddenly too much to bear. "Thank you," I stutter. "For your discretion. For Junie's sake. I—I need to go."

"Maisey—"

"I need to go," I repeat as I dash toward the back door, which is propped open for me so I can continue helping set up homecoming decorations for the kids for this weekend.

This can't happen again.

It can't.

No matter how much I want it to.

Chapter 17

Flint

The worst thing about having a best friend is that he can see right through your bullshit.

Second worst is that my particular best friend thinks everything's hilarious.

"Ah, the look of Flint Jackson in the throes of obsession is a beautiful thing," he says with a smirk as I take the seat next to him at my favorite table at Iron Moose after soccer practice.

Light's fixed overhead.

Maisey was here.

"I'm not obsessed," I mutter.

I am 100 percent obsessed.

Kory cackles.

I consider knocking him out of his chair.

He scoots just out of reach.

"You wanna talk, or you wanna take out all of your frustrations on a meatloaf?" he asks.

"Not frustrated."

"Gotta get out of the river if you want help, my friend."

"The river? What the hell are you talking about?"

"The river. Da Nile." He cracks up.

I close my eyes and breathe deep through my nose. "Another day, another woman," I tell myself out loud. "This will pass."

"Oh, hey, did I tell you I had a stretch of fence come down last week?" He leans back and tips his cowboy hat back on his head.

"Fuck. When do I need to show up?"

"You don't. Your landlady came by and already helped me patch it."

My brain processes the words.

But something deeper processes the relief.

Utter. Fucking. Relief.

She doesn't even know she's helping *me*, but *she is*.

"Heard she took care of the Hancocks' chicken coop too. Does the woman sleep? Does she? Because I know she's taking her kid to school and picking her up every day, and she's at every soccer game, and she's the PTA superstar, and she's making progress on shit on her own land . . . It's like she's you but a single mom doing even more than you do."

I'm supposed to reply to that, but I can't find a single thing to say.

So instead, I flag down George, the owner, and order a beer and a meatloaf.

For the past six years, I've been *the guy*. The one everyone in town calls when they need something.

And now, Kory's telling me Maisey's fixing all the things that I would've normally gotten a call to come help with.

And she's not doing stuff that takes away from the local electrician or plumber or painters or roofers. She's helping with the projects they can't get to for months, for the families that can't afford to wait or can't afford to pay for repairs.

"Tony's kickin' back up there at his palace in the sky, getting a big ole hootin' chuckle out of watching you lose your shit over a woman who beats you at your own game," Kory says.

"What the fuck does that mean?"

"Means you volunteer everywhere because you never got over feeling like the bad kid for running away from home when it was the only option you had left to take care of yourself, and now you're still afraid nobody will like you if you don't bend over backward to try to make them, and here she is, moving to town after a big, ugly, public divorce, with an angry teenager, doing the exact same."

Should've gone home.

Should've. Fucking. Gone. Home.

But I was afraid that was where Maisey was going, and I didn't want to follow her, or have her follow me.

"I don't do it so people will like me," I say to Kory. "I do it because it's the right thing to do."

"Is it?"

I stare at him.

"You like coaching soccer?" he asks.

I twitch.

I actually fucking *twitch*.

He lifts his massive hands and spreads them in a *Don't shoot the messenger* gesture. "Community isn't built by a single man. You step back, someone's gonna fill your shoes. Will they do it your way? Nope. Will they do it better or worse? No telling. But will the kids get to play? Yep. Yep, they will. You don't show up to help patch a chicken coop *that doesn't even have chickens in it right now*, world won't end. Skip helping on someone's moving day, the moving still gets done because there's more of us around to do stuff. You get crankier and crankier and resent your friends because you don't *let* yourself say no to anything, that's on you, man. That's on you. All I'm saying."

George puts a beer in front of me while I stare out the window at the bluffs. "How about that light?" he says. "Maisey knew exactly what was wrong with it, and it hasn't blown a bulb for us since she fixed it right up."

I wince. "Sorry I couldn't—*ow*."

"Flint says he loves it," Kory tells George, like he didn't just kick me in the shin with his damn boot. "And he says thank you."

George grins.

Kory grins back, but his is full of *Told you so*.

"Why do I pick asshole friends?" I mutter to him.

"Being honest isn't being an asshole, and you know it. Bigger question is why I keep putting up with you, Mr. Martyr."

I slink back in my chair.

Considering he doesn't need me to fix his damn fences anymore, that's a really good question.

"It's because you're a good dude," Kory stage-whispers. "Sometimes, all people want in a friend is someone to shoot the shit with over a beer."

Hell.

That was my favorite part of hanging out with Tony.

Didn't mind helping with the upkeep of the ranch. I was *using* Wit's End. Only right to help keep it in good shape.

"You remember when Tony bought that box of lamp pulls?" I ask Kory.

And yeah, I waited until he was taking a sip of his own beer.

Means I'm wearing it now.

Worth it.

"You ever talk to him about those?" I ask while he wipes his face.

"If the old man didn't talk to you about them, I'm not either."

"Was he . . . he wasn't lonely, was he?"

"He was." All the smirk is gone from Kory's face. "He was fucking lonely, and he was fucking up in his own head, and he spent his whole life trying to feel like he was worthy when all he really needed to do was look around and see that he had friends who loved him and didn't care who he loved. Sound familiar?"

Not so sure I can stomach that beer after all. "Yeah," I mutter.

"That why you're asking, or were you planning to tell me you know where Tony hid those artful lamp pulls?"

"I don't like having a crush on a woman I can't date."

He rolls his eyes so hard, they should've gotten stuck in the back of his head. "Who says you can't date her?"

"I do. She does. Her daughter does. *You* do."

"Fine. There you have it, then. Can't date her. So just get over her."

Nope.

Definitely not stomaching that beer.

Kory heaves a sigh and leans his chair back on its back two legs. "Since you're clearly not interested in my advice about *not* dating her, and since she's way more than even I gave her credit for when she got here, let's try this the other way. You can't go through life without getting hurt, my friend. So you choose. Do you take the risk that it's worth it, or do you keep hiding behind all the lies you've told yourself about being happy alone and not deserving someone to love you?"

I don't bother denying any part of his analysis of me.

He's not wrong.

"You let Maisey and June know you—the real you—and neither one of them will be able to argue that you're bad for anyone. So make up your mind. If you're in, go all in. If you're out, quit being a grumpy asshole and go back to just being an overcommitted crank."

I grunt. "Where's your love-muffin?"

He beams. "Chicago. Got a special invitation to a big show. And don't think for a minute that me pulling out my phone to show you pictures means you're off the hook and I'm forgetting about this conversation."

"Sure."

"Also, your landlady and I jointly ordered, like, six cords of wood, and she mentioned making sure her tenant had enough, since you're ridiculous and insist on renting a place heated only with a woodburning stove all winter like we live in the Dark Ages. So you can rest easy that you won't need to stock up on her behalf. Oooh, look. Have I shown you this outfit yet? He spent *forty-six days* tweaking it and driving me up the wall, but how awesome are those sequins?"

I pick up my beer and pretend I'm drinking it while Kory flips through photos.

I get it.

I hear him.

The problem with me and Maisey? It's me. It's all in my head. And the part that isn't me isn't something I can fix.

She's not wrong to put June first.

She's not wrong to put *herself* first.

So I'll pull my head out of my ass, accept that I have the world's largest crush on the world's most unavailable woman, and that if I still feel the same way about her in two years that I do today, *then* maybe I'll act on it.

But not a day before.

If I survive that long.

Chapter 18

Maisey

The day I decided to divorce Dean, I also decided I would never, ever, *ever* let another man into my head, my heart, or my vagina.

The day my mom was arrested, I realized just how much I needed to straighten out my priorities with Junie too.

So dealing with Flint Jackson and his constant presence in my life, in my head, and in my dirty fantasies is *not* convenient. He's not my top priority. He's not even in my top dozen priorities.

So I'm keeping him at arm's length for Junie, and it's a sacrifice I'll happily make. Especially knowing it's probably best for me long term anyway.

Even if it's completely wearing me down to be back here, at the edge of the soccer field on a cold Saturday morning, watching as he huddles with the group of kids during a time-out in a very tight first playoff game in late October.

"How's the dog situation?" I ask Charlotte, who's beside me with a steaming coffee tumbler.

She huffs. "As expected, my ex thinks the dog's better at my house, which means I now have five children to manage. But the kids love her. They really do. So it's . . . just one more thing that one day will pay off when they spend all of their holidays with me instead of him."

I lift a brow.

"I'm so tired, Maisey," she whispers. "So fucking tired."

I loop an arm through hers. "If you ever need to drop the pup off for doggy day care, I have this giant fenced-in part of my yard and enough cow patties left over that it won't matter if there's a pile of dog poo in the midst of it."

"Do you know what I want?" she says.

"A week-long spa trip where you come home to a housekeeper and a chef?"

She laughs, but it's strained. "I want to ride a horse. Just for, like, fifteen minutes. Until my thighs get chapped and I remember why I gave it up. But book club the other day? When Libby was talking about learning how to refinish her cabinets to freshen everything up once her twins leave for college? And Opal saying she'd always wanted to learn to play the flute? And Regina saying she could soak all day in the bathtub doing logic puzzles, because she's a freak but we love her?"

"Mm-hmm," I say.

"I want to ride a freaking horse."

"I'll call Kory next door to me. I'm *positive* he'd let you ride a horse."

"But then I'd owe him a favor."

"One, I doubt it. And two, he can cash it in with me."

"I wish—" She stops herself, shaking her head.

"You wish?" I prompt.

Her nose wrinkles, and then she makes a face that I'm starting to recognize after hours and hours working with her on PTA things and soccer-team things and book club.

Discussion closed.

"I hate playing this team," she says, sealing that we're moving on. "It was Coach Jackson's high school before he came back here a few years ago."

"Isn't your oldest a freshman?" I reply.

Far easier to deflect than to discuss Flint.

"Yes, but my niece graduated last year after four years of soccer, and my kids *loved* to watch her." She wrinkles her nose. "Just look at them. Half of them are making eyes at him, and the other half look like they want to murder him."

I peer across the soccer field to the area where the parents for the other team are standing.

And I think I can see what she's talking about. "Why?" I ask before I can help myself.

I want to know.

God help me, I want to know. And I hope it's bad so that he can go permanently on the *bad guy* list in my head, and then I can forget that he kisses like he invented kissing, and that his body feels like it was made to mold against mine, and that he spent an entire day cleaning out my uncle's sex-toy collection before my daughter could find it.

And she *did* find the root cellar.

Yesterday, in fact.

Thank *God* she came running to tell me. When I was her age, running to tell my mom I'd found the perfect spot for a secret clubhouse would *not* have crossed my mind.

Charlotte takes an audible sip of her coffee, then sighs happily. "He left after a bad breakup with the PTA president."

"*What?*"

"Mm-hmm. He noticed her son was falling asleep all the time in class, so he did what he does: reached out, tried to solve it, found out the mom had just quietly signed divorce papers, did that thing where he tells her he only screws around, but then found out . . . things . . . about her ex, got worried, but did that thing he does where he says he's not getting involved, even though he clearly was, and things got ugly."

I gape at her.

"The husband was into some illegal things," she whispers. "I know nothing. Nothing at all."

"You know *everything*."

"It's really not an interesting story."

"Charlotte."

"Wow, you're really interested in small-town gossip."

I take a gulp of my own coffee, which is way too hot, and scald everything from my tongue to the back of my throat. I rasp out a cough, my eyes watering.

Charlotte smirks over her own delicate sip.

"If there's reason to be concerned about my tenant—" I start.

"No one's buying that. And I saw how he looked at you when you pulled up with June."

"I'm not dating."

"And he doesn't date students' parents. Anymore."

"That's completely irrelevant."

"You brought it up."

"So we're in enemy territory, even though we're at home," I say, desperately trying to get this train back on a track where I can find out everything I want to know without actually asking.

And that I don't want to know.

But do.

But am happy to pretend I don't.

"Flint lost his job there. It was billed as a voluntary resignation, but Opal said it wasn't. Not really. Since the divorce happened so quietly— the husband was always out of town to begin with—everyone thought he was the *reason* they got divorced. Then parents of other kids that he'd been working with after school started questioning his intentions and why he cared so much about *their* kids and what he was teaching them, and if he was playing favorites, and basically a million other things that really boiled down to it turning into a crowd with pitchforks who forgot why they had them in the first place but were determined to burn it all down, and the rest is history."

I stare out at the field as our kids trot back out.

Junie's played exactly two games this season, so I did get to see her play once.

I won't today. But she's still out there managing water bottles and towels and balls without complaint.

And she's doing more than that too. All season, she's been the team's biggest cheerleader from her spot on the sidelines. Today, though, she took it one step further and actually bumped Flint out of the way at halftime, grabbed his whiteboard and markers, and apparently gave orders on a play.

The team scored two minutes into the second half.

I sip my coffee again, slower this time, and keep my eyes trained on the action on the field while I ask my next question, which I *should not* ask and technically already have an answer to, but Charlotte knows things.

If there's more than what I've been told, she'll tell me. "Why's it so important to him to watch out for the kids falling between the cracks?"

"He *was* one of those kids."

I wince, even knowing that part was coming. Junie could've been one of those kids. I still go to bed half the nights of the week worried that she hates me, even when I know she's been happier here where what my mom did hasn't impacted her social life.

I'm seeing her less and less because she's hanging out more and more with her classmates.

And for the record, yes, I know all their parents and what she and her friends do while she's gone.

"Was he?" I ask like this is new information. I want to understand more, even though I know I shouldn't.

"There's a lot I don't know," Charlotte murmurs as voices swell around us. The other team is charging down the field toward our goaltender, and that makes all of us nervous. "The most I've ever gotten out of Opal is that his father was toxic, his mother bent over backward to try to get his dad to love her, and by the time Flint was, like, twelve, his father was never home, his mom was in a pretty bad state of depression, and he was having to do things like shop for groceries and sneak money to buy himself clothes. He ran away when he was sixteen. Opal found him and brought him here to finish out high school. He had remarkably good grades through all of it, so the town put together a scholarship fund for him."

I try to make the surprised sound that slips out of me pass for a hiccup.

I did *not* know that part.

"But I think it embarrassed him," she adds, ignoring my not-so-subtle stifled gasp of surprise, "because he didn't want to come back once he got his degree. At least, not until everything fell apart at his last school."

She stands straighter. *"Run, Abigail, run! You can stop him!"*

Our team is bearing down on the other team, converging as their player lines up to take a shot.

I go up on my tiptoes and watch as the ball sails toward the net.

At the last second, while all of us hold our breath, our goaltender dives and deflects the ball.

All of us erupt in cheers while Charlotte's daughter claims the ball and dribbles it back up the field.

"Way to go, Viv!" Charlotte cries.

We all whistle and cheer and yell, then groan together as the other team steals the ball again and kicks it out of bounds.

"So, anyway, he's never been the settling down type," Charlotte says to me. "I don't know a lot about his dating history in college and his early years of teaching, but I know if he had a choice between running a camp for kids who needed a solid adult in their lives or having a family of his own, he'd pick the camp for kids any day."

I study her. "That's a lot of detail for not knowing a lot of details."

"You seem interested."

"Just like knowing who's living down my driveway and teaching my kid."

"Sure." She lifts a shoulder under her oversize Hell's Bells Demons hoodie, which is one more thing I love about Charlotte.

She might be an attorney by day, but she's all in with comfy clothes on the weekends.

"I don't *want* to be interested," I mutter.

"Safe choice."

"I missed a lot of Junie's—" I don't finish.

Instead, something drives straight into the side of my face.

Stars dance in my vision.

I hear people gasping around me.

There's something wet and hot soaking through my own Hell's Bells Demons sweatshirt.

And I'm on my ass on the wet ground, taking entirely too long to process that I've spilled my coffee all over myself.

Bodies crowd around me.

"Mom!" Junie yells.

"I'm okay," I gasp out. "I'm okay."

"Is there a medic?" Charlotte calls above me.

"*I'm okay,*" I repeat.

"Mom!" Junie yells again.

Her voice is tinny but close.

Oof.

That hurt.

Actually, are my brains swimming right now?

And why do I have three hands on my left arm?

"Back up, give her space," Charlotte orders.

"I'm okay," I try one more time, but actually, I'm not sure I am.

Chapter 19

Flint

"Is she sleeping?" I ask Charlotte roughly twelve hours after the kick of doom.

That's what the kids are calling it.

The kick of doom. The penalty of bad. The murder ball.

All the phrases that they used to cheer June up when we joined her and Maisey and Charlotte at the hospital after we pulled off a miracle and won our first playoff game.

We were swiftly informed we needed to remove ourselves from the premises for being too rowdy.

So now I'm back at Maisey's house, hat in hand, my heart in overdrive, asking if Maisey's still okay.

"She's in her room. And no, you can't go see her there."

"I don't—"

"Want to make her life more complicated?" Charlotte supplies.

I sigh.

My heart's still operating like a piston on a runaway train. I don't know if Charlotte's judging or trying to see through me. I shouldn't be here, but I can't be anywhere else.

"You have a type, don't you?" she murmurs.

"I'd check on any kid's parent who took a ball to the head like that."

"You still have a type."

I do.

I like the wounded, unavailable ones.

But that's not Maisey.

Not entirely.

She's *more*, and I can't fight it the way I need to.

"Coach Jackson?" June steps into the foyer under the chandelier that Tony used to claim he'd made from antlers he found himself. "Did you run out of firewood or get a clogged toilet? Sorry. You'll have to handle those yourself for the next few days."

Charlotte sucks her lips in.

"I'm checking in on your mom," I tell the teenager.

"She has me. She's fine."

"If *you* need someone—"

"I just talked to my dad and my grandma. They're both on the way. Thank you."

I'm just off my game enough that I almost miss the subtle hint that she's lying. And if she'd left it at *My dad's on his way*, I might've believed it.

Definitely would've had some fun body twitches while I believed it too.

Or maybe I'm *hoping* she's lying.

Does Maisey have a good relationship with June's paternal grandmother? I haven't heard anything about her.

"Your mom's mom is on the way?" I ask.

"Yep."

I frown at her.

She doesn't budge in her story. "Isn't she, Ms. Charlotte?"

Charlotte looks at me, then back at June. "Was that your mom calling for me? I think it was. Hold that thought, kiddo. I'll be right back."

She dashes deeper into the house.

June lets her pass, then takes a wide-legged stance in the entryway from the foyer into the living room, her expression telegraphing that she doesn't appreciate being abandoned by the only other adult in the house.

I lift my brows at June. "You're pissed at me."

Her eyes narrow.

I slouch and lean in the doorway, going for nonthreatening, which is a challenge but necessary. "Not gonna flunk you or tell you that you can't be our extra on the team if you don't like me. Talk to me. What's on your mind?"

"I don't like it when you come to my house. My teachers never come to my house."

Fair. I wouldn't have liked it when I was her age either. "I live in your gatehouse. Used to come up here to hang out with your great-uncle all the time."

"Did you look at him the way you look at my mom?"

I have a love-hate relationship with teenage brains. So much potential. So much intelligence. And when we want them to aim it at things like math and learning to drive and mastering the art of power tools, instead, they get up in our business. "Usually worse. He thought he was handy around the house, but unlike your mom, he tended to cause more problems than he fixed."

"Abigail says she saw you two hiding out while you were supposed to be coaching practice a few weeks ago."

Fuck. Also, *phew.* I have zero doubt if they'd seen us kissing, this story would be bigger than *Someone saw you two hiding.* "Ran into her right after she got off a call with your grandmother and wasn't too happy about me overhearing any part of it."

June freezes, and her dark eyes go momentarily wide, then narrow into tiny slits.

I lift my hands. "Not gonna do anything to hurt either one of you," I say quietly.

Charlotte has to be listening in.

Not a soul in town that wouldn't be.

"How would that hurt me?" June's coiled tighter than a rattlesnake facing a honey badger.

"I ever tell you I was about your age when I moved here and had to finish high school in a new place too?"

"Back in the Stone Age."

I almost smile. For all that teenagers can be brilliant, they're also unoriginal at times. "Not quite the same—I'll give you that. Had to carve my letters to my old friends in stone and roll them up the hill to the chiseled-message horse-and-buggy delivery service back then. None of this newfangled email and text technology twenty years ago."

She rolls her eyes.

Fair. We had technology when I was her age, and I think she knows it.

"Moved in with my aunt, actually," I add quietly. "And my parents never called to check on me either."

"I just told you, my dad's on his way."

"Took me ten years to realize that just because I couldn't count on my parents, it didn't mean I couldn't count on my friends."

"So you're slow. That doesn't prove anything."

She's quiet at school. Does her work, turns it in, gets good grades.

At practices and games, she's gotten bolder with speaking up when she thinks I'm calling the wrong play or putting in the wrong player.

She runs with the team. Helps when I ask her to. Doesn't complain about refilling water bottles or cleaning the same balls over and over again. And all season, she's been a quiet presence behind the bench, telling everyone else they've done a good job, or that everyone makes mistakes, or that she knows they can shake it off and get back in there, or what an opponent's weakness is.

She's not quiet in the cafeteria. I see her laughing with a small group of friends. Hear her telling stories or watch her flirting with a boy here or there when she passes in the halls sometimes.

But here?

Here, I'm on her territory.

Here, I get to follow her rules.

Teenager or not, this is her home, and she deserves to feel safe here.

I lift a shoulder. "I'd check on any parent who got hurt at one of our games."

"I can vouch for that," Charlotte says from the living room.

I want to go in and see what's changed. If Maisey's removed the dark leather furniture and the moose head mounted over the fireplace that weren't included in the estate sale, or if she's left a lot of Tony in there.

If the wool blanket he got on a trip to Scotland seventeen years ago is still there, or if she put it in a giveaway pile.

If she figured out there's a secret compartment in the end table closest to the kitchen and that if you hit it just right, you'll find a stash of butterscotch candies.

Or if she knew that all along, or if she knew it once upon a time when she'd visit and has forgotten now.

"And I'd check on any of my kids whose parents got hurt, or any of my students or players who got hurt," I tell June. "So if you need anything while your mom's recovering, I'm right down the driveway."

"Mom's fine. I'm fine. We're all fine. Thank you. You can go."

The dismissive phrase is so familiar that my gut aches in a way it hasn't in years.

This is why I don't get involved with parents.

It's messy in ways that dating women without kids isn't. But that dating pool is shallow in these parts.

Which isn't the point.

Point is, I'm ridiculously attracted to Maisey, and I can't be.

Not until June's not my student or player anymore.

I slowly straighten. "Offer stands no matter what. Glad your mom's doing okay. Glad you are too."

She looks pointedly at the door, so I go.

Not happy about it, but I go.

I want to see Maisey. I want to know she's okay. I want to tell her I'm kicking someone off the team so June can play next game.

I want—

I just want.

I want in ways I haven't in years.

And I don't know what to do with that.

Chapter 20

Maisey

The day after the soccer game of mortification, I'm up early. My head aches slightly but not so badly that popping an over-the-counter painkiller can't take care of it. The bruise on my face is fine, so long as I don't accidentally bump it.

And I have boundless restless energy.

I want to *do* something.

Go out and *be* somewhere.

Anywhere but here, with Flint right down the driveway and his desires for the ranch looming in my head anytime I look out the window at the sun rising over the bluffs and lighting the clouds with a brilliant pink-and-orange show.

I have my coffee while I research something that's been niggling the back of my brain but hit stronger after talking to Charlotte at the game yesterday, fix myself pancakes and eggs and a bowl of fruit, and check on Junie seven million times before I finally wake her at eleven o'clock.

Or try, anyway. "Junie-June," I whisper. "Wake up. Wanna go shopping and get lunch in town?"

She mumbles in her sleep and rolls away from me.

I plop down at the edge of her bed in the bedroom that she's some-how made filthy despite telling me she feels like she hasn't settled into it yet.

We've hung her favorite pictures and drawings on her wall. We ran-domly stopped at an antique mall on our way home from an away game a few weeks ago, just to look around since she was so charmed by the old covered wagon sitting out front when we drove past, and we found hidden treasures of a chest of drawers and an old wooden shelf that we brought home and refinished for her room. Her bed has updated gray sheets and a new blue damask comforter. Three of her favorite old stuffies, Mr. Lion, Mr. Turtle, and Ms. Giraffe, are all on the unused pillow in her queen-size bed. Her low antique bookshelf is covered with team photos and trophies from her past eight years of playing soccer.

And her floor is a hazardous-waste site.

"C'mon, sleepyhead. Wakey-wakey," I sing.

"Ungghh."

"No plans for us today. We can do whatever you want. Doesn't have to be lunch and shopping."

"Mph."

"Where did you get all these clothes? I feel like I only bought you half this many. And I had no idea you had enough shoes to fill a storage unit."

"Sleep," she grunts.

"But we can do *anything* today."

"Want sleep."

I eyeball the phone tucked half-under her spare pillow, and then I stifle a sigh.

I don't want to take her phone away from her every night, but I know she'll sleep better if I do. Or maybe she'd be like this anyway after adjusting to a new school and sitting on the sidelines most of the soccer season.

"If you could build your perfect *awake* day, what would it be?" I ask.

One brown eyeball slides open and peers at me. "Anything?"

This is a trap. "I'm curious what you want to do."

She stares a beat longer, and for three seconds, she's six again. Open and vulnerable and trusting that whatever she wants, I can make happen.

"I want to get a dog," she says.

"Like a circus dog?"

"Mom."

I bite back the questions. *Can you care for a dog? What would the dog do while you're at school? Do you know what kind of shots and medicine dogs need? A big dog or a little dog? Will you train the dog? Will it sleep with you? Who'll take care of it?*

God, I feel for Charlotte so much right now. When she told us her ex was getting a dog for the kids, we all knew.

We knew.

We knew he'd drop it with her, even though she doesn't have room for *one more thing*, because that's what they always do.

And now Junie wants a dog, which is *one more thing*, but for her, I'll do anything.

"I thought you didn't like dogs," I say quietly, which is the truth. She had a bad experience when she was little and hasn't asked for one, or even talked about dogs, ever since.

She grunts.

I put a hand on the blanket covering her calf. "What kind of dog?"

"Never mind."

"Junie. C'mon. What kind of dog would you get?"

"Not practical," she mutters.

"What's not practical about a dog?"

"College."

Hello, knife. That's my heart you're getting a little too close to.

She's right.

If I get her a dog, what happens when she goes to college in two years?

Do I keep the dog? Does she take the dog with her? Could I handle losing a dog *and* my daughter? Could I handle keeping her dog and making her separate herself from it?

Oh God.

She's leaving me. I have literal *months* left. Like, *twenty*. Maybe *twenty* months left with my daughter before she leaves me.

"Stop it," she mumbles.

"Stop what?"

"Panicking."

I'd say I'm not panicking, but my eyes are stinging and my voice is already high pitched and I'm having a massive anxiety attack because I'll be alone in less than two years.

Junie would take the dog. She would absolutely take the dog. I couldn't keep her dog and not let her play with it and see it every day.

We don't even *have* the dog, and I'm panicking at the idea of both of them being gone.

"Are you getting up?" I ask.

"No."

"Okay. Okay. If you change your mind, I'll be out in the bunkhouse working on a few things. Call if you need me."

She doesn't answer.

She's already asleep again.

Maybe faking it. Maybe not.

"I feel a lot better today, and I won't push myself or hurt myself," I whisper quietly as I rise off her bed.

Her shoulders melt just a little more into her mattress.

Swear I'm not imagining that.

And I suddenly freeze at one more thought that I hadn't considered about her sleeping in so late.

Was she up checking on me all night?

Did she fall asleep *at all* before dawn?

I should've let Charlotte stay over when she offered.

"Love you, Junie," I whisper. "Thanks for being the best Juniper on the planet."

"Only Juniper," she mutters.

"Damn right."

I toss on work clothes and head out the door and across the scraggly field toward the bunkhouse. My phone's in my pocket. It's borderline chilly, and I heard one of the parents say yesterday that we could get our first snowfall sometime in the next couple of weeks.

Junie's right.

We should get a dog. One dog for her now, and when she goes to college, I'll get another dog to keep me company.

Or a cat. Or maybe a talking bird.

Or maybe you'll have guests on the ranch after fixing it up to its full potential, the voice I've been ignoring all morning whispers in my head.

And that's why I'm at the bunkhouse.

I need to see it. Envision what it could be. Figure out which walls are load bearing. What the plumbing situation really is out here. Heating too.

Can I make this work?

Can I do it?

Could I turn the bunkhouse into a retreat center for women just like me?

For women like Charlotte and Regina who have been so consumed with taking care of their families that they've lost the rest of their identities to motherhood?

For women like Opal who clearly have stories of pain and hurt in their past, too, but don't talk as openly about it?

Could I fix up the barn and keep a couple of horses here?

Run shop classes?

Hire artists to help women just like me, like Charlotte and Regina and Opal, sample painting and pottery and knitting to see if those are things that could give us joy?

I'm measuring a wall in the galley kitchen when I sense someone behind me. "That was quick," I say to Junie. "Missed me already?"

"You're okay," a deep, rumbling voice answers.

I spin, momentarily jarring my head a little too much, and then my panties go wet.

Flint's standing in the doorway to the long hall, his eyes tired but intense while he searches my face.

"You're okay?" he repeats, this time as a question.

"Just a little soccer ball to the head. I'm fine."

He nods once.

I watch him while he watches me right back.

He shouldn't be here. I got the vibes off Junie last night that she didn't like him here. She doesn't *know* we had a moment of bad judgment, but she's not stupid.

She knows there's a level of attraction here, and she doesn't like it.

Flint's gaze shifts down my body. He's not ogling. It's like he's taking inventory. Arms? Check. Shoulders? Check. Chest?

There's no amount of self-talk in the world that could convince me he's simply making sure I don't have a gaping wound anywhere.

His eyes darken. His mouth tightens. His *biceps* tighten, and I watch him curl his fingers into fists like he's trying to keep himself from reaching for me.

I self-consciously curl my own fingers into a fist, then shake them out while he continues to let his gaze drop lower on my body.

"June's light was on all night." His voice is husky, and I don't know if it's exhaustion from watching the house all night himself or if it's desire. "I promised her I'd leave you alone, and I swear, I'm not here because I want to break my word, but I was . . . I was worried. About both of you. I didn't think she'd come get me if anything was wrong, and I hate that, so I just—I needed to see for myself that you're up and about and okay today."

When his gaze lands on my hips, then lower, I have every belief that it's desire.

Not simple concern for a fellow human but an all-consuming, desperate need.

But he doesn't come any closer. He stays in the doorway, clearly doing his best to balance respecting his promise to my daughter while also fulfilling his own clear need to make sure I'm recovering.

And possibly ogle me.

"She okay too?" he asks.

I nod.

Swallow.

Nod again. "Y-yes."

His hooded eyes lift to mine, sharp and focused.

I clear my throat. "She's sleeping. Thank you. And Charlotte told me you stopped by. I'm fine. Truly. Not the worst I've ever had. Once on set, Dean and our roofing guy were tossing off old shingles right over the front door, and the sign wasn't up inside warning us that things were falling like it was supposed to be, so I walked out and right into a rain shower of bad. Tetanus shots are fun, let me tell you. But I was okay then too. The nail in that one shingle missed the crucial veins and arteries, and really, it was barely a nick."

"Saw that episode," he says quietly.

I fiddle with the tape measure, pulling it out and letting it snap back in. "So thank you. I'm fine."

"You've said that."

"You keep looking at me like you don't believe me."

"I—"

He cuts himself off with a growl, but I swear I hear what he wanted to say anyway.

I'm here because I want to tear your clothes off and inspect every inch of your body for myself, then kiss where it hurts, then kiss where it doesn't hurt, and then treat your body like my own personal playground of pleasure.

I shiver and shift my stance to subtly press my legs together against the throb growing between my thighs.

"Last time I dated one of my student's parents, it didn't end well," he says gruffly.

"I heard."

"And June doesn't want me here."

"She's had a rough year or six."

"But I can't stop thinking about you."

"I'm very think-aboutable," I joke.

He doesn't laugh. Doesn't snicker. There's no amused twitch of his lips under that thick dark-copper beard.

Just golden-brown eyes telegraphing that yes. *Yes.* I'm very think-aboutable.

Much like he, too, is very think-aboutable.

I thought about him in the shower last night after I heard his voice rumbling through my house, when Junie wouldn't let him enter.

My shower has *seen things*.

And I would do them again, because *oh my holy God*, is this man talented in my imagination.

I spin and point to the ancient refrigerator in the corner. "It occurred to me that Uncle Tony would've loved the idea of converting the bunkhouse to an artists' retreat, and whatever liability insurance I'd need for that should also cover letting you use a small corner of the ranch for giving the kids a place to practice being ranch hands and learn how to do practical things. Out here, for the retreat, we could update the kitchen to turn it into something more workable. Then redo the plumbing and separate the main bunk room into private suites. Just basic bedrooms with functional bathrooms. The secondary bunk room could be a workroom. Maybe put in extra windows, and then have anyone who needs to be inspired by nature. Writers. Painters. Weavers. Artists. Or anyone who needs—"

I cut myself off with a small gasp as he places a large, warm hand on my shoulder. "Maisey."

"—an escape," I finish on a whisper. "A safe escape to explore who they are."

"You're exploring who you are."

"We all should."

"I want to explore with you."

"We—"

"Shouldn't," he cuts me off again. "Shouldn't. But shouldn't isn't *can't*."

"Shouldn't is still *shouldn't*."

"I wouldn't take this kind of risk with anyone else." His voice. *God*, I love that rumble. "But you—I thought I'd despise you, and instead, you're so much more than I expected."

"Junie—"

He jerks his head to look over his shoulder, like he thinks I'm saying she's *here*.

"—doesn't want me to date," I finish.

"I don't want to hurt her, Maisey. I swear to God, I don't. I get it. *I get it*. But I have never—*ever*—in my life put my own needs and wants in front of a teenager. And this would be so much easier if I thought I was bad for either of you. But I don't. *I don't want to hurt you*. And it's fucking killing me to know I want to do something good and she doesn't trust me. And it's killing me that I want to do something good for *you* and she doesn't trust me."

God.

He knows exactly what to say.

He understands.

And knowing how much he worries about her makes me like him even more.

"I don't know what her *needs* are and what her *wants* are, and I don't know if it matters," I whisper. "I just know I *want* you, and I feel like I shouldn't, even though it's also the most natural thing in the world to like someone who *gets it*."

His head swivels back until he's looking at me. And then his lips curve up in a naughty, dirty, promising smile. "So maybe we just fuck for a while."

That should not make my vagina sit up and cheer. Or my brain short-circuit with lust. Or my panties go so wet that I can smell my own arousal.

"You know there's no such thing as working someone out of your system," I whisper.

He angles closer, our bodies separated by the width of a feather, and *yes yes yes*, I want him closer, but *no no no*, I've made a thousand excuses to my daughter about why I won't do this no matter how much I want to.

My brain is so scrambled anytime I'm near him. And as much as my heart and brain whisper *Junie first*, sometimes they also ask, *Who do you become when you never put yourself first?*

I did that with Dean.

He was first, and what did I become?

But I'm responsible for Junie. She's my *daughter*.

Where do her wants end and my needs begin? Or are they her needs and my wants?

I don't know.

"I can't in good conscience say that we should test that theory, but God, do I want to," he says.

Yes yes yes, my clit is chanting. My nipples are hard and aching, and I can't remember the last time a man looking at me made me this hot and wet.

Yet here we are, and it's taking every ounce of self-control I possess and more to not jump him. "And I can't in good conscience say that you would have to be terrible in bed for us to prove that theory wrong, and I have to warn you, novelty turns me on. So you'd have to be *extra* bad."

"I could be fast. Right now, I'm pretty sure I wouldn't last three seconds in your hot, wet pussy."

The idea that he'd be done before we even started should be a turnoff.

Instead, the idea of my own raw sexual power making him lose control and talk dirty to me is making my breath come in small gasps, and I very, very much want to slip my hand into my pants and finger-fuck myself.

"That would be very disappointing," I manage to choke out.

"I'm very clumsy with my fingers too."

One, he's lying. Two, *yes*. Yes, I'd very much like to feel his hands and his fingers on my body. Stroking my breasts. Pinching my nipples. Teasing my clit. Thrusting in my vagina.

Making me come.

Over. And over. And over again.

"If we do this—" I start.

His eyes flare wide for a hot second, and then his pupils dilate, until I feel like I could see the universe in their depths if I looked closely enough. His hand moves to my waist, and then I'm backed against the chipped green countertop. "If we do this?" he prompts.

His erection is pressing against my lower belly, and that is *not* where I want it.

I want it lower.

Between my thighs.

"If we do this"—I repeat, arching my hips into him and making him swear out a soft oath—"it's one time only. When Junie isn't here. There's no dinner. There's no talking. There's no staying. There's no acknowledging this ever happened in public."

His fingers are digging into my hips while we rock our bodies against each other through the clothes. "Agreed."

"And you have to leave. Now. Before Junie sees you out here."

"Maisey—"

"*Now.*"

"Are you going to blow me off?" His rough question hits a spot in my heart that's ached entirely too much in the past year or so. Usually that part only activates for Junie, but here it is, wanting to hug a man who's dry humping me in a run-down bunkhouse.

"Maybe."

"Maisey—"

"Maybe." My bra is too tight. I can't get enough air. And I don't want enough air. I want him to touch me and make me feel good and lose my mind. "I won't lie to you. I'm turned on and ready and willing and *I cannot do this while my daughter is home.* I can't. I *shouldn't* do it at all, and I'm honest-to-God afraid I'll hate myself for giving in, but *I want you.* I want you, but I promised her stability, and I won't—I can't—"

He cuts me off with another of those searing kisses that I feel from my lips to my toes.

I don't know if he's trying to stifle my *I can't*s or if he's turned on by me being ridiculously overprotective of my close-to-grown daughter.

I just know when he grips my hair and tilts my head back and thrusts his tongue in my mouth while he's rocking his hard cock against my pubic bone, I want to strip myself naked and ask him to feast on my pussy the way he's feasting on my mouth.

I want him to be rough.

I want him to be thorough.

I want him to eat me like he's starving and only every last drop of my climax will satisfy him.

I whimper as I kiss him back, clutching his shoulders, trying to push myself up onto the counter so I can spread my legs and rub my clit against his hard, thick length.

Not enough.

Not *nearly* enough.

He breaks out of the kiss with another *Fuck me, I want you.*

I can't catch my breath.

And when I look up into his dark, hooded, slightly unfocused eyes—

Oh God.

I'm in so much trouble.

Junie first, I remind myself. *Junie first. I can't do this.*

She's not here, silky-smooth temptation whispers back. *One romp in the sheets when you know it's a one-time thing to work an emotionally unavailable man out of your system will not hurt her.*

Is my libido lying to me?

Or can it be as simple as having sex with a man to scratch an itch and let it go at that?

"Name the day. School day. I'll take off. Personal day. While June's in school." He's panting as hard as I am. "We'll fuck. We'll feel good. We'll go our separate ways."

Yes. This is how he operates. Everyone knows it. This is safe.

It's a one-time thing.

No emotions.

Just physical sensations.

"I'll email you," I gasp.

"Text it."

"Okay."

He grips me by the chin and kisses me again, but instead of hard and fast and deep, he softly brushes his lips over mine, then sucks ever so gently at my bottom lip. "Text me soon," he says.

And then he's gone, striding out of the bunkhouse like he doesn't have a steel pipe in his pants, he's not struggling to breathe, and he can see straight.

I can barely make it to the bunkhouse bathroom to unzip my jeans, slide my hand into my panties, and work out all the built-up tension.

I wonder if he's headed home to go rip his pants off and stroke himself too.

Nope.

Nope nope nope.

Not thinking about that.

This thing between us?

Passing infatuation.

I have to let it go.

Not just because I told Junie I wasn't dating.

I have to let it go for me too. When she leaves, I want to stay here. I want to have a home. I want to see if this ranch can give me a greater purpose. And I don't want ghosts haunting me.

Especially the very alive, very virile, very sexy, very unavailable kind.

Chapter 21

Flint

I never knew torture until Maisey Spencer moved in up the driveway.

When Tony was alive and running the ranch, he'd stop to chat every time he passed the gatehouse if I was outside. He'd invite me up to the house for a beer after school. We'd do dinner with Kory and a few others at Iron Moose every other week or so.

He was a good friend when I needed one after I moved back to Hell's Bells.

And now images of his niece—watching me, kissing me, clinging to me, the color high in her cheeks, her breath coming in short pants, her eyes dark with craving—haunt me with every waking breath.

Tony was never a prude. Clearly.

But I don't know what he'd think of my wanting to strip Maisey naked to work her out of my system.

At least you know it's public knowledge that this one's fully divorced, a not-helpful voice in my head offers.

And are you going to marry her? Tony's voice adds.

Jesus.

Fuck.

Neither one of us wants to get married.

That's why blowing off steam is good. Friends with benefits. Clear rules. Boundaries. We can do this.

We can blow off steam. Privately. Won't hurt anyone.

That's what I'm telling myself while I follow the sound of nails being hammered somewhere on the ranch early Saturday morning.

Our next playoff game is this afternoon, and I know Maisey never sits still, so this isn't a surprise.

The barn comes into view, along with Maisey's rear end.

June's dribbling a ball around cones on the far side of Maisey's truck. That helps my body's instant reaction to Maisey's ass.

As does the reminder that June's really good.

She's had solid coaching. More, she puts in the work to improve her natural talent. If they'd been here two weeks earlier, she'd be on the team.

I'd tell her that if I didn't think it would get me an eviscerating eye roll.

Also probably won't tell her how much of her mom I see in her on the field. She's been the first person to trot over and talk up a player who has fucked up. The loudest cheerleader. The quickest to jump in with a quip that clears the tension when things are rough.

Coaching a coed team is no joke.

She's made it easier without realizing it and probably without intending to.

She spots me, frowns, and finishes her run with a solid kick to the ball that sends it sailing into the side of the barn, where it connects with a hard thwack, then continues right on through the wood.

Maisey drops her hammer and leaps to her feet, her head swiveling first to the barn, then to her daughter. *"Juniper."*

"Sorry, Mom. Guess I forgot my own strength. I'll go—"

Get it.

I assume she's about to say she'll go *get it*, but an ominous creak from the barn cuts her off.

Her eyes go wide.

Maisey takes two steps back, then darts toward June.

The building sways.

Oh, *fuck*.

It's swaying.

The barn's swaying.

"Get back!" Maisey yells at June. "Back! *Back!*"

"I'm sorry," June gasps.

"It's okay. *Back. Back!*"

I'm dashing toward them as well, but I have nothing on Maisey's speed.

Jesus.

She's fast.

She's fast. She can hammer. She can paint. She can fix fuse boxes and roofs and plumbing and doors.

She can do anything, and she does it *well*.

Fuck, competence is hot.

But the barn is not.

The boxy, two-story, formerly red building creaks and groans and leans. The sound of dry, old wood splintering crackles through the crisp fall morning.

"I didn't mean to." June's voice is high and tight, her face flashing with horror.

Probably afraid of how much trouble she's about to be in.

But Maisey grips her arm tighter and pulls her farther and farther away from the barn. "It's okay. I know. I know. Back. Get back."

"It's falling the other way."

Maisey pauses and looks back at the barn. Then she spots me as I reach them. She looks at the barn once again, her lips moving quickly.

June does that in class.

Maisey's doing math in her head.

They both move their lips like they're saying the problems out loud.

Maisey likes math.

Maisey does math.

That's as hot as competence.

The barn creaks heavily again, and four rapid-fire snaps get my brain out ahead of my hormones.

She grabs June's arm with one hand, drags her three feet to me, grabs *my* arm, and hauls us both another fifteen feet away.

"Mom," June whispers.

"I don't want—" Maisey starts, and then she stops talking altogether as the barn gives one final groan and collapses on top of itself with a racket like ten loads of lumber being dumped on each other at once.

Dust and wood splinters billow into the air, sending a cloud of dirt debris swelling out from the base.

June squeezes her eyes shut and holds up an arm, but the flying dust scatters and dissipates approximately where we were just a minute ago, settling to the dry ground with small swirls of final joy.

Maisey lets out a loud *hooo*.

June squeezes her lips together, but a noise still slips out, like she's trying not to cry.

"Well, that was fun," Maisey says.

Dust is still swirling around her truck. A small cloud of it, but still enough that we can't see yet if there's any damage from splintered wood that might've flown off the outside of the structure.

I look at her.

She slips an arm around June's waist. "It astonishes me that with a kick like that, the soccer coach wouldn't take you on. His loss. You're *amazing.*"

Now I'm not just looking.

Now I'm *gaping*.

Did she seriously just do that?

"He's such a dick," June says around a sniffle.

"If your plans to be a professional soccer player don't pan out, we can still get you a job taking buildings down."

"*Mom.*"

"What? Do you know how much work you just saved me trying to figure out how to get that thing safely pulled down? One kick and *boom*. Now it's just a salvage job. I'll even buy you a new ball until we can find the one lost in there."

"Stop," June whispers.

Maisey visibly squeezes June's waist tighter. "Okay," she says quietly. "So long as you know I'm not mad."

"Dad would've yelled."

"He's the last thing I'd ever want to be."

June's eyes go wide as she looks at Maisey. And then she chokes on a laugh that turns into another sob. "I'm going home," she whispers.

"Make sure you take the shortcut," Maisey replies. "None of that weaving around all of these open plains to get back to the house. Never know what kind of questionable characters you could run into."

"You are such a dork," June mutters.

She doesn't say a word to me. Or look at me, for that matter.

"I'm your dork," Maisey says to her as she sets off for the house.

June spares me a glance then. "Don't look at my mom wrong."

"I'll get my hammer if he does," Maisey says cheerfully.

This time, June doesn't respond at all, and soon, she's out of earshot.

Maisey looks at me.

I make a point of looking at the barn like I don't know she's looking at me. "Glad no one was inside."

"I was going to reinforce a few beams in there and set it up like a haunted house for Junie and her friends before we tear it down—reinforcement would've only been a temporary situation given how much snow apparently usually lands here—but I suppose having it fall wasn't bad. That was some kick. She must've been really pissed to see you. You give a pop quiz this week that I didn't hear about?"

"You're avoiding me again."

"The hot-water heater broke Monday morning, and the dishwasher I had scheduled to be delivered Tuesday to replace the one that went possessed showed up without any working sprayers, which you'd *think* they would've checked before it left the warehouse, but didn't, and *yes*, Mr. Deliveryman, *the water was on and flowing into the dishwasher*. Jesus, I hate men who don't believe I know a thing about appliances. And then Charlotte called because the PTA's fall fundraiser got dorked, so I helped her with that, and while I was at her house, I noticed a draft, and considering how cold it's been getting at night, I couldn't leave without finding where it was coming from. Heating bills suck when your house is drafty."

"Maisey."

"And did you know the tavern's been doing patch jobs on their roof all summer while they wait for some contractor from Laramie to come up and finish it? Took us all of a day on Thursday to get the manpower to reshingle it once I drove down to town to get the shingles."

"Maisey, if you don't want—"

My words die on my tongue as she steps into my view. She doesn't touch me. Doesn't grab me by the face to make me look at her and to make sure I'm listening. The intensity in her blue eyes holds me captive without her even trying. "I want. I want *very much*. But I'm *busy*, because I also *want* to belong here and I *want* Junie to belong here, and I *need* to be able to explain this to her if we get caught, and I *want* to make sure I don't have any regrets. Okay?"

I swallow.

Hard.

And then I nod.

She sighs and turns around, surveying the barn. "And it appears I'm tied up for the next few days getting this cleared. She must've put that ball through a support beam or knocked it just right. It shouldn't have fallen this easily."

I can't remember the last time I let fear run my life the way it's clearly running Maisey's.

She's afraid to have too much liability on the ranch.

She's afraid of doing anything that would make June uncomfortable or unhappy.

She's afraid of not fitting in here.

"You're allowed to make mistakes as much as you let June make mistakes," I say quietly, ignoring that voice in my head that sounds a lot like Kory lecturing me about how I can be a good friend without showing up for every volunteer effort anyone in town needs. "And I don't mean doing things like fucking around with someone she doesn't like. I mean *all* of the mistakes. *Any* of the mistakes. So long as your heart and intentions are in the right place."

She shakes her head. "I've used up my quota of mistakes as a mother. Tell me that again when she's off to college and her bills are all paid and I never miss one of her phone calls. Until then, I *cannot* afford to screw up with her again."

I rub my neck and sigh, looking back at where June's figure is steadily shrinking as she gets closer to the house and farther from us. "I'd vouch for her to any college soccer scout in the nation," I tell Maisey. "She's been as much a coach this year as I have."

"You don't say."

She smirks at me, and it's hot as hell.

I cross my arms. "You didn't know she'd be good as a self-appointed assistant coach, too, when you bribed me with cherry crisp."

"I did. But I was too stressed to remember it at the front of my brain. The *back* of my brain knew it the whole time."

Not smiling at her sass is impossible. "You listening to the front or the back of your brain when you keep worrying that you can't fix things with her?"

"Yes."

"Take it from someone who spends every day with teenagers. You're getting credit for trying. You're getting credit for being honest with her. You're doing the right stuff."

"It's really hard to not jump you right here when you say things like that," she whispers.

"It's really hard not to be jumped."

She cracks up. So do I.

But it's hard to keep being amused at not being able to touch this woman.

Chapter 22

Maisey

I recognize that it's probably overparanoia to assume someone's going to come onto the ranch and go digging around in the fallen barn while I'm with Junie at the soccer game, but I still rope it off with yellow caution tape before we leave for the hour-long drive.

The team pulls off another improbable victory, and we all celebrate at Iron Moose when we get back to Hell's Bells.

I make sure to sit as far as humanly possible from Flint.

Charlotte notices, but other than a knowing look, she doesn't say anything.

But it's Sunday morning that surprises me.

Sunday morning, Junie and I are awoken by the sound of multiple cars pulling to a stop in our circle drive.

We meet in the hallway outside our bedrooms, then make our way to the front door together.

Half of Hell's Bells has arrived, most of them in trucks, led by Flint. "Got a few helpers to clear out the barn debris," he says.

As if it's that simple.

As if it's that easy.

As if none of these people has anything better to do on a cold Sunday morning than come out here and haul away the barn.

He shoves a stack of papers at me. "Liability waivers," he adds.

Six months ago, when we were living in Cedar Rapids, I couldn't get a neighbor to return a simple phone call or email about if I could sign up to deliver a meal as part of a meal train for a friend who'd had a baby.

Now, half a town has turned out to help me with what would be a major headache if it were just me but will be an easy day job with this many people.

I will not cry.

I will not cry.

I will not cry.

"Thank you," I stutter. "I'll get coffee going, and—"

"We brought coffee and donuts from town," someone interrupts.

"Gonna ask that we get to keep whatever wood we take," someone else says.

"Weird stuff, too," yet another someone pipes up. "I live for the weird stuff."

"Of course," I reply. "Of course. Let me get dressed. I'll come help."

I shut the door before my eyeballs start leaking.

Junie watches me.

And then she does the last thing I expect, and she wraps me in a hug. "They don't hate us here."

I laugh into her shoulder. "They don't hate us," I agree.

"It's a really nice change."

"So much so."

"I'm still going to college on the East Coast. Or in California. It's not even snowing yet, and I already don't like the snow here."

"Okay."

"And you'll have to visit me for the holidays because there's no way I'm coming back here when it's already ass-cold."

"Okay." I still have some time with her at home. And when she goes to college, I can sell the ranch and move closer to her.

Not on top of her.

But close enough to visit.

Being here is about giving her stability until she's ready to spread her wings. It's not about forever insisting that we stay here.

But even as I think it, I know it will kill me to give up the ranch before I get a chance to see if I can turn this into a women's retreat.

Why can't I do both?

Why can't I live both here and also right where Junie is for college?

"You're getting snot on my sweatshirt, Mom."

"I have to while you're still here. I won't be able to when you leave me for college."

She lets me go and flops off with a sigh that I know she's affecting just for me, but when I've finished pulling on my work clothes, she's waiting for me next to the door in work clothes of her own.

I don't say a word.

I won't complain if she wants to help, and I won't tease her about it and make her change her mind.

"I broke it," she mutters. "I might as well help fix it."

"It was the best kick of the day."

She rolls her eyes, but she also smiles a little. "I know."

I'm laughing as we both head out to help our friends help us.

And with so many trucks out there at the barn and so many helping hands, it really is all done in under a day.

Someone shows up with a load of sandwiches from the deli right about the time I'm starting to realize I should feed all these people.

The trucks keep coming, then going with loads of wood and shingles and whatever tools and equipment we uncover in the barn. Someone's even brought us a massive dumpster too.

Several of Junie's classmates show up, and they all laugh and gossip and tease each other as they work together. I overhear stories about Uncle Tony and his cows. More stories about Gingersnap. Someone asks if we marked Gingersnap's grave, because she wants to leave a token in memoriam to the time she caught Gingersnap eating the laundry off her line.

A few people ask me about doing handyperson work. They've heard I'm good and haven't been able to find a local business with availability for a patch-and-paint job or sealing concrete or a few other small things before winter sets in.

And the minute we find Junie's soccer ball?

It's Flint.

He finds it under a panel of boards, lifts it in the air, and calls, "Hey, June, you wanna frame this?"

After a beat of total silence, Junie does the last thing I would expect, and she cracks up.

"What's the story with the soccer ball?" It's a murmur going through the whole group of ranchers and teachers and residents of Hell's Bells who have come out to help us today. Junie's friends too.

I'm sure many of them know she wanted to be on the team but that we got here too late and Flint wouldn't bend the rules.

And I'm sure those people who know suspect there's tension there, and they'd be right.

But Junie strides right up to Flint, takes the ball from him, tucks it under her arm, and faces the crowd. "I was out here kicking it around yesterday, and when I turned one of my cones, it whispered, 'June. Juniper. That barn is so ugly. If you kick me, I'll take it down,'" June answers dramatically.

A few people share nervous glances, but more laugh or giggle.

"So I was like, 'No, ball. No. That's bad. That's wrong.' And the ball whispered, 'But if you don't use me to take it down now, someone could get hurt if they're inside when it falls. You need to do this. You need to do this to *save lives*.' And so I trusted the ball, and I trusted the universe. I knew if the ball was lying, it would bounce off, but instead, it went right through the wall and took down the whole barn."

A few people look at me.

I shrug. "She took the barn down with the ball. That part's true."

"Saw it myself," Flint says.

"She had to have hit the side at exactly the right weak spot to do it," I add, "but she did it. I actually think the ball *did* talk to her."

"I have a way with balls," Junie announces. She blinks, her face goes redder than a tomato, and Flint and I both rush in to save her at the exact same time.

"She's such a great soccer player," I say too loudly.

Flint, unfortunately, takes a different tactic. "She's the ball whisperer."

My eyes fly to his.

He blinks twice, and now *he's* the color of a tomato.

An uncomfortable giggle goes through the crowd.

"Who needs a drink?" I say, again too loud, but now more comfortable ripples of laughter flow around us. "Water? Lemonade? I can make sun tea. And cookies! I'll call in an order of cookies to the bakery."

"Already on their way," someone calls.

One of Junie's friends nudges her in the ribs, and they lean their heads together, whispering and giggling and sharing in her mortification.

Her friend squeezes her shoulder and grins, and the color eventually fades from my daughter's face.

Let's be real.

Who among us *hasn't* accidentally said something embarrassing?

Do I want the entire town talking about *balls* with my daughter?

Nope.

But I'm well aware she knows the double entendre. Her friends too.

And as they giggle together and more teenagers approach her with smiles and hugs and laughter, I realize this is good.

Being here is right.

For the first time since my mom was arrested and I missed Uncle Tony's funeral and I realized I had to divorce Dean, I know Junie will be okay.

We all get back to work, and gradually, I find myself working right next to Flint as I help load boards into the back of his truck.

"The *ball whisperer?*" he mutters to me. "You know how much shit I'm gonna get from my students for the next week?"

I stifle a chuckle and resist the urge to lean into him and soak up the heat of his nearness. "I'm sure you've had worse."

"Not like this. And not for a while. Jesus. *The ball whisperer.*"

"It's genetic, you know."

He slides a look at me, then glances around.

Closest other person is over ten feet away, loading up another truck. "Soccer?" he says flatly.

I smile. "Whispering to balls."

His mouth sets in a grim line, and he shifts to glare at the wood—heh—in the back of his truck. "I'd tell you you're evil, but I suspect I wouldn't be the first."

Is it wrong that simply teasing him here is turning me on like the full sun over the desert on a summer day?

Nope, I decide.

It's a perfectly rational, valid response to being near a sexy man who's made it clear he wants me, and who brought not just help but a sense of community to our home. "Definitely not the first. But it's been a while since anyone's called me evil for the same reasons you would."

I feel someone's attention on me. Sure enough, when I glance over my shoulder, Junie's staring.

I shove away from the truck bed and dust my gloved hands together.

I'll thank him later.

Properly.

But in the meantime—"Back to work for me. Gotta pull my own weight at my own house."

"No one doubts you're pulling your own weight. And no one would care if you didn't lift a finger."

That hot prickle hits the backs of my eyeballs again.

I was on the road too much to feel like a part of my community in Cedar Rapids for the six years we filmed Dean's show, and then the bombshell with my mom dropped, and there was no community after that.

Flint studies me.

I blink quickly. "I don't take it for granted."

He lifts his dark-copper brows.

"Feeling like I belong," I explain. "And Junie too. I will *never* take that for granted. We needed somewhere to belong."

He nods. "Good place to belong."

It is.

It really, truly is.

Chapter 23

Flint

I'm working on lesson plans late Sunday night by the light of an old desk lamp over my small kitchen table when someone knocks at my door.

Sun set hours ago.

Opal would've called before coming over. Most friends in town too.

So who's knocking softly, as if they're half hoping I'm already asleep and won't hear?

Definitely not Earl.

The bear would just crash through the door if he smelled something in here that he wanted.

Which means my suspicions about what's waiting on the other side have my blood pumping and the hairs on my arms rising and my cock half-hard before I flip on the light and peer through the pane-glass door.

And there she is.

Maisey.

Standing on my small stoop, in a long-sleeved thermal covered with a puffy vest, her short hair just long enough to be tucked behind her ears, her eyes bright and alert, her arms crossed just under those gorgeous breasts.

Not an angry crossed.

More an uncertain *I don't know what else to do with my hands* crossed.

She lifts one bare hand and gives me a small finger wave.

I turn the door handle and tug on it, only to have it stop short when the chain lock catches.

I'm so fucking excited that this woman is on my doorstep that I forgot to undo the chain.

I close the door, unhook the chain, and open it again.

Maisey grins at me. "That was adorable."

"That was embarrassing."

"Adorable."

I stop arguing and step back, gesturing her inside when I'd love to grab her by the waist, haul her against the wall, and kiss the ever-loving hell out of her.

But I don't know why she's here. If she's alone. Even if she thinks she's alone but June followed her.

She stops barely inside enough for me to close the door. "I just wanted to say thank you. Again. For bringing help. I feel—*oof.* I can't even tell you how much better I feel having the barn mess all cleaned up."

I nod.

I'm starting to understand her *why*. So it was a no-brainer to gather a few helpers from town to clear away the debris.

Maisey arrived here every bit as lost as some of the kids I work with at the school.

Looking for where they fit in and belong in this world, with not enough support at home. Their parents are often in over their heads, doing the best they can but not nearly good enough for what their kids need.

"So I was going to bring more cherry crisp to say thanks, but the truth is, I bribed Regina to make her recipe in Uncle Tony's old dishes so it would look like I made it, and I didn't have time to do that again today," she says in a rush.

Now *I'm* grinning. "Guess you're useless, then. Get out."

She gives me a playful shove in the biceps. "What I lack in cooking skills, I make up for with knowing how to use a hammer."

Yep. Contemplating my cock as her hammer, and there's no *half* about how hard I am anymore. "I have some hammering that needs to be done."

Those baby blues meet mine, go wide, and then smoky. Also smoky? Her voice. "That was terrible."

"You alone?"

"Junie's talking to friends on her phone. I told her I had to run to Charlotte's to pick up a cookie platter for next week's PTA Halloween party."

"And she thinks you're walking?"

"I *did* go to Charlotte's. I'm back now."

"Didn't hear you go past."

"Stealth mode."

I crack up, but with every word she's saying, I'm angling her deeper into my house.

It's not big. A cozy living-slash-dining area with a table for two pushed under the window and a couch on the opposite wall, with my woodburning stove between them. A bare-bones kitchen with a small oven, small refrigerator, and no dishwasher. And the single bedroom just big enough for a king-size bed.

We're headed toward the bedroom.

She rests her hands on my chest as I walk her backward, heat radiating from her palms. "I can't stay long," she whispers, "but I had to say thank you. Thank you is important."

Can't stay long.

That's what her words say.

The way she's stroking her hands all over my pecs says, *But I want to.* "How long is not long?"

"It was a *really* fast trip to Charlotte's."

I'm grinning again as I dip my head to nuzzle her jawline. "So June thinks you're gone for a little bit longer."

"Just a—*oh God*—bit."

That *oh God*? That was me, licking that sensitive spot on her neck right beneath her ear.

I do it again.

Her body shudders against me while she curls her fingers into my shirt.

"Maybe a bit longer?" I murmur against her skin, my breath on the wet spot I left beneath her ear.

She arches into me. "I won't take long."

Fuck me.

Images of Maisey with a hair-trigger orgasm are making me sweat.

We're in the doorway to my bedroom, and I'm so hard, it hurts to take another step. So instead, I turn her against the frame and roam my hands over her curves while I nibble a path along her jawline, and she gasps and pants and grabs me by the hair and hooks one leg around my thigh.

Yeah.

Yeah, I know the feel of Maisey in my arms. The way she fits. The way she wraps around me.

"I'm going to touch you," I murmur.

"Oh God, I think I'll die," she whispers.

"In the good way?"

"The best way."

I reach for the button on her jeans, feeling her belly quivering beneath my hands as my lips connect with hers.

I'm in control today.

Mostly.

I can take this slow and steady and not be a damn neanderthal like I have the last times I've kissed her.

But she whimpers and grips my hair, pulling my head closer to her, and strokes her tongue into my mouth, asking for—demanding—more.

Jesus.

I'm about to have a hair-trigger reaction.

My hands shake as I inch down her zipper. She makes a mewling noise as she arches her hips into my hands, still kissing me like I'm the missing piece to her life, and *fuck*.

I should not be this attracted to this woman.

To *any* woman.

But I want to slam into her and feel her vagina clench around my dick and listen to her scream my name, and then I want to do it all over again.

I slip my hand into her pants and stroke her over her cotton panties.

She's wet.

She's wet for *me*.

Wet, and wrenching out of the kiss with a moan. "More," she pleads.

"How much more?"

"All the more."

Chuckling is painful, but *God*, she's funny and sexy and strong and smart, and I want this to last forever, but I also want to get her off before she decides she has to go. I stroke her center again. "All the more? I'm a math teacher, not an English teacher, but I don't think that's right."

"Flint—"

She cuts herself off with a curse as I tease the edge of her panties. Her hips buck, and she twists like she's trying to help me find her clit.

"Yes, Maisey? Tell me what you want. Tell me what you want me to do."

"Stroke—under—panties—touch—me—bare."

"Like this, baby?" I push the edge of her panties aside and stroke in her curls, knowing I'm not where she wants me to be.

I want to get her off.

I want to get her off with my fingers. With my mouth. With my cock. With toys. I don't care how—I want to get her off.

And I want to make this last as long as possible.

"More—middle," she gasps.

"Here?" I stroke her hot, wet labia, and she moans, her eyes crossing just before her lids shut.

"Oh God, *yes*," she moans.

She bucks her hips into my hand, still pinned to the doorframe, her head back, her lips parted, while she pants and writhes in my touch.

If you'd told me this summer Maisey Spencer would be the easiest woman in the world to please, I would've laughed in your face.

But here we are with her riding my hand, gripping my shoulders so tightly I'll probably have fingerprint bruises tomorrow, while she moans and rocks against me.

I circle her clit with my thumb while I enter her with one finger. Her hips jerk, and her moan goes high pitched. "More," she chants. "More. More fingers. Touch me—*oh God*, keep playing—*oh yes*—my clit, and—*ooooh God*."

"Like this?" I thrust two more fingers inside her while I press my thumb to her clit, and it's like I've hit her on button.

"Yes. *Yes*. Oh God, *yes yes yes*, I'm coming, I'm—*ahhhhhh*." Her inner walls clench hard around my fingers. Her hips jerk erratically. She shifts to grip me by the hair again, and *fuck me* again.

The color high in her cheeks. Her unfocused eyes. The sound of her voice as she chants incoherently. Her plump lips. Her pussy in my hand.

This.

This is what I've wanted for weeks in a way I've never wanted any woman before.

I've never *waited* this long for a woman before.

I hold her, still teasing her clit and thrusting my fingers into her as she rides the waves of her orgasm until she sags against the doorframe.

I catch her before she slides all the way down it.

"Oh God," she whispers again between pants while I angle her more against the wall than the doorframe and hold her up. "What time is it? Can you do that again? Take your clothes off. I want to lick your tattoos. Will you really come fast if I ride you right now? I have seven minutes before Junie will notice I'm running late."

I half blink, half laugh. "You—"

"I'm equal parts determined to return this favor and terrified we'll get caught. I know I get things for me, but she's still—she's so—okay. Done talking. Take your pants off."

"Maisey—"

"Turnabout's fair play. But my hands don't work. That orgasm broke them. So you have to do the unbuttoning for me."

I'm smiling as I drop my forehead to hers. "Am I going to have to jerk myself off too?"

"No, but you will have to throw me on your bed and have your way with me. With your penis. In my vagina. For the record. Are my eyes still crossed? I feel like my eyes are still crossed."

"Your eyes are closed, sweetheart."

Closed and getting wet at the corners.

Shit.

"Maisey?" I touch the tear slipping out of the corner of her eye. "Did I do something wrong?"

"No. No! It's been a long time since . . . someone else . . . took care of me," she whispers.

I open my mouth, then close it.

That she hasn't had a man-made orgasm in a long time probably shouldn't be a surprise. Much as she's nothing like I would've expected after watching her show, everything I've heard about her ex suggests I haven't read him wrong at all.

He doesn't deserve her.

Probably never deserved her.

Also, I need to quit reading the tabloids, and yes, I know I'm lying to myself when I say it's so that I know if one of my students might be having an extra-rough time at home.

"Lucky you have me right down the driveway," I finally murmur.

That earns me a laugh that I'm nearly certain is real. She blinks her eyes open, swipes at them quickly with her apparently not-useless hands, and then squirms in my arms. "I should go. We can—Junie's

219

planning on going to a sleepover next weekend at Abigail's house with half the soccer team. You can come up to my house then, and we can, erm, finish what we started. Unless you want me to jerk you off real quick. I could. I'm *very* good with my hands, and I think they're working again. Oh God. That sounded totally lame and porn movie-ish, didn't it? I'm really—I haven't—it's been—*gah*."

I kiss her forehead.

Can't help myself.

This Maisey?

She's *real*. She's not a made-for-TV inept repairperson. What you see is what you get. I wonder if there are pockets of the internet devoted to Maisey-stan because of that show.

There should be.

"Next weekend," I murmur. "Text me."

"But you—"

"Know that you deserve champagne and roses and bubble baths, and I'm going to do this right."

I feel her shiver. "Are you trying to impress me?"

"If I haven't already, I'm fucked."

She laughs again. It's a soft sound, almost hesitant, and there goes my heart again.

Wanting to save the injured damsel.

For the first time in my life, I don't mind that saving takes work.

She's worth the effort.

Chapter 24

Maisey

Normal.

I can act normal.

It's not easy sneaking back into my own house when I can still smell my orgasm on me, knowing my teenager's like a bloodhound when anything's out of the ordinary. But I call out a cheery, "Hi, Junie, I'm back," as if everything's normal, because if I believe it's normal, then it's normal, right?

That orgasm was *not* normal, but I'll contemplate that later.

Along with how much I need a time machine so that I can both leap ahead to this weekend and come right back here because my time with Junie is limited and I don't want to miss a moment.

She appears in the doorway to the kitchen, a pint of ice cream in hand, a spoon sticking out of the treat. "What's with you? You look weird."

Dammit dammit dammit. Hello, guilt. Lovely to see you. "What? I don't look weird. You look weird."

And now I'm cringing.

Probably not just to myself.

Junie's face twists in a classic teenage *Adults are so weird and confusing, and I'm not going to be that dork when I grow up* look. "Dad called.

He invited me to spend Thanksgiving with him and Grandma and Grandpa and my next stepmother."

Happy orgasm glow all gone. *"What?"*

She pulls a face. "I'm not dumb, Mom. He hasn't proposed yet—unless that's why you're being a total weirdo—but he will. He couldn't even tie his shoelaces without you. There's no way he can survive being a bachelor. Plus, it'll improve ratings on his show if he's all over every magazine while she's planning the wedding."

I can't find words.

I know I have them.

But she's rendered me unable to find the right ones.

"Ah—oh. Um. So. Do you—do you *want* to go spend Thanksgiving with your dad?"

She shrugs.

Yes! My inner scorekeeper crows. *She still likes me more!*

Won't last long once she figures out where her least favorite teacher just had his tongue and hands, my inner guilt monster replies.

I shut them both down—the more important part here is that Junie knows she's loved and feels confident in whatever decision she makes.

I can compartmentalize. I can have a fling with Flint and also be a good mom.

I get to be both.

Don't I?

Out of your head, Maisey. Get out of your head.

I remind myself I could ask her if she wants cookies for dinner and get the same shrug, and I decide the important thing is making sure she's comfortable with whatever decision she makes. "Well, think about it, and if you do, that's okay with me. I'd love to have Thanksgiving with you, but I understand and support you getting to see your dad too."

She stares at me. "Don't you hate him?"

I shrug right back at her. "It takes a lot of energy to hate someone. Why spend it there when I can spend it making up for all the time I missed with you the past few years?"

She watches me while she stabs a spoonful of ice cream from the carton and then shoves the whole thing in her mouth. "Don't you ever want to be petty?" she asks around the ice cream.

"Only when you can't hear me. I'd hate to set a bad example." I shift toward the hallway to the bedroom. "I need to pee. But I'll be back, okay?"

"Vivian said you left her mom's house, like, forty-five minutes ago."

Dammit again. "I had to make a few stops on the way home, and then I got stuck in elk traffic."

"Stops for what?"

"Gas." Mental note: run out for gas when she's asleep so she doesn't notice my truck's under half a tank. "And then I wanted cookies, but I didn't want to scarf them in front of you, so I sat in my truck and texted old friends for a while."

Too far.

Her eyes narrow while she licks her spoon. "What friends?"

"Charlotte."

"She's not an old friend."

"She *feels* like an old friend, and it *felt* like it had been ages since I talked to her as soon as I left her house. Do you ever connect with someone and feel like you've known them for years?"

"The only people I've ever known, until we moved here, are people I've known for literal years."

She shoots. She scores. *No, Mom, I haven't made any super-tight besties that I'll be so sad to leave when I go to college. You and Grandma fucked that all up for me.*

"Well, trust me when I say, when you meet that friend and have that instant connection, you'll know it, and you'll love it, and it'll make your life better."

"You look at Mr. Jackson like he's your *instant friend.*"

She knows.

She knows I stopped by Flint's place, and she knows I'm making up an elaborate story so I don't have to tell her the truth, and I am screwing this up all over the place.

I'm a grown woman and I like sex and I like Flint and this should be okay, but it's not, because Junie's not okay with it.

And I get it.

I neglected her for her father.

Why wouldn't it be even worse when it's for a man who's new and exciting? And she's already getting bombarded with images of her father spending more time with another woman than he spends with her. And I count phone, text, and email time as *spending time with her*, for the record. I'm willing to give him that.

But I'm smarter now. I know what I have to lose. And I will give my libido a stiff upper finger before I let working Flint out of my system interfere with being a good mom to Junie.

Maybe it's an excuse.

But it's the truth.

I know what's important. I know I won't let a man get in the way of my taking care of my daughter. If he hasn't caught on to how serious I am about that, then he's an idiot. I'll figure it out, and I'll move on.

Nothing could be *less* attractive than a man who doesn't respect my daughter.

And I think Flint does.

I think he truly does, and he's battling his own wants and needs against a teenager's wishes.

"Life's complicated," I say to her stubborn *Tell me I'm wrong* look. "But nothing will ever change the fact that you come first. Okay?"

Definitely not helping.

"I really need to pee," I say before she can continue. "Hold that thought, and I'll be right back, okay?"

I actually need to shower before I get close enough that she can smell what I've been up to.

Dammit, libido. Dammit dammit dammit.

I shouldn't have stopped at Flint's place. Now I feel like *I'm* the rule-breaking teenager and *she's* the mom, and I don't like it.

She watches me while I dart to my bedroom.

As soon as I'm locked in my bathroom, I pull out my phone and flip through my text messages, looking for someone—*anyone*—I can message for support right now.

Probably shouldn't tell Charlotte. She already suspects, and I don't know enough about how the gossip network operates here yet. Like, can she tell her besties with one glance that she knows who the most eligible teacher at the school is boinking?

Can't text my mom. Clearly. Three years ago, yes. No-brainer. This was something I would've taken to her because she really was that mom who was there with all the answers when I was growing up. Now—now, I don't know who she is, not fully, but I know I can't take this to her.

Even if I could, no cell phones in prison, so I can't reach her.

I scroll through the other names of friends I've made through the PTA or by eating out at all the restaurants in town.

Nope, nope, nope.

Which leaves one person.

Dammit.

I hit Flint's contact info and pull up our text thread. He gave all the soccer parents his contact info, and I had to use it one time to let him know I'd be a little late getting Junie from practice, and her messages kept bouncing like her battery had died.

That's it.

Two messages.

I type out and delete a new message fourteen times before I realize I can't send it.

And not just because I'm pretty sure Junie knows how to break into my phone.

It's more that I don't know how to say what I need to say.

I am so in over my head, and I like you and I want to have sex with you, and I don't know how this fits into my plan of figuring out who I am before I consider getting into a relationship with another person again, and also I have horrible guilt at the idea that I've betrayed my teenager by coming to see you tonight when her father is openly dating a woman she's never met and I know she peruses gossip sites looking for updates and information about them. So I want to tell her, but I don't want to be one more parent that makes her feel like she's coming second in their lives. That's my hard line. Junie first. Junie first. Junie first.

My phone dings in my hand, and it's so sudden and unexpected, and it's *Flint.*

I shriek and drop it on the tile floor.

And then I snatch it up again and look at the message.

Our striker had a fender bender. Two other players with him. All okay overall, but initial exam says he's out for the rest of the season. Have J ready to step in Saturday just in case.

I sigh. My shoulders sag.

If ever I needed a reminder that he, too, needs to put Junie first, here it is.

My phone dings again.

And quit overthinking.

That's it.

Quit overthinking.

"Are you still peeing?" Junie calls from my bedroom. "What are you, a racehorse? You didn't drink *that* much today, did you?"

I pocket my phone and get to work cleaning myself quickly. "Got distracted thinking I need to redo the bathroom," I call back. "Hold on. I'm changing into jammies. Wanna watch a movie?"

"It's a school night, Mom."

"Wanna watch an episode of *SpongeBob SquarePants* and pretend it's a movie?"

"You are such a dork."

"I am. And wouldn't you rather have a dorky mom than a militant mom?"

For the record—that was my own mother coming out of my mouth.

And despite where she's living right now, I think I'm okay with that. And despite her dabbling in white-collar crime, she's still the best mom I could've ever had. So as long as I never decide to take a leap to the wrong side of the law, Junie and I will be fine.

I snort softly to myself.

Yes, Junie, I banged your coach because a woman has needs, but at least I'm not in jail, right?

Worst part?

My daughter would probably mostly agree with that.

Doesn't mean I don't feel terrible for sneaking around behind her back, but this time, I'm not doing it to make a man happy.

This time, I'm doing it to make *me* happy, and I know I'd stop in a heartbeat if I thought Flint was truly bad for her.

And for me, that makes all the difference.

Chapter 25

Flint

The only thing more frustrating than waiting to get Maisey alone again is being eliminated from the state finals after a bad call that ultimately cost us the game.

"You were totally not offside," Abigail says to June as we drown our sorrows at Iron Moose with fried cheese sticks, bison burgers, and root beer floats. The team took over the entire dining room, and most of the parents are scattered at tables around the long table the kids rearranged so they could sit together. "That was the worst call in the history of worst calls."

June doesn't answer.

She's still slunk over her untouched plate.

I can *feel* Maisey biting her tongue down at the other end of the table.

"And it was great that you were there to play so we weren't short-handed," Vivian chimes in.

June shakes her head and sits up straighter. "You did really great," she replies. "That goal was the best *ever*. It's awesome that the scout got to see."

Yeah.

That's the other issue.

The entire team figured out we had a college scout watching today.

"Who wants another root beer float?" Regina calls.

"Can I get a brownie sundae instead?" Wade, one of our defensemen, asks.

The parents crack up.

Regina pats him on the shoulder. "Of course you can, hon. Anybody else?"

Season's over. Got a few months before spring ball tryouts. And every last kid who's been aiming to eat as healthy as possible, especially since we started advancing in the playoffs, wants more dessert.

"Teenagers," Charlotte says.

She's sitting next to Maisey, across the room, and I still hear it.

I don't think Maisey does, though. She's still watching June like she wants to swoop her up in a hug and take her to get a thousand puppies.

"Hey, now we don't have to worry about staying up too late for Xavier's birthday-blowout party next weekend," one of the kids says.

Most of them are taking it pretty well.

This is as far as we've gotten in playoffs in *years*.

Possibly since before I was a student myself at Hell's Bells.

This is a thing to be celebrated.

Unless, I suppose, you're a kid who's used to getting all the way to the championship game.

"You gonna give 'em a pep talk?" Kory asks me. He came out to cheer us on today. Even brought one of his cows in homage to Tony bringing Gingersnap the one other year we made it to the playoffs.

Considering we lost that first playoff game, too, pretty sure nobody's gonna want to bring any more cows after that.

Cows are officially our playoff curse.

If you believe in curses.

I shake my head. "Already did. Lot better watching them all give each other pep talks."

"Afraid you won't say anything as intelligent as the teenagers?"

"Pretty much."

He grins over his glass. "So long as you know your place."

June shoves up from the table and heads toward the bathrooms.

Maisey watches her the whole way. Charlotte leans over and says something to her, and she nods.

Then Maisey glances across the room.

Our eyes connect, and I know exactly what she's thinking.

I can't do this. I can't do this tonight. Junie needs me.

Takes every ounce of self-control to pretend I don't see it.

Thing is, I *get* it.

Hurts me, too, to send kids home knowing they're in a bad mood, that they're disappointed, that they're disappointed in themselves.

Maisey rises.

Charlotte pulls her back down.

Maisey scowls at her.

Scowls.

Maisey.

Charlotte doesn't seem offended. She sucks in one of her cheeks like she's trying not to smile, then turns to someone on her other side.

Conversations keep rolling all around the room. Most of my players are in pretty good spirits. Their parents too. We talked a lot after the game about how great it was to get this far.

They know.

They get it.

I'm about to agree with Maisey that June's been gone too long to not be checked on when she reemerges from the bathroom, eyes downcast, cheeks pink.

Maisey's half out of her chair faster than I am.

Several of the kids notice. Parents too.

I know June's supposed to hang out with Abigail at her house tonight. Half the team is. But there's no mistaking the look on either of their faces.

Maisey grabs her coat.

June heads for the door, so Maisey grabs June's coat too.

She doesn't look at me.

Neither of them do.

Fuck.

And not *Fuck, I'm not getting laid tonight.*

This is pure *Fuck, one of my kids feels shitty.*

"Right back," I mutter to Kory.

"Take your time. Don't cut her hair again."

I don't know all of what my face telegraphs to him, but he grins way too widely in response.

The parking lot's well lit, so it's easy to see Maisey and June hunched over against the wind as they cross the pavement quickly. I stride even quicker, and I catch up to them as they reach their truck.

"Hey," I say.

Both of them turn to look at me.

June has two inches on Maisey, but she's slouching so they're basically the same height. Maisey's eyes flair like she wants to know what the *fuck* I'm thinking talking to them alone. June's shoulders visibly stiffen like they normally do anytime I talk to her.

"Yes, Coach?" June says tightly.

"You know you're the reason the team went as far as they did, don't you?"

Huh. Parking lot lamps really exaggerate teenage eye rolls.

I squat enough to get down to her eye level, because this is important.

"You know what every team needs to succeed? It needs *heart.* It needs *belief.* You think you stood on the sidelines most of the season and didn't do anything, but the truth is, you were the glue holding the team together."

She snorts.

I shake my head and cut her off before she can argue. "Hey. Listen. How many times did you help one of your teammates shake it off when they got called for offsides or missed a kick? How many times did you step between Bella and Hugh when they were arguing over a play and helped them find the middle ground? Those two have *never* gotten along, but did you see them tonight? Playing like teammates."

She's finally listening. Her eyes are fixed on me, getting shiny under the streetlamps.

I clap her on the shoulder. "*You* are why we made it as far as we did. You made a massive difference to this team, despite knowing you wouldn't see much action on the field. You know how many other players in your shoes would've done what you've done? Not many. You took what you were given, and you made yourself the best damn equipment manager in the history of equipment managers. And *that* is what makes a player great, and *that* is why every last one of your teammates inside that building right now has told me you need a place on the team this spring, even if they get cut. Don't doubt your power. Don't doubt your value. You're a damn rock star. Okay?"

She swipes the back of her hand over her nose and steps back. "Okay. Whatever. Mom, can we go home?"

"Of course," Maisey says quickly.

She shoots a look at me, mouths *Thank you*, and blinks rapidly herself.

I nod. "Really proud of her. I mean it—not many kids in her situation would've stepped up like she did."

I don't need June to believe me right now.

But I know she needed to hear how important she's been. And I know Maisey will find a way to reiterate it in whatever way June needs to hear it again and again.

Maisey flashes me another half smile, this one loaded with complicated emotions and a clear resistance to saying whatever it is she thinks she needs to say, then heads around her truck to join June inside without letting anything slip.

I don't watch them leave, even though I want to.

No need to push it.

Don't head right back inside, either, though.

I'm crazy to be thinking about having a fling with Maisey. The last time I got involved with a student's parent, the situation was completely different, but that doesn't mean it's not still a bad idea.

But as far as bad ideas go, it's my favorite in a long, long time.

She's the one who's sticking.

Not because I want in her pants.

But because for the first time in my life, I trust that I've found someone who knows what it's like to be abandoned. Who knows how hard it is to fit in. And who's still willing to put themselves out there no matter the pain if it ends terribly.

For the first time in my life, I think I've found someone I *want* to love.

Chapter 26

Maisey

We're halfway home before Junie says anything, and when she does, it cracks my heart in two.

"Do you think he meant it?"

I know what she's asking. I know *exactly* what she's asking. "Who meant what, sweetheart?"

"Coach Jackson. That I—that I mattered."

"He doesn't strike me as the type to offer up false flattery," I reply slowly. "I think he genuinely appreciated everything you did for the team this year, and he genuinely believes every word he said."

"This season sucked." Her voice cracks. "Do you know how hard it was to stand on the sidelines and tell everyone they were doing a great job when you know—*you know*—you would've been so much more effective on the field? But you also know if you're on the field, someone else isn't, and I can say all I want, that I would've made that goal or I wouldn't have been sloppy in my ballhandling, but I don't know that *for sure*."

"Junie—"

"*I lost us the game tonight,* Mom. Sometimes I need to be irrational just to be irrational, but *I lost us the game*. So I've earned this. Okay?"

I squeeze her knee. I get it. I need to work through feeling irrational sometimes too. I wish she didn't, and letting her sit with her feelings is one of the hardest things I've ever had to do as a mother, but I know she's right.

She needs to work through this on her own. "Okay. Let me know when you want me to talk you off the edge."

"I don't know if I can be good anymore. *Offside.* I was freaking *offside.* And I don't know who'll hate me for taking their place in the spring if I make the team and they don't. I don't know who liked me *because* I wasn't a threat when I was just the stupid equipment manager and who'll turn on me if I get to play."

Scratch that thing about letting her hurt being the hardest thing ever. Biting my tongue to keep from telling her that I will personally destroy any child who dares to be an asshole to her after all she's done for them is harder.

And facing that I am not, in fact, heading home to prep myself for a night of wild monkey sex with Flint while Junie was supposed to be at a sleepover isn't the greatest.

Especially after the way he just went full-on *You were the linchpin to our team and didn't even know it* on her.

Is it wrong that watching a man be amazing to your kid makes you want to jump his bones even more?

Dammit.

Now *I'm* the asshole.

I am *such* an asshole for thinking of my own physical wants when Junie's in so much pain, and no amount of *Seeing my child hurt makes me hurt and want to feel better too* can erase the guilt at thinking it.

"I love soccer," she whispers. "It's where I'm *me*. I don't know if I'm *me* here anymore. But I can't be *me* back in Cedar Rapids either. I don't know if I'll ever be *me* again."

"Oh, baby."

"I don't want to go back. I don't. I hate it there. I didn't do anything wrong, and everyone treated me like it was *my* fault for what Grandma did, or like I have criminal genes and can't be trusted. Like it's *my* fault I was born into our family."

My throat goes tight, and my eyes dampen again. Have to get home. *Have to get home.* I can do this. "It's not your fault, Junie."

"I *want* to like it here. I do. But it's just—it's hard. It's so hard, Mom. Why is it so hard? And don't say *Life's hard sometimes* or *You'll be so much stronger for having gone through this.* I don't care if it's true. It feels like shit. It feels like absolute shit."

I open my mouth and shut it six times before I find anything worthwhile to say, and even when I do, it doesn't feel right. Just slightly more right than anything else. "Want to go throw axes at the side of the bunkhouse? I found rotting wood in the floorboards. Might as well take that down too."

She sob-laughs.

I'll take it as a win. "I want you to know how grateful I am that you've been so amazing through this move," I tell her quietly. "I know it's been hard on you. I know it sucks. If I could wave a wand and make it easier—"

"Stop, Mom." She sniffles. "It's hard on you too. I know it. And I know Grandma was running *your* fake homeowners' association too. I know she stole from you too. And I know you're putting half of what you get from Dad aside to try to help her pay it all back."

I'm so startled I actually jerk the car when I look at her. "How—"

"I know your passwords," she mutters. "And I don't want you dating Coach Jackson because I don't want you to get hurt. You're infatuated. It's not good for you in the condition you're in."

"If you think that's going to distract me—"

"You're infatuated with the first man to give you attention in a way Dad hasn't in years, and it's not good for you. He's a total player. Everyone knows it."

"Who's *everyone?*"

"*Everyone,* Mom. The students. The teachers. The principal. Regina at Iron Moose. Ms. Charlotte. *Coach Jackson.* He was fired from his last job for sleeping with a student's parent."

"How do you know all of this?"

"We're teenagers, Mom. Everyone's sex life is basically all we gossip about."

I whimper.

The theory of knowing teenagers *do things* and the reality of having my daughter gossiping about people's sex lives are two different things.

"I'm not having sex, Mom," she grumbles. "There's no one worth sleeping with. They're all too immature, and I'm out of here in a couple of years, so why bother getting attached?"

I don't need sex tonight.

I need a drink.

A very tall, very stiff drink.

"You have your phone and email and all kinds of ways of keeping in touch with anyone you want to keep in touch with," I say. "Who knows? You could go to college with someone *else* here who wants to see California or the East Coast."

"And that's the other reason I don't want you dating Coach Jackson," she says, completely ignoring my very obvious solution to her objection to making good friends. "I'm leaving in a couple of years, and there's so much work to be done on the ranch, and you like it, so you'll stay, and then you'll have people you're avoiding because your relationships ended poorly."

"*Juniper.* I have no intention of going through the entire single male population of Hell's Bells in the next two years. What I *intend* to do is to call Charlotte and a few other single PTA members and invite them over for book club meetings that aren't actually about books so that I can make tighter friends with the single *women* in town. And maybe I'll move across the country to somewhere like an hour or two from wherever you go to school when you leave me."

"Nope. You're gonna fix up the whole ranch and make it an escape for women who are recovering from having spouses who treat them like shit, because *that's your mission*, and that's great. You *should* have a mission. You *should* have a life. And then you'll also fix up the old cabin and put Grandma in it when she gets out of the slammer so that you can keep an eye on her and limit her internet access."

It's a really good thing we're almost home.

My eyeball is twitching too much for me to keep driving.

"Bear!" she yells.

I slam on the brakes, sending both of us flying forward to get caught by our seat belts and making the truck shudder as the back end swerves and the antilock braking system kicks in. *"What? Where?"*

Freaking Earl strolls out from among some scraggly, dead underbrush on the side of the road and crosses three inches in front of my bumper, my headlights illuminating his dark fur and the look of disgust he gives us.

I'm gasping for air like I just ran a freaking marathon.

Junie's audibly panting too. "Okay," she says. "Okay. You can move when I move. Somewhere—somewhere without Earls."

"Freaking *bear.*"

"He's kinda cute."

"He's kinda *almost dead.*"

She giggles.

My daughter, who's had the most up-and-down experience of her life the past few months, and more so today, is giggling at our almost taking out a bear.

"If that's funny, does that mean you're willing to try driving sometime before you go to college?" I ask.

"Nope. Still holding out for you to get a sugar daddy that you're not attracted to, who's also old so he'll die soon, too, and leave you enough money for you to afford for me to have a driver."

"You know sugar daddies. I'd probably actually have to have sex with him."

"Ew, Mom! Are you serious? *Don't say that to me."*

She's laughing again, though, and it's music to my soul.

"You really hate it here?" I ask her softly as I slowly press the gas to get us moving toward home again.

"No," she replies, even softer than I asked it. "It's pretty. The people are nice. And I wish you'd left dad before he started his stupid show and moved us here so I could've met your uncle and helped take care of Gingersnap and so everyone wouldn't have to stop and explain every single inside joke to me ever at school, but they stop and explain it, Mom. They stop and explain it. I never would've done that for a new kid back in Cedar Rapids. But they do it for me, even when I don't think I deserve it."

I don't dare take my eyes off the road again, but I reach over and squeeze her knee again. "Uncle Tony wouldn't have picked a place to live if it was only populated with dicks."

"Can we go back?" she asks as we approach our gate. "I think I want to go to the sleepover, after all."

Yes! My heart yells.

Yes! My vagina joins in.

Fucking Earl better be fully across the damn road, my brain sighs.

"Of course, sweetie."

"We'll tell them I forgot my overnight bag and had to go get it."

"I'll never say otherwise."

"I'm glad you had this place for us to go when the whole world turned on us," she whispers.

"Me, too, baby. Me too."

Chapter 27

Flint

I don't get nervous around women.

Just don't.

Have to care to get nervous, right?

But tonight, when I get the text from Maisey that June decided to go to the sleepover, after all, and I should feel free to stop by the house to discuss *that thing* we need to talk about, every cell in my body goes into panic mode.

What if that wasn't code and there *is* something we need to talk about?

What if I say something wrong before I get her naked?

What if I get her naked and then I can't perform?

What if I can perform but I'm too fast?

What if I have to leave in the morning and still want to come back?

Moron, my dick scoffs. *Of course you're gonna want to go back. You have it bad in a way you've avoided having it bad for decades. She's not a fling. She's the woman you've waited for your whole life, and you need to take this leap or you will regret it to the end of time.*

It's annoying when my second head is the smarter of the two.

But I won't let nerves stop me. Not when I've wanted a night to myself with Maisey for weeks.

Possibly months.

So an hour after her text, I'm standing at her doorstep. She hasn't yet pulled down her Halloween decorations, so her covered porch is decorated with pumpkins and cornstalks and those funny cloth scarecrows. The light above me is glowing orange, like she changed it out for the season too.

I'm reaching for the doorbell when the door swings open.

And there she is.

Maisey, with her short hair tucked behind her ears, her eyes cautious but hopeful, biting her lip. She's in an oversize Hell's Bells High sweatshirt and black leggings. No makeup. Bare feet. "You're early," she blurts.

"Sorry." My voice is raspy, so I clear my throat and try again. "Didn't know you wanted me to wait."

"I was going to . . ." She trails off, then jerks a hand up and down, gesturing to her body like there's something wrong with it.

"Don't let me stop you. But can I watch?"

Her eyes flare wide for half a second before she grabs me by the lapels of my open coat and hauls me inside.

And then Maisey's kissing me.

I vaguely hear the door click shut, and I hip check a side table that wasn't in the foyer the last time I was here. But I ignore the pain because *Maisey is kissing me.*

She moves her hands to hold my cheeks, her chilly fingers exquisite on my skin while her lips suckle on mine. I shake my coat off, then wrap my hands around her ass cheeks and lift her.

Her legs go around my hips, and she licks the seam of my mouth. I part my lips, and her tongue dives in, and *Jesus.*

Yes.

Yes.

I run into everything a man can run into while I kiss her and knead her ass and carry her into the living room. I dimly register candlelight.

A new sectional where Tony's beater leather sofa used to be. A furry rug in front of the fireplace.

Yes.

Furry-rug sex.

I want furry-rug sex with Maisey.

I drop to my knees with her still wrapped around me, and she breaks the kiss with a laugh. "Sorry. I didn't mean to be—I mean, do you want a drink?"

"No. Take off your clothes."

I nip at her ear.

She moans.

God, that moan. I love that moan.

I sit back on my haunches, Maisey still straddling my thighs but starting to slip.

She repositions herself across my hips and pushes me onto my back. "I almost didn't text you."

"Glad you did."

"Worried—Junie—but you—*thank you.*"

"Not a dick."

I'm helping her pull off her sweatshirt, and my mouth goes dry at the sight of the skimpy white tank underneath.

No bra.

Just full, lush Maisey breasts with hard nipples poking through the fabric and a hummingbird tattoo at the front of her shoulder.

I sit up to suckle one nipple through the thin cotton, and she gasps as she fists my hair in her hands again, holding me there, incoherent noises coming out of her throat and making my cock harder and harder with every sound.

"Want—you—naked—inside—me," she gasps.

She rocks her center against my dick, and I swear to God, jeans have never been more painful.

And also never more worth the pain.

I'd sit like this forever if it meant Maisey peppering my head with kisses while I suck her nipple into my mouth, her hips rocking against my raging erection, every little noise she makes telling me I'm making her feel good.

But the lady wants me naked inside her.

Who am I to deny her?

I stroke my hands up the silky-smooth skin covering her ribs, pulling her tank up until I can switch to her other, now-bare nipple and taste her sweet flesh in my mouth.

She cries out like she's basically on the verge of an orgasm just from one little tease to her breasts, and yes—*yes*—I need to be inside her.

It takes more effort than it should to flip her onto her back, peeling her tank top the rest of the way off as I go. She wriggles beneath me, legs spread wide and keeping me from easily tugging off her leggings, while she unbuttons my jeans and slides my zipper down.

My cock springs semifree, still held in check by my boxer briefs, but *Christ*, it's a relief to not be trapped in denim anymore.

"Help me here, Maisey," I grunt, still unable to get her pants down.

She pulls her knees to her chest, yanks, does some acrobatic thing beneath me, and suddenly she's completely naked and exposed and open to me.

I swallow. Then swallow again.

She's so fucking gorgeous.

Long neck. That tattoo. Round breasts tipped with deep-rose nipples. Soft belly. Trim hips and strong thighs. Light brown curls covering her pussy. A scar near her ribs that I know she got from getting whacked with a two-by-four, because yes, I saw that episode of her show. The shimmer of stretch marks lit by the fire, more evidence of just how strong and capable she is, how much she's *lived*.

"Fuck me," I whisper.

She reaches into my boxer briefs, pulls out my cock, grips it in both hands, and strokes, then cups my balls and squeezes. Goose bumps erupt all over my body.

"Maisey—". I can't finish.

My voice is too hoarse, and I don't want to do anything to interrupt the sensations that come with her hands stroking and cradling me.

"Mine," she says, squeezing harder on her next stroke.

Hers.

All hers.

I should touch her. Kiss her. Bury my face between her thighs and lick her until she's screaming my name.

But all I can do while she explores and teases my cock is close my eyes, drop my head, and breathe while I try not to collapse on top of her.

"I am so wet right now," she whispers.

I'm still wearing my boots. My jeans are hanging open but still covering most of my ass. My breath is ragged, and it's taking every ounce of control to not come all over her belly. "Maisey—"

"Condom?"

I grit my teeth. "Back pocket."

She rolls my balls together one more time before stroking her hand over my hip to my ass, which she squeezes before digging into my back pocket.

"A whole roll, hmm?" she murmurs.

My eyes are still closed, but I can see her smile.

"Otim—oppom—optimist," I finally force out.

"You like me touching you."

"Feels—so—good."

"You feel so good in my hands. I have to know how you feel inside me." Foil tears, and then she's stroking me again, this time to roll the condom down my length.

Instinct takes over as soon as she's done, and she gasps as I push deep inside her.

"Can't—slow," I grunt.

"Don't—*oh God*—want you—*yes yes yes*—slow. Want you—*there*. Oh God, yes, *there*."

My body is on fire. My hips jerk erratically as I pump into her tight vagina, heat radiating around my dick, which is so hard and primed and ready that I don't know how I'm not coming inside her after two thrusts.

Fuck, she feels good.

"Flint, *yes*, there, ohmygod, *there*," she chants, bucking her hips to meet mine, her hands wrapped around my back, her legs hooked around my ass, everything about her driving me wild.

I'm teetering on the edge, and I don't think it's just the edge of coming.

This edge is much more dangerous.

Much more risky.

Much more worth it.

And terrifying as hell.

I should be telling her she's beautiful.

I should be worshipping her whole body, not just slamming into her like a wild beast staking a claim.

I should be ordering her to come for me.

But all I can do is squeeze my eyes shut and let my cock do all the talking.

Which is the last thing this woman deserves.

"Oh God, Flint, *oh God oh God oh God*, there, I'm—I'm—*yes yes yes aaaaahhhhhh*," she moans.

Her vagina clenches like a fist around my cock while her legs strain and straighten, her pussy pushed up against my hips.

She's coming so hard around me that dots dance in my vision, even with my eyes closed, and I finally let go.

I let go, my own pent-up orgasm railing out of me like a runaway train while I moan into the sensation.

My cock is pulsing. Her vagina keeps squeezing and releasing me, clenching and relaxing, spasming around me while I come harder and longer and deeper than I can ever remember.

I feel it in the pit of my stomach.

In my balls.

In my toes.

In my biceps.

Everything—*everything*—straining into release in the grip of this woman who has utterly bewitched me and whom I'd happily follow to the very ends of the earth.

"Oh God, you're good," she pants. "*So* good. So so good."

Her fingers are curled in my hair again. Her legs go limp, but I can still feel aftershocks squeezing my cock inside her as the last of my own orgasm rolls through me.

I don't know if I'm breathing.

I don't know if I'm still alive.

All I know is that if there's meaning to life, it's this.

It's Maisey, beneath me on a furry rug in front of a fireplace, her breath coming in sweet little gasps while she peppers my head with kisses.

This is it.

This is everything.

This is home.

And it's terrifying as all fuck.

Chapter 28

Maisey

It takes me a long time to catch my breath.

Even longer to catch my emotions.

If I've ever come that hard before, I don't remember it. I don't know if I'll even remember sex before this.

Every inch of my body is satiated. Every nerve at ease. Even my brain is mostly a calm, happy soothing slate of blankness.

The fire crackles and pops next to us, and the rug I almost didn't get for it being completely impractical is warm and soft beneath my back, almost tickling my neck, but not quite.

Flint eases off me and settles in beside me, looping an arm over my belly and pressing a gentle kiss to my temple.

No hurry.

Nowhere else to be for either of us.

I let my eyes slide closed and tilt my head so it's touching his and listen as his breathing evens out.

He doesn't ask if it was good for me. Dean used to do that all the time. *Wow, babe, was that as good for you as it was for me?* He never listened to my answer, so I quit saying anything beyond *mm-hmm*.

But Flint doesn't ask.

Because he knows it was good? Because he knows if I need or want something different next time, I'll ask? Because there won't be a next time?

Because it wasn't good for him?

Dammit.

Brain has engaged.

I told him it was good, didn't I?

Did I?

Everything that came out of my mouth while he was inside me is a blur.

Yet despite the insecurities settling in, I'm stroking the back of his hand with my fingertips as if I'm claiming him. This hand. I love this hand. The thick veins. The strong bones. The soft skin and rough hairs and long, blunt-tipped fingers. This hand is mine.

"Junie says everyone knows you're a player," I whisper.

He makes a noise that's not a full grunt.

I don't say anything else, and eventually, he makes another noise that's not quite a sigh and not quite a grunt.

I still don't say anything.

And eventually, my patience is rewarded with a quiet confession.

"I know what it's like to feel abandoned," he says slowly. "I wasn't physically abandoned as a kid, but emotionally . . ."

I shift just enough to be able to look at him.

His eyes are still closed, but he keeps talking.

"It's easier to keep people at arm's length than to risk letting them hurt me."

Forget his hand.

I need to touch his face. His cheeks. His temple. His lips. "That's a lonely way to live," I whisper.

"I look at you, and I see me." His lids flicker open, and I lose my breath at the raw vulnerability shimmering in his beautiful hazel eyes. And yes, they're hazel. Shimmering in golds and greens tonight. "Hurt so much by the people who are supposed to care the most. Afraid to open up to anyone again. But so desperate to fit in that you'll bend over backward giving and giving and giving until there's nothing left for yourself."

Heat prickles my eyes. "You fit here. You're loved here."

"There's understanding the logic of it, and there's feeling it, and they're not the same."

His voice is getting husky, and it's taking everything inside me to not give in to the urge to let tears fall.

This man doesn't want my pity, and I don't want him to think that's what I'm feeling. "That's a little too relatable."

"You get it. Nobody else—" He stops, clears his throat, briefly closes his eyes, and then he looks at me again, his thumb lazily stroking my belly. "I've never trusted anyone else to get it."

"Why me?"

"Because it wasn't until you started showing up to fix chicken coops and paint nurseries and organize roofing jobs that I would've done if you weren't here that I realized what I was doing." He squeezes his eyes shut again and lets out a massive sigh. "And I didn't realize it. Someone pointed it out, but they weren't wrong. Everything you've done for Hell's Bells—you took over what *I* was doing to fit in. You get it. You know how it feels to want so desperately to belong that you'll sacrifice everything you want for yourself to know that the people around you like you, even when you're telling yourself you have to do all of the things because no one else will and this is where you're needed."

A few months ago, this would've left me feeling naked and raw and attacked.

But all I feel right now is a bone-deep connection to a man who understands me more than I understand myself, and who *likes* me because I understand *him* more than I thought I possibly could.

"We're a mess, aren't we?" I say.

"Little bit." His eyes flicker over my face. "But for the first time in possibly forever, I don't feel alone in it."

This isn't *Let's work this out of our systems.*

This is *I could be very serious about a relationship with you if one of us had the slightest nudge to get there.*

"Are we friends?" I whisper.

He studies me, and I find myself holding my breath like the fate of my entire life depends on his answer.

But when he finally answers, it's everything. "I want to be more than your friend, but I know it's complicated, and I know we have to go slow, and I know there are people in your life who need to come before me."

"For a while," I acknowledge.

"I spent my entire childhood wishing someone would do for me what you're doing for your daughter. I get it, Maisey. I do. She needs to come first. So whatever it takes—however long it takes—for her to get comfortable with the idea of us, I can wait."

"You know what you said to Junie tonight?" I whisper. "That was a superhero speech. Do you have any idea how badly she needed to hear that?"

"Yeah. I do."

"And do you know the worst part?"

"There . . . was a worst part?"

"Her own father wouldn't have done that for her."

His jaw tightens, and a feral growl emanates from deep inside his chest.

And I swoon.

I know I'll have to explain this to Junie at some point. I know it won't go the way I hope it does.

But I also know that this man will champion my daughter and build her up and go out of his way to make sure she's comfortable if he wants to have a part in my life.

He knows I'm a package deal, whether she's in high school or beyond.

And I trust him.

I trust him to care for her feelings and her needs and her wishes, and I'd trust him even if he weren't lying on my living room rug half-naked with me.

"She doesn't hate you," I whisper to him.

He grunts.

"She doesn't," I repeat, stronger. "She just doesn't want you to hurt me."

His thumb stills. "I don't want to hurt you either."

"And I don't want to hurt you. But I also don't want to let you walk out of my door without a promise that we can do this again. Because I like you. Naked. Clothed. Tearing down barns. Cleaning out secret foot-fetish shrines. Talking. Listening. Understanding. Seeing my daughter for who she is and building her up for what she can do. I like you."

He studies me in the flickering glow of the firelight. "You told me not all that long ago that you need to figure out who you are before you get involved with anyone else."

"Sometimes figuring out who you are and who you want to be involves figuring out who to trust to go on the journey with you."

His lips part and then slowly close again.

"Junie says I'm having a rebound and you'll hurt me. But *I like you*. I like you a little more every day, and I like when you trust me, and I like when you let me see you. Whatever happens tomorrow, or next week or next month or whenever, I won't regret that you've been part of my journey."

He blinks and shakes his head.

"I know. I'm a little ridiculous."

"No. You're not." He blinks again. "You just have a lot more Tony in you than I thought you did."

"Oh."

He lifts his brows.

"Does that mean this just got awkward?" I whisper.

His grin is slow, but *oh my God*, does it take my breath away. "Rest assured, at no point tonight have I felt like I'm naked with your uncle."

I cringe. "You're making this worse."

His chuckle reverberates through my soul. "How about I make it better?" he murmurs as his hand slides down my bare hip and he leans in to press a kiss to my jaw.

My nipples tighten in excitement, and my already-satisfied vagina starts to smile in anticipation again. "I suppose you can try."

This time, I get a full-on laugh.

It's beautiful.

Much like everything he does to my body for the rest of the night.

Chapter 29

Flint

The last day of school before Thanksgiving break is always hellacious. It's long. The kids have the energy of caffeinated squirrels. The PTA always brings in snacks to help us get through, but I don't want snacks today.

I want the day to be *over*.

It's been too many damn days since I've seen Maisey alone, and I want her. I want her at my house or hers, naked, in my bed or hers, my shower or hers, my living room or hers.

What I don't want?

Her walking through the hallways handing out gingerbread turkeys and miniature pumpkin pies.

And I want to not feel weird every time I catch June Spencer looking at me during second period.

All my classes had tests yesterday, which served the double purpose of giving the kids a fighting chance at doing well and also letting me have today to grade the tests in class while they play math games in small groups.

Or so the theory goes.

In actuality, my students are far more interested in asking me questions all day than they are in entertaining themselves while I do my grading.

Especially in second period.

With June right there in the second row.

"Mr. Jackson, what are you doing for Thanksgiving?"

"Mr. Jackson, will you be at the parade?"

"Mr. Jackson, are you boycotting the shopping again this year?"

"Mr. Jackson, what should I get my boyfriend for Christmas?"

I finally give up, toss down my grading pen, and prop my feet on my desk. "Okay. You win. Go around the room. What's everyone doing for Thanksgiving?"

It's the usual stuff.

Going to Grandma's. Someone's hoping their dad doesn't catch the garage on fire again when he fries a turkey. One family's going skiing. Another's hosting out-of-town family.

And then there's June. "I'm going to see my dad and his snack of the week," she announces.

She has a cool delivery that says she wants to not care, and she wants to not care what anyone else in the room thinks about it, but she also shoots me a look like she wants to know what *I* think of that.

"Does he have a new one?" Hugh asks her.

She shakes her head.

"Ew," someone else says. "Do you think they're going to *get married?* I saw last week's *People*, and *People* says he's gonna pop the question."

June flinches, but she also sets her jaw the same way I've seen Maisey set her own jaw dozens of times. "He's just being a guy."

"Abigail," I call. "Your turn."

"Isn't that just like a man to have to get married right away again because he can't take care of himself?" Abigail replies.

June lifts a single shoulder.

"Abigail, your turn is up. Next? Sariah?"

"Do you think she's actually nice?" Sariah says to June. "Like, I always thought your mom was a total airhead from watching her show, but that was all fake. Your mom's really cool. So is your dad's girlfriend actually as nice in real life as she is on TV?"

"Your own Thanksgiving plans or we're having a pop quiz, please," I interrupt.

The kids all groan, but they quit peppering June with questions and start talking about things in town instead.

The parade coming up the day after Thanksgiving, which half of them will apparently be missing. Our football team is still in the playoffs, so everyone's heading to that game before our weeklong Thanksgiving break. The tour of lights that's normally out at Tony's place will be hosted at an alternate ranch this year instead, and anyone still in town is *definitely* going to that.

When the bell rings, nobody has anything to gather because no one's gotten anything out. I'm behind on grading, which will cut into my time with Maisey this week, but she has to sleep sometime.

And she's helping friends on the PTA with side projects for all the holiday festivities coming up in Hell's Bells.

I'll get the grading done.

June's the last person to leave my classroom, which is unusual.

She pauses at my desk, and for a second, I think she's going to lose the nerve to say whatever it is she wants to say.

But she doesn't. "I can handle that my dad's dating again. Abigail wasn't wrong. He can't take care of himself. He never could."

Warning bells are going off in my head.

I don't like it, but I know these warning bells.

They're hitting a spot inside me that I don't like to remember and I don't like to let other people see. *Flint, take care of your father. I don't feel good this week, and you know he can't take care of himself.*

"You gonna be okay with him for a week?" I ask her.

She rolls her eyes. "He's my dad."

"That's the most nonanswer answer ever."

Her brows knit together, and she scrunches her nose, then quickly schools her face into a blank expression.

Still picking at one of her fingernails, though.

"You're not obligated to like your parents, June."

"That's a weird thing for you to say."

I lean back and shrug at her. "I ran away from home when I was your age because my father was a prick, my mom struggled with depression, and I finally realized a sixteen-year-old shouldn't be responsible for managing a household with people who didn't even want him there."

She blinks twice at me.

I keep talking like I don't want to throw up.

Still isn't something that's easy to say out loud, but if I owe *any* kid the truth, it's this one.

"You're allowed to feel how you feel about things that are out of your control," I tell her. "And picking your parents is always out of your control."

"How do you know? How do you know there isn't, like, this soul nursery in heaven or wherever, and you get to pick the parents you want?"

"If there is, you must've known something great's coming. Wouldn't have picked them otherwise, right?"

She stares at me like I'm an alien.

"Look, I get the *Woe is me* routine to get sympathy from your friends. I know you haven't seen your dad in months. I know you're probably excited in a lot of ways. But you know if you don't want to go, your mom will throw down and take half the state with her to give you what you want, right?"

"How do you know that?"

Maisey's voice rings somewhere down the hallway, cheerful as she tells a kid to take a cookie. I slide a glance at June as her lips flatline and then tip up in a reluctant smile.

"You're right, I'm wrong," I deadpan. "Your mother hates doing anything for you and is undoubtedly counting the hours until she doesn't have to make excuses to be close to you anymore."

It's astonishing to me that teenagers have yet to develop a more advanced reaction than an eye roll.

"Hey, about soccer—"

"I don't get to make it in the spring either?" she says.

"I am truly sorry that I didn't find a way to get you more playing time this fall. You're good, and you're a good leader. I should've made more of an effort to rotate you in."

I get the hairy eyeball of teenage doubt, followed by her reshuffling her backpack. "Thanks. I guess."

"Enjoy your Thanksgiving, June," I call as she heads for the door.

"You, too, Mr. Jackson."

Huh.

That's a win.

She sneaks out around the third-period students starting to filter in the door. I hear Maisey call her name, and I can't stop myself from smiling.

June's getting on a plane first thing in the morning, and once Maisey pulls herself together, she's all mine.

For the next week.

I don't know what it means long term that I'm head over heels for her. I don't know how June will eventually react when Maisey decides it's time to tell her, which, knowing Maisey, will be sooner rather than later.

I don't know that I won't end all this with a severely broken heart.

But I know without a doubt that it would be far more painful to *not* see Maisey this week than it would be to walk away and miss having her in my life, no matter how much it might hurt later.

Chapter 30

Maisey

This isn't the first time I've put Junie on a plane solo, but it's the first time I haven't been able to walk with her through security and be with her until the minute she boards the plane.

She's sixteen now.

Old enough to be treated as an adult by the airlines.

I, on the other hand, am not too old to sit in my truck in the parking lot and sob as I wait and watch for her plane to take off.

And yes, there are cookies involved.

So many, many cookies.

My phone rings as I'm shoving one more in my mouth, and I almost hit *ignore* until I realize it's the prison.

"Haawoo?" I sob into the phone.

Cookie crumbs dribble out of my mouth and onto my lap.

Dammit.

Need to get the truck cleaned now, before Earl smells the snack and helps himself to my leftovers.

"Happy Thanksgiving to you, too," my mother says dryly. "Did your warden also put you on laundry duty?"

"Junie—flying—Dean—*saaaad*." I drag out the last word on another sob.

"Awww, sweet Maisey. Honey. It'll be okay. What you need to do is go sow your wild oats while she's gone, and then you'll forget it's even Thanksgiving. While your mother is in prison and you get to enjoy pumpkin pie. Do you have my recipe? You know no one else's recipe comes close."

I sniffle a few times. Take a deep breath. Tell myself I'm okay. Junie will be back soon, she's not leaving me for Dean forever, and I *do* have some fantastic plans for this week. "You make the recipe on the side of the pumpkin can."

"But I put *magic* in it."

"Mom."

"Oh, that's right. You can burn water. Probably don't have the magic in your genes. Skips a generation. Do you think Junie will make pie for Dean and his floozy?"

"*Mom.* We are *not* calling her that."

"Why not?"

"Because *she* was not the one who was *married* when they started sleeping together."

"She knew he was married, though. And he's a man. They can't—"

"So help me, I will hang up on you and not talk to you again until next year if you finish that thought."

"Not crying anymore, are you?"

I pull the phone back and gape at it. "You are the worst."

"And the best," she chirps.

My phone dings in my ear, so I put Mom on speaker while I check to see what's up.

And then I get teary eyed all over again. "Junie says they're shutting the boarding door and she'll ping me from Florida."

Yes, *Florida.*

Dean and his parents decided that Junie deserved a warm beach getaway for Thanksgiving, so they rented a condo on a beach in *Florida.*

Where there are no bears. Where it's warm. Where there's a beach. No dead cows. They'd probably let her on the soccer team, even if she was late for tryouts.

"She's never coming back, is she?" I whisper.

"Junie's a smart girl. She can't be swayed by beach trips and piles of early Christmas presents."

"Oh God. She's going to be swayed by the beach and presents."

She snorts. "No, she won't."

"What if she's miserable? She's not stupid. She notices Dean only calls about every fourth time he says he will. She's getting tired of the excuses. And he says this is to make it up to her, but what if she's secretly resentful and she doesn't feel right and she's utterly miserable?"

"It's only a week. She's a strong girl. She'll find her way through. Did I tell you that one of the guards was making eyes at me last week?"

I don't even pretend I'm annoyed at the idea that she'd flirt with her prison guard. I'm too grateful for the distraction she's providing.

And don't tell me she didn't know to call *right now*.

She probably pulled prison strings to switch call times. Because that's exactly the sort of thing my mom would do.

She's there with me while I stare at the runway as the plane that I know is Junie's finally takes off, and she talks to me as I start my drive home, not warning me she's about to be cut off, as usual, which happens about five minutes into my hour-long drive.

I stop in Hell's Bells to grab a sandwich from the deli and to smile at the picture of Uncle Tony and me still hanging on the wall. I wish Junie had memories of him, but she's settling in at the home he left us, so I'll have to be satisfied with that.

"You okay, Maisey?" Izzy, the deli's owner, asks me as she hands me my sandwich.

My eyes are dry and sore, and I probably look like crap, but I nod. "Just dropped Junie off," I whisper.

If I say it any louder, I'll cry again.

She nods once, grabs three chocolate chip cookies, and throws them in my bag and then pats me on the shoulder from across the counter. "Call if you need anything."

I blink and nod and dash for the door before simple kindnesses make this worse.

But when I get home, it's no better.

There's a massive basket of treats sitting on my doorstep.

And it has *all* my favorites. Kit Kats. Twizzlers. Oreos. Peanut butter cups. A bag of Cadbury Mini Eggs that are completely out of season. Cans of hard kombucha and a bottle of my favorite red wine. Candles. Bubble bath. Body lotion. And a carton of Tums.

In the middle, there's a card tucked in, with a short message in bold, masculine handwriting.

To help if you're down. Call if you need me.

It's seven days.

Seven days when I'm supposed to be so excited about having no responsibilities beyond doing whatever it is I want to do to make me happy, and I know *exactly* what I want to do to make me happy.

But I'm a mess.

I sink onto my front step, survey the light dusting of snow on the ground and up on the butte, zip up my jacket, and dive into the basket.

That's how Flint finds me fifteen minutes later.

Sitting on my porch, basket in my lap, my sandwich uneaten beside me and my stomach starting to hurt from the cookies at the airport topped with the Kit Kats and the kombucha.

"I miss my baby," I blurt, and then, to my utter horror, I start to cry.

He nods to the front door. "She have access to that on her phone?"

"Why could she control the door with her phone?" I sob.

"The doorbell, Maisey. Your video doorbell that you installed last week. Can she see who's coming and going on her phone?"

"Oh. No. Unless—crap. Unless she stole my password."

He lifts his brows.

"No," I say, more firmly. "My bank account passwords, yes. But not the doorbell camera."

He squeezes his eyes shut, then smiles and joins me on the porch. He's not wearing a coat—just jeans, boots, and a big flannel—and I wonder if he's cold.

"She worries about you," he tells me.

I swipe my eyes and swear this is the last time. She's going to be fine. "That's not her job. It's *my* job to worry about *her*."

"And you're doing great." He loops an arm around my shoulder, and I feel something I never felt when I'd worry about her while I was on the road with Dean.

True compassion.

Comfort.

Understanding.

Patience.

There's no *Suck it up, Maisey. Our parents raised us—they've got our daughter.*

Not that Flint would use the same line as Dean, but he might express the same sentiment.

And she's not spending a few weeks with her grandparents while her father and I are on the road this time. This time, she's spending a week with her father and his girlfriend and her grandparents, who will all act like I'm the bad guy for keeping her from them.

"I don't want to be the bad guy," I confess while I lean into his heat.

"To her or to everyone else?"

"To her."

"She knows you're not the bad guy."

"You're just saying that to get into my pants."

He snorts in amusement. "Is it working?" he deadpans.

"Clearly. Didn't you see them just go flying?" I sigh and drop my head into my hands. "Look, I'm a total disaster. Maybe—maybe come back in a few hours?"

"Nope. C'mon, Maisey. In we go. Time to watch your favorite movie and wait for Junie to call and say she landed."

"You called her Junie."

"So do all of her friends when you're not around, even if she tells us teachers to call her June."

I don't know why that breaks me again, but it does. Flint hauls me to my feet and pulls me into my house and then directs me onto the couch in front of the fireplace with the television over it. He disappears for a hot second but returns with the basket of goodies from the porch.

"Superheroes, fast cars, sci-fi and aliens, romantic comedies, or dude-bro fests?" he asks while he grabs the remote.

"You don't have to—"

"There's this completely awful movie I saw once when I was little. *The Pickle*. Heard of it?"

"No."

"Guess we better rectify that. If I'm hanging around, I can't have a memory of a horrible movie that I can't share with you."

There it is again.

Warmth.

Patience.

And it makes this place feel like *home*.

Not just home. But the home I always wanted.

The only thing missing is Junie.

He settles onto the couch next to me and points the remote at the television once more.

It's not *The Pickle*.

It's *The Princess Bride*.

I blink up at him.

"Tell any of my kids I like this movie and I'll let mice in your house," he murmurs.

"No, you won't."

His lips tip up behind his beard. "I'll want to."

I press a kiss to his cheek, then snuggle up next to him while the opening credits roll. "Thank you," I whisper.

He wraps me tighter. "Worth it."

Chapter 31

Flint

June texts that she's made it to Florida and is safely with her grandparents around dinnertime.

Maisey scowls at the phone. "Are you serious right now? Dean couldn't even be bothered to pick her up? Just because I want to be her favorite parent doesn't mean I want her to feel like she only has one parent."

I run my fingers through her hair. "She'll be a very discerning adult when it comes to who she trusts when she grows up."

That earns me a look I'm not prepared for. "Is that what you are?"

"You hungry? I can cook."

She bawks softly like a chicken.

It's the funniest, cutest, most unexpected noise she's ever made, and it cracks me up.

She leans back on the couch and smiles. "And that's one point for me . . ."

"I'll give you three," I reply, still chuckling.

"Three . . . points?" She wiggles her eyebrows.

My dick goes hard in an instant. "Is that what you want? Points?"

Her nose wrinkles like she's thinking hard, but those eyes—they're sparkling with mischief and fun.

Not the most mischief and fun I've ever seen on her face, but enough.

"Are you offering three of something else?" she asks.

"Suppose that would depend on what that *something else* was. I have my standards. And my boundaries."

"So you won't give me three impressions of your coworkers?"

That grin.

That grin is utterly irresistible, and I want to kiss it.

I lean in close to her. "I only do my impressions for people I need to scare away."

"Are they that bad?" Her eyes dance as they dip to my mouth.

"They're terrible." I brush my lips against hers, softly, rubbing them back and forth, teasing her without taking the kiss any further.

She strokes my cheek and beard, and her eyes drift shut. "This is not terrible," she whispers against my lips.

"It can get better."

She shivers. "I know."

But instead of leaning closer to kiss me, she suddenly leaps to her feet. "Oh! I forgot. But I didn't. I didn't forget. I didn't. Just . . . temporarily. Stay. Right there."

"I—"

"*Stay*," she repeats while she scoots to the front door and shoves on her boots.

I start to rise.

She snaps her fingers and points me back onto the couch. "Can you *please* let someone else do something for you and trust that it'll be a good thing?"

And there go my dirty librarian fantasies again. "You naked is a good thing."

She blushes.

She actually blushes.

And fuck me if that isn't *also* a massive turn on.

"I'll be naked soon. But I don't want to forget this. Two seconds, okay?" She darts out the door before I can answer, shrugging into her coat as she goes, and I watch out the side window as she dashes around the house.

I jiggle my foot.

My cock is aching.

She needed to watch a movie and hear from June and *not* have me be a horndog, but *I want*.

Jesus, I want her.

And she's been gone for more than two seconds.

More than a minute . . .

More than two minutes . . .

Yeah.

I'm timing her.

And at three minutes, I'm about to ignore her orders and leap out of my seat to follow her when I hear the back door open.

"Are you still sitting down?" she calls.

"Against my will," I reply.

"Good boy."

I stare down the hallway.

And then I snort with laughter.

Being with Maisey is like being with one of my best friends, but better.

Not just because sex with her is amazing, and I want more, but because I see so much of me in her.

The way she views the world. The things she'll do for the people she loves. The way she's afraid it will never be enough, and the way she goes above and beyond to support everyone around her. Her hopes for June. Her mission for herself. Her fears that she'll never be enough.

She gets me, and with her, I don't feel quite so alone.

Or so broken.

Something crashes in the kitchen.

"Don't you dare move," she yells. "I've got this. Everything's fine."

"I ever tell you how much I like that you're not the best in the kitchen?" I call back. "You're unstoppable everywhere else. I like that you have a weakness."

"I have many, many, many weaknesses." Something clinks. Then something else. And then I hear a squeaky sound I haven't heard in about a year and a half, and it has me going still.

The squeak gets louder until Tony's old dinner cart with the fake gold handles and the one unpredictable wheel comes into view a split second before Maisey does.

And when I realize what's on the tray, my gut clenches.

She's not supposed to know.

"No frowny faces," she informs me. "In town, you might get away with *It's no big deal*, but here, in this house, we celebrate what makes people fabulous. And you, Flint Jackson, are *fabulous*. So. We have ice cream cake. Cherry crisp—yes, Regina made it—and a package of Little Debbie Oatmeal Creme Pies."

I gape at her. "I don't—"

She clears her throat and cuts me off. "We also have cards from basically everyone I've ever met in town, but don't worry. They think I started a Ten Most Amazing Residents of Hell's Bells project, so no one knows what this was so that you, and you alone, would feel appreciated and valued on a day that you happen to hate."

I have to blink back some heat in my eyes and clear my throat a few times before I can talk. "Someone told you it's my birthday."

"Psh. Birthdays. They're just days that sometimes come with a lot of bad memories. *This* is a Top Ten Best People in All of Hell's Bells celebration. It's officially a thing. And since I created it, I get to pick the winners."

There's an ache in my chest, but it's not pain.

It's not regrets.

It's not old memories.

I think this is gratitude.

Belonging.

Respect.

Appreciation.

I think this is what falling in love feels like.

"You made up a whole award just so that you could give me a not-birthday birthday present," I force out.

She smiles at me as she pulls a basket from the lower rack of the dinner cart and hands it to me. "You do so much for everyone else here in town. You deserve to feel appreciated too."

"Do you sleep?" I should say *thank you*, but I'm terrified I'll cry if I do.

She slips back onto the couch next to me, tucking her legs up and resting them on my thigh next to the basket, propping her elbow on the back of the couch and resting her head on her hand while she watches me. "Every once in a while. You?"

"Not enough."

She reaches into the basket and plucks the top envelope off. Unlike the rest, which are all colorful greeting card–shaped envelopes, this one is plain white, the right size for a letter. "About this one," she says slowly.

"Eviction notice?" I'm desperately trying for light.

I *need* to stay light.

Otherwise, I might tell this woman that I love her, and I'm not ready.

I'm not.

She shakes her head. "Junie sort of called me out on something a while ago, and I realized I was putting resources toward something that isn't mine to solve when I could be putting them toward something that will bring a lot more joy to someone very important to me."

I study the envelope. The full basket of cards. My favorite desserts, all laid out on an old dinner cart that Tony used to use for rolling out Super Bowl snacks or his favorite whiskeys for tastings. "Maisey, I don't think I—"

"It's no strings," she interrupts. "All of this is no strings. You've been here for me and for Junie since the moment we arrived. You were here for Uncle Tony, and I have so many—but not nearly enough—emails from him talking about the things you two used to do together. Everyone in town adores you. Your students adore you. And I know you live for what you do for other people, but you deserve things too. So I made a call, and the ranch has liability insurance now. You can bring anyone out you want, for whatever you want. I'm covered. I can't bring Uncle Tony back, but I can do this. He would've wanted me to. But more, *I want to*. For you. And this doesn't mean that I *expect* you to bring kids back onto the ranch. I just want you to know that *if you want to*, if it makes you happy, the ranch is yours to use however you want."

Words won't come. They're buried under a flood of emotions.

Gratitude.

Overwhelm.

Grief for myself for all the times I've felt not good enough.

A blossoming awareness that, just like Maisey is more than enough but doesn't feel like she is, I, too, am good enough.

That I'm worthy of being first sometimes.

"You—" I start, but my throat is too clogged for words.

So instead, I do the only thing I know to do that's better than words.

I set the basket aside, I haul her into my lap, and I kiss her until neither of us can breathe.

Chapter 32

Maisey

I miss Junie, but Thanksgiving week does not suck.

If Flint and I aren't in bed together or off with the few other commitments we each have this week, we're walking around the ranch together while I tell Flint more of what I'd like to do with the land, and he offers complimentary suggestions that only make it better, on top of showing me work that he's had some of his high schoolers do out here over the years, and tells me more stories about Tony and Gingersnap and his students.

We watch movies. We cook together. I can chop vegetables and measure ingredients, even if I don't have the patience or skills to put the rest of the package together as well as he does.

We even spend an entire night playing strip puzzle.

It's like strip poker, except when one of us finds the exact piece we're both looking for, we pick which piece of clothing the other has to take off.

The puzzle, erm, doesn't get done.

I gradually relax about Junie being gone. She texts a couple of times a day, frequently with an eye roll emoji over a planned family activity, but overall, she seems good. She tells me that the Florida weather is awesome, and her grandparents are spoiling her, and her father wouldn't let her wear a bikini and is pressuring her hard to practice driving.

Everything sounds normal.

And I miss her, but I also like this opportunity to get to know Flint better without pressure.

We avoid each other in town. I get knowing looks from my PTA friends that suggest I look like I'm getting laid, so I go out of my way to talk about how much I love the facials and spa supplies I picked up from the local apothecary, and I wear my muddy boots in town too.

Working hard and taking time to pamper myself while my daughter's gone is the message I'm trying to portray.

Charlotte lets me get away with it during Thanksgiving dinner at her house.

Flint's having dinner with Opal.

Whom I saw for a haircut a few days ago, and who didn't say a word about what I've been up to with him.

The minute I pull into the driveway after Thanksgiving dinner, though, and spot Flint's truck next to his house, I happily pull in beside him.

He meets me at the front door. "You alone?" I whisper.

He answers me with a soul-searing kiss, drags me inside, slams the door, and proceeds to strip me and then feasts on me like I'm the Thanksgiving dessert he's been waiting for.

This isn't Thanksgiving week.

It's Orgasmgiving week.

And it's amazing.

We're lying in bed together in the wee hours of the morning, tired but so, so physically satisfied, his heartbeat strong beneath my ear, my fingers playing with the hair on his chest, his fingers stroking the hair on my head, when I can't hold in the lingering insecurity anymore. "Are you going to dump me after this week?" I whisper.

He stills. "You think I'd dump you?"

"We're . . . hiding. And when Junie gets back—"

I'm suddenly flipped on my back, and a moment later, the lamp switches on. He looms over me, his face inches from mine, his body covering all of me, and he growls. "I am *not* dumping you."

"So how—"

"And I am *not* embarrassed to be seen with you. And I don't *want* to hide with you."

"Okay."

"That didn't sound like a real *okay*."

I sigh and rub my hands over my face. "I don't know what Junie will think, but I know I have to address it. I can't *not*."

"So we'll go slow." He brushes a strand of hair off my forehead. "You want me to ask her permission to date her mother?"

"The soccer team—"

"If anyone has the nerve to suggest I'd play favorites after what I put her through this fall, they can go fuck themselves."

I feel a smile peeking out. "You're kinda adorable when you go caveman."

"Cavemen are not adorable."

"And yet, here you are, being a caveman and being adorable . . ."

"You're deflecting."

"You spend seventeen years married to someone who takes you for granted, the last six neglecting your daughter, move across the country, get obsessed with your grumpy but adorable neighbor with understandable commitment issues, and tell me you wouldn't want to deflect too."

He studies me in the soft glow of the lamp. "I like you, Maisey Spencer," he says quietly. "I like you enough to tell you I like you, and that's more than I've admitted to any woman in years."

"I like you, too," I whisper. "And it's scary. And I don't know what Junie will think."

I kiss her forehead. "So ask her."

"I put a man's needs ahead of hers for *years*. More years than I have left with her before she goes to college."

"I'm not Dean."

I huff. "I'm *well* aware. You've done more for my daughter than her own father has lately. But that doesn't mean she sees it that way."

He settles onto the bed, still half leaning on me, and kisses my shoulder. "Tony used to talk about you like you hung the moon. I didn't understand why he bothered when he'd always tell me you had your own life, you had better things to do than visit an old coot like him. But I get it now. You're a star, Maisey. Not a TV star. A celestial star, shining bright, bringing hope and inspiration everywhere you go. You say you neglected June the past six years. But did you? Did you call her every day when you were gone? Did you send her things that made you think of her while you were on the road?"

"Of course, but that's the absolute bare *minimum* of what a parent should—"

"Did Dean do it?"

"I did it for both of us."

He doesn't answer right away.

And I know why.

He's letting me think about the fact that Junie will remember those details. She'll know I did the best I could with the choices I made.

"Three years ago, when we got home after wrapping up the season and had two solid months at home, I refused every job offer that came our way. Dean got super pissed at me, but that summer, I took Junie everywhere. We went to the pool. We went to three different amusement parks. I made Dean take off work, and we went to the beach. We shopped. We gossiped. We ate too much ice cream. And I did it all out of guilt, and I have no idea if she liked it or not, and I don't know if she remembers. I just know it never felt like enough. I feel like I'm finally in a place where I know I'm giving her enough, and it's hard and draining but *so worth it*, and I don't want to go back."

"I heard a rumor there are people who start dating single moms and engage with their kids because they know they're getting a package deal."

"I hear the words you're saying, and I want to believe them. And that's the best I can do tonight."

"I'll take it."

I twist my neck so I can look at him. "Seriously? That's it? You'll take it?"

"No rush, Maisey. Can't do the math if you don't read the whole problem, and you can't wave a wand and make a person's feelings go away. If you could, my job would be a fuck ton simpler."

"You like your job."

"Love it."

"Teenage hormones and all?"

"They're a puzzle. Every one of them. If they leave my classroom happier and more confident, even if they can't math to save their lives, I've done my job."

I stare at him.

He gives me a lazy smile.

I know what that smile means. It means *And yes, Maisey, I'm working on making you see what a good person you are too.*

"Who regularly tells you what a good person *you* are?" I ask him.

"I do."

An unexpected laugh rolls out of me.

His smile goes soft as he strokes my hair again. "Apparently there's this woman in my life who's bound and determined to tell me too. Funny thing, though—the more she tells me I'm good, the more I want to be even better."

"Hmm. I have something that I think you might be able to do better."

"Do you now?"

I slide my hand over his chest, soaking up the view. The wolf tattoo on one biceps. The geometric designs on the other. The hair over his broad pecs, narrowing down to his fit stomach and his belly button.

My hand drifts lower. And lower. Until I'm gripping his hard length and stroking my fist slowly over it. "Yep. And it starts *right here*."

"You're gonna kill me, woman."

"You're welcome."

He pounces again.

I laugh, but not for long.

Because when Flint kisses me and touches me and makes me gasp and moan, he takes me somewhere even better than laughter.

Chapter 33

Flint

I'm happily dozing Friday morning, vaguely aware that the sun is peeking through the blue checkered curtains Opal insisted on putting in here for me when I moved in, under the massive quilt that was a gift from a student my first year of teaching, playing big spoon to Maisey's warm, lush body, when she bolts upright with a gasp. "My phone."

"It's here," I mumble. I smack my nightstand on her other side, find it, and hand it to her. "Why?"

"This is *your* phone."

"Hmm?"

She sighs. "Go back to sleep, goofy."

The mattress shakes as she climbs off it. I watch through half-closed eyes, enjoying the view of naked Maisey moving around my bedroom, but not so much enjoying the sight of her pulling on her leggings and her sweatshirt. "I think I left it in my truck when I got here last night. Right back."

"Better," I say through a yawn.

My favorite thing about Maisey?

She doesn't hold back. She doesn't play games. She says what she's feeling. She tells me what she wants. She's not afraid to talk about her insecurities and what she views as her failings, and she's not afraid of the work it takes to get what she wants and needs.

Yeah, that's a lot of favorite things.

But they're all true.

My stomach grumbles, so I pull myself out of bed, dig into my dresser for a pair of pajama pants while Maisey hunts around my living room and kitchen. "I'm running outside quick," she tells me when I step out of the bedroom. "I really do think I left it in the truck."

"I'll be here to warm you up. Coffee's coming."

She smiles over her shoulder, her hair a disaster, her cheeks pink, and her lips whisker burned, and dashes outside. I yawn through realizing I should've offered to go get her phone out of her truck for her, but it's too late.

Plus, one other thing I like about Maisey?

She'd tell me that I do enough for other people and she can do this for herself.

So I start coffee instead.

I've just hit the button on the pot when I hear a strangled noise that wakes me up faster than caffeine ever could. I'm out the door before I register that I'm barefoot, but the frost and subfreezing temperature don't bother me.

Not after one look at Maisey's face.

"What?" I stop on the freezing gravel driveway right next to her. "What?"

She gulps for air while she lifts her phone to her ear. "Junie's missing."

"*What?*"

"Shh."

June's voice comes through the phone. I can't hear her words, but I can hear her tone, and it's a punch to the gut.

She's crying.

No, she's *sobbing*.

Maisey's blinking rapidly, her chin trembling, while she listens. "That utter *asshole*," she chokes out.

I cup her elbow, straining to get close enough to hear June's words. My heart's in my throat, and I can't imagine what Maisey's feeling right now.

She pulls the phone from her ear, looks at it, and goes sheet white.

"Maisey?"

"She went to the airport at midnight last night," she whispers. "Midnight. It's—it's after ten a.m. there now, and my credit card got declined when she tried to buy a plane ticket, and Dean can't find her, and her phone goes straight to voice mail, and—*and my baby is missing*."

My stomach rolls over.

"She needed me, and she's missing," she whispers. "I have to go. I have to go find her."

"Let me help—"

She doesn't answer. She's dialing a number on her phone, climbing into her truck as she does it.

"Where. The *fuck*. Is my daughter?" she says before she slams the door.

She jerks her seat belt on, hits the button to start her truck, and nothing happens.

Of course nothing happens.

Her purse is inside.

June's missing, and Maisey can't start her truck. I turn to head inside, intending to grab shoes and a shirt and go with her, but before I've finished turning around, Maisey's leaping out of her truck and hustling around me to my front door.

"No, Dean, she's not being *a brat*. You're being an asshole. You don't call when you say you will, you cancel weekend trips to come see her, when you email, it's all *Look at the cool places I am that you're not*, and now you fly her to Florida, bully her into driving when *you know she's terrified*, and top it off by telling her you're *getting married and having a fucking baby* with the woman you were cheating on me with, and you think our neglected daughter is supposed to be *happy* about that? You have exactly fifty-eight minutes to call me back and tell me you've found her before I'm boarding a plane to come tear you apart piece by piece by—"

The rest of her sentence is lost as my front door slams behind her.

It opens again nearly instantaneously, and she marches out with her purse in hand. *"No, I will not calm down, you fucking bastard.* You lost my daughter. *You lost my daughter."*

"Maisey—" I start.

"Thank you, I've got this," she says to me.

"I can help—" I try again.

"Yes, Dean, that's a man," she says into the phone. "A man *I'm not marrying,* and a man *whose baby I'm not carrying,* and a man who *does shit for our daughter,* unlike you, so you can just take a goddamn flying—"

She slams herself into her truck again, still yelling.

Wonder if this is the first time she's let it all out.

But I don't wonder how she's planning on getting to the airport and on a plane in fifty-eight minutes.

I know better than to doubt a mother on a mission.

She flings the phone down, and I hear the truck shift into gear, but before she puts on the gas, she looks down, and she crumples.

Head to the steering wheel.

Truck shifted back into park.

And she crumples.

I cautiously reach for the door and open it, doing my best to not let her see that my heart's in my throat and I'm terrified for her. She needs calm.

She needs confidence.

She needs belief.

Fuck.

I need all those things too. "Maisey?"

"I'm on empty," she sobs. "I can't—"

"C'mon. Let me grab my shirt and get us both coffee. I'll drive you."

"Flint, I can't—"

"You're Maisey fucking Spencer. You can do any goddamn thing you want. And right now, you can let me drive you to the airport while you make some phone calls, okay?"

Her eyes meet mine, and she doesn't have to say what she's thinking. I know.

You can't know Maisey and not know.

I wasn't there when Junie needed me because I was having fun with you.

And as she's having her own guilt attack, I realize what I did.

I told June I ran away when I was her age.

I fucking told her.

Did that stick? Did she remember? Did it inspire her?

Is she okay?

My stomach knots. Chest too. My eyes get hot, but I turn and head to the house before she can see.

I can't tell her this might be my fault.

I can't.

The more important thing is finding June.

"Right back," I repeat over my shoulder. "Do *not* hot-wire my truck. Five minutes. I'll make it up on the road."

"I can't go dressed like this," she whispers. "People will think I'm crazy."

"Right back, okay? Just—just stay."

I get us both coffee and grab Maisey's clothes from yesterday. By the time I'm back outside, wearing pants, a shirt, shoes, and a jacket, she's huddled by the passenger door of my truck. She makes eye contact barely long enough to acknowledge I'm there. "My phone's almost dead, too," she tells the door. "The cold—the battery—it—"

She cuts herself off as she pinches her lips shut tight like that's all she needs to hold herself together.

I unlock the door, help her inside, hand her a coffee cup, and reach across her to grab the charging cable that I keep ready in here.

"Thank you," she whispers.

I squeeze her forearm, close the door, and head around the truck to climb into the driver's side.

We both smell like we did exactly what we did last night, and I have regrets. Not about a single minute with Maisey, but that I can sense her pulling away.

And I don't blame her.

Even if she doesn't know what I told June, I don't blame her.

The minute I pull the truck onto the highway, she's on her phone. First call—the local law enforcement for the beach town June's supposed to be in. *Yes, please, I'd like you to go talk to my ex-husband about why he hasn't called you yet to report her missing. He's Dean Spencer. Home Improvement Network star? Yes, feel free to alert the news that his daughter is missing because he's a twatwaffle.*

Mama bear is on a mission.

And all I can do to help is drive her to the airport.

I figure out when she's rejecting calls from her ex. I figure out when she's trying June's cell again, which she does between every other call. It takes me a minute to realize who she's called after we get out of a dead zone for cell signal about twenty minutes from the airport, and when she suddenly bursts into sobs, I wrench the truck over to the side of the road.

"Maisey—"

"Junie?" she gasps. "Junie, baby, I'm so sorry. Are you okay? Are you hurt? Did you sleep? Have you had anything to eat? I'm almost to the airport. I'm on my way. I'm coming to get you. Oh, no. No no no, sweet Junie, don't say sorry. It's okay. It's okay."

I suck in a breath I didn't know I needed and press my palms into my eyeballs while I process what I'm hearing.

She found her.

Maisey found June.

"No, no, shh. Shh, sweetie. It's okay. It's okay," she repeats, over and over.

There's June's voice on the other end of the phone, high pitched and upset, too, but it's June.

June's okay.

"*Juniper.* Do not *ever* apologize for standing up for yourself. You deserve *so* much better than that. So much better than that. You hold tight, sweetheart. I'll be there as fast as I can get a ticket." Maisey turns a desperate *Please get me to the airport right now* look to me, and I clear my throat, nod, and pull back onto the road.

Twenty minutes later, I drop her at the front door.

Twenty-three minutes later, I've parked and am walking in the door myself.

"No, please, I don't care what it costs," she's saying to the clerk at the counter for the lone airline that flies out of Laramie. "I need to get to Tampa *today.*"

"Ma'am, we don't have any more flights out with space today that can get you—"

"I can drive you to Denver," I interrupt quietly behind her.

The clerk looks at me.

Maisey does, too, but there's anguish in her face that wasn't there when she was talking to June. "Thank you, but you don't—"

"I can get you on a direct flight out of Denver in three hours, but I don't have anything leaving for Denver between now and then," the clerk says.

"I'll rent a car."

"Maisey—" I start.

She cuts me off. "I can't—"

"Take help from a friend when it's the fastest and easiest way to get you to June?"

I know what she's fighting.

I know *exactly* what she's fighting.

And it fucking *sucks.*

The worst part?

I understand.

To the very pit of my soul, I understand.

At the end of the day, you're the only person you can depend on.

And sometimes, you have to feel like you're the person meeting the needs of everyone around you to feel like you have any worth at all.

My very, very, very favorite thing about Maisey?

It's that she turned her whole damn life around to make sure her daughter knew she was loved, protected, and safe. She's doing for June what I desperately needed my entire childhood and never got.

I can't judge her for that.

Even knowing what she's thinking.

Even knowing she's thinking it without knowing that *I told June I ran away.*

And what would it solve if I did?

I'll tell her. I will. I'll apologize.

Later.

When she can handle hearing it.

If she'll give me a chance and let me be what she still wants once she and June come home.

If they come home.

I hold up my hands. "I won't say a word the whole drive. You can pretend it's a self-driving car. Just—just let me get you to where you need to be to get to June."

"Next best thing from here won't get you in until about seven tomorrow morning," the clerk says.

Maisey squeezes her eyes shut. "I'm paying for gas."

"Okay," I agree quietly.

She hands the clerk her credit card, and five minutes later, she has a paper ticket in hand. "I was always Team Maisey," the clerk says as Maisey tucks the ticket into her purse. "Dean was such a pompous ass, and I knew there was no way you were as dumb as they made you look. I hope your daughter's okay."

Maisey blinks once, then reaches across the counter to hug the woman. "You are a good person, and I will never forget this. Thank you."

We hustle out of the airport and back to my truck.

Maisey shoves her credit card at me to use for parking.

I don't argue, mostly because I know she needs a win. And she sees paying for parking as a win.

"Okay?" I ask her hesitantly as we get back on the highway and head toward Denver and its massive airport.

"No," she whispers. "Not yet. And probably not for a long time. But thank you."

"Anytime."

She buries her head over her phone, thumbs flying. June must've gotten her phone plugged in. Or else Maisey's activating the gossip chain back in Hell's Bells to explain why she won't be at the parade.

A very, very long two hours and one bathroom stop later, I drop her off at the Denver airport. "I'll put your truck back at your house," I tell her as she climbs out of my truck at the curb. "Can you let me know when you get there?"

For the first time all morning, she looks me straight on. "Thank you. And I'm sorry. And thank you."

I don't let her drop the eye contact. "I will be here."

"That's ridiculous. You should get home. Enjoy—enjoy the parade. The festivities. Sleeping. Whatever you need."

I sigh. I don't mean *here*, literally, and I think she knows it. "I'll be *there* too."

Her chin wobbles. "You shouldn't. Not if—not if you find a better . . . there."

"Been looking for twenty years and haven't yet."

"Flint—"

"Go get June. Bring her home. Do what you need to do for you. But whatever that is, Maisey, you don't have to do it alone."

She doesn't believe me.

Or she's afraid.

I know today sucks. I know it does. But she's not alone, and I need her to know that.

Mostly because I need her to come back.

I can't be there waiting if she doesn't come back.

Her phone dings, and she steps up onto the curb. "It's Junie. I have to—thank you. Again. For the ride. And—you deserve so much better, Flint. You really, really do."

She shuts my truck door and turns to dash inside the airport.

I wait in the parking lot until I know her plane has departed, and then I start the long drive home.

Alone.

Chapter 34

Maisey

I move Junie's flight home and book myself on the same flight before I land in Tampa. Everything gets crazy as soon as I'm on the ground. There's airport security. Sheriff's-office paperwork. Dean and his parents and the woman who's apparently on her way to being Junie's stepmother.

And there's Junie.

Hunched in on herself, looking like she would've rather a whale swallowed her whole last night.

"I told you not to come," Dean says to me.

He's thinner than he used to be. Either that, or I've gotten so used to Flint's bulk that anything looks small now. "I'm not here for you."

I step around him and kneel in front of Junie, taking her face in my hands until she looks at me. "I have missed you so much. And I am so glad you're okay."

There's absolutely no point in yelling at her for running away. She's beating herself up enough over it, and I'd imagine Dean's laid into her already a time or two.

Let him be the bad guy.

"You stink," Junie whispers.

"I haven't showered in four days, and I rode on an airplane," I whisper back.

"This is *my* time with my daughter," Dean says. "Go. Away."

I sigh. "Sorry, Junie, but I'm not sitting this one out," I tell her.

And then I rise.

And I turn.

And I draw myself up taller than I've ever been in my entire life, and I open my mouth, and—

"I don't want to visit you anymore."

And Junie takes all the wind out of my sails.

I turn and look at her, but she's not in the chair.

She's standing right behind me.

"That's no way to speak to me, young lady," Dean growls.

The hairs on the back of my neck stand up.

The police officer takes two steps toward me, and the airport-security agent's eyes flare in alarm.

Junie puts a hand on my shoulder before I can attempt to eviscerate her father once more. "The divorce agreement says I get to choose where I live and who I see and when. Go to hell, Dad. Good luck, Samantha. He's a shitty father and a shitty husband, and I never want to see him again."

I choke on my own tongue.

She's sixteen. Caught in that age where she understands how the world works but isn't allowed to participate fully as an adult. Strong but still so vulnerable.

"Can we go?" she asks the officer.

He looks at me, then Dean, then Junie. "You got that divorce agreement?" he asks me.

"Carry it with me everywhere I go." I pull up the documents on my phone and hand it to him.

Junie grips my hand tight while he skims it.

"Mr. Spencer?" he says. "You got any proof otherwise?"

Dean glares at me.

"Take that as a no," the officer says. "Smidge of paperwork in this office over here for you, Mrs.—Ms. Spencer, and then we'll let you be on your way."

An hour later, we're at a hotel not far from the airport. Junie shoves me into the shower as soon as we're checked in and takes my credit card to the gift shop to buy me clothes while I clean up.

I debate texting Flint but decide I shouldn't.

I can't see him anymore.

Not until Junie's out of the house.

I can't risk not being there if she needs me again.

I don't even want to shower while I know she's leaving the room, but I know I have to show her that I trust her.

And sure enough, when I'm all cleaned up, she's there.

Waiting.

With brand-new sweatpants, thong underwear, a sports bra, and a tourist T-shirt. "I picked the least gaudy stuff I could find," she tells me.

"I believe you."

"I didn't know your credit card wouldn't work at the airport last night," she says, and then she bursts into tears all over again. "I just wanted to go home, and I knew you'd understand, and he was so arrogant, thinking I'd be so thrilled to have a stepmother and a half-sibling when *he doesn't even call me*. I don't call anybody, and I have friends in Hell's Bells that I've talked to more on the phone than I've talked to *my own father*."

I hug her tight. "I know, baby. I know."

"Why doesn't he like me?"

"Oh, Junie. Sweetheart."

"Don't tell me he likes me, Mom. Don't lie to me."

I squeeze her tighter.

Her father *should* like her, but I can't make him. Neither can she.

"Am I going to do it, too, one day?" she asks. "Am I going to pick a man who's a total narcissistic asshole too? You did it. Grandma did it. Am I doomed, Mom? Or should I just figure out how to be happy alone? Can I skip ahead to that part?"

"Absolutely."

"Mom."

"You can. And you *should* like yourself first. Junie. You are the strongest, bravest, smartest, kindest person I know. And I am so proud of you. I know what it took to look your own father in the eye and tell him you deserve better. And *you do*. Do you have any idea how many people wouldn't have the strength to do that? You're *sixteen*. And you're taking a stand for yourself. I wish I'd had half your bravery and confidence when I was your age. You're gonna kill it in adulthood, sweetie. You will absolutely slay."

"Don't say *slay*, Mom," she grumbles.

"Aww, there's my teenager. I missed you."

She eyeballs me.

I know that eyeball.

That's the eyeball of *I got your password for your doorbell app, and I know what you've been doing, and I don't think you missed me at all.*

Or possibly my overactive imagination, guilt complex, and coming down off the adrenaline that's gotten me across the country today are wearing me down.

"Can you put your clothes on?" she says.

"Yes! Of course. Absolutely. Want to order takeout and watch a movie? Our flight's early tomorrow, but we have all night—"

"Mom."

I sigh.

She's not crying anymore.

And she's staring at me like she knows there are things I'm not telling her, even if she picks me and wants to come home with me. "I . . . went on a few dates with Coach Jackson while you were gone, but I won't—it's not going to work. He's a professional, and we're both adults. This won't impact you at school or on the soccer team at all. I just want to be honest with you, and I want you to know that you come first. Always. For me, you will *always* come first. And I will *never* put myself in a position to miss a call from you again. Okay?"

She stares at me for a long time. My towel is slipping, but even if it fell off, I don't think I'd feel more naked than I feel right now.

Maybe I *should* let it drop.

Then I'd be embarrassed enough to let myself cry over this too.

Later. I'll mourn *later.*

"Thanks, Mom," she finally says softly. Then she shoves my clothes at me. "Now go get dressed. I don't want to see you naked."

So.

That's that.

My daughter knows I won't be the same kind of asshole her father is, and she's worth it.

If I stay in Hell's Bells after Junie leaves for college and there's still something there with Flint in a few years, then there's still something there.

But right now, I really don't see that happening.

I told him he could trust me.

I told him we were friends.

I told him I wanted to be more than friends.

And then, just like everyone else in his life, I left him.

This one's on me.

Chapter 35

Flint

I'm at Iron Moose when news breaks that Maisey has landed in Tampa to pick up her runaway daughter. No TVs in the place, but everyone's checking their phones.

Takes about thirty seconds to get the scoop.

Dean's mistress is pregnant. They're engaged. And June threw a fit and ran away because she's the same brand of selfish narcissist as Maisey.

Yeah, that one makes me come out of my seat.

"Sit down, Mr. Neanderthal," Kory drawls. "You know the only people in here who believe that are the same people who think aliens are coming to kidnap us tomorrow."

"I dare them to come here to Hell's Bells and say that about our Junie and our Maisey," Regina says.

"I'm getting bored. Might branch out into libel-and-slander law," Charlotte adds.

Libby is growling like I haven't heard her growl since the drama department was disbanded at the high school. "I'm starting a petition to block any site that says bad things about Junie from Hell's Bells forever. First Hell's Bells. Then all of Wyoming. And then *the world*. Maisey, too, for that matter. She brings good treats. But Junie—she's such a good kid."

"Send me the link," Regina calls. "I'll share it with my cousin up in Montana. He's, like, TikTok viral for splitting logs or something. We'll get the right side of this story out."

"She dump you?" Kory asks as I lower myself back into my seat.

"It's a temporary thing."

"Temporary dumping or temporary fling?"

"Dumping."

"How temporary?"

"June has another year and a half of high school."

He snorts in his tea. Chokes on it, actually. "Oh, wait. You were serious."

I don't answer.

"You're serious," he repeats.

"I'm a sucky soccer coach, and I need to step aside and let someone else run the program."

He drops his fork. "Excuse you?"

"A fucking *teenager* brought those kids together in ways I never could've. A teenager who had every reason to hate all of us and not a whole hell of a lot to gain, but she did it anyway. And you know why? Because *that's what her mother taught her to do.* And you know what's sexy as hell?"

His face twists into a horrified grimace. "Single mothers?"

"People who fucking *care.* People who *try.* People who get back up. People who can look beyond what you do when you're down to who you're trying to be. People who—"

"Are hard to get?" he supplies.

I glare at him.

And then I take my bison burger to go, and I head home, where Maisey's truck is still parked at the gatehouse.

Dammit.

I peek in the truck.

No keys.

Can't get it back to her house.

Not that it matters.

After an hour of trying to force myself to eat the burger while I'm not hungry, I get a text from her.

> I told Junie we went on a couple dates and that it's over. I'll move my truck when we get back tomorrow. Apologies for it being in your way until then.

"You're not in my way." I toss the damn phone across the room, knowing she can't hear me and wouldn't listen even if she could.

Not today.

Maybe tomorrow.

Maybe not.

I give up on dinner, head into my bedroom, and spot the crumpled sheets plus the spare pillow on the floor, since we shared mine last night, and I almost walk away again.

Still smells like Maisey in here.

And I want it to *always* smell like Maisey in here.

But if I want Maisey, it's not *just* about Maisey.

Which means I know exactly what I need to do.

I stay scarce on Saturday, and when I get home, Maisey's truck is gone.

Keep to myself Sunday too.

Monday's a bitch and a half. None of the kids want to be back in school. All of them are counting the days until winter break. Since Thanksgiving was early this year, they still have *weeks*.

I hand out test results, and we start new units in every class. I act like I had a great Thanksgiving break. Interrupt trash talk about who got more candy at the parade. Steer them back on course. Ignore the questions about if I have a stick up my butt.

And get really pissed myself that the winter break is so far away.

Most of the rest of the week is the same.

Me pretending like I'm not a grumpy bastard. The kids hyped up but mostly able to focus. Fellow teachers avoiding me the same way they did when I got here six years ago, before I pulled my head out of my ass.

Even the PTA volunteers flinch when I step into the teachers' lounge and find a holiday spread laid out for us.

I skip it without being force-fed anything by Libby and spend my time getting looks from my horse out in the school's stable. I've been riding Parsnip instead of driving, to use some of my pent-up energy.

Not like there are any projects around town I can volunteer to help with to get out of my own head.

Maisey's either working them or has them done.

And then it's Thursday.

A week since the best night of my life. Six days since I let Maisey walk away from me. Six days when I haven't changed my mind.

She makes my life better. She makes me want to be happy. She makes me want to be better for her. For Opal and my students and my colleagues. For everyone around me.

And having June sit there quietly in class, not looking at me the entire week but turning in perfect homework every day, is utterly killing me.

I keep it together during my classes, but I'm in the foulest of foul moods by the time Thursday's over.

Logically, I know why I have to wait for winter break to go see Maisey again.

I need to give her space. I need to give June space to finish the semester without added stress if I have any chance of accomplishing what I need to accomplish with both of them.

The logic makes sense.

Emotionally, though, I'm a wreck.

I don't know if Maisey's okay. I don't know if she saw the tabloids. I don't know if she's hurting. I don't know if she's *not*, and I really do need to move on.

But I know that when I'm standing on a chair, reaching up to rehang the damn Einstein poster that fell off my wall in fifth period today, I don't want to hear footsteps behind me, and I don't want to deal with *one more thing*.

"Study hall hours are over," I say shortly without looking back.

"My mom misses you."

I almost fall off the chair. "June."

She hovers in the doorway, arms wrapped around herself, looking at me like I might bite. I don't know how it's possible that she looks even more like Maisey now than she did in class this morning, but she does, and it makes the wrench flung through my heart twist even harder.

I climb off the chair slowly, sit on it, then gesture for her to come in.

I didn't mean to imply that you should run away probably isn't the best start here.

No blame.

And knowing that she wasn't so much running away as trying to get home—and seeing that she's back home and acting normal in the cafeteria—I'll still own my part if I need to, but I'm also so fucking proud of her that I can't bring myself to ask if it was my fault.

"My dad's a total dick," she says.

There is literally no good answer to that, so I don't say a thing.

"But my mom—she's always tried to make everyone around her happy. I know she didn't like doing my dad's show, but she wanted him to be happy. And I know she didn't love roller coasters, but she'd ride them with me because she wanted *me* to be happy. And the thing is, she deserves to be happy too."

"She does," I agree, but I stop talking when I get the teenager look of *You are not in charge here, so be quiet and listen.*

"She's not happy," June continues. "And I hate when she's not happy, even though I'm supposed to be a teenager who doesn't care, because you always hate to see the people you love hurting. Always. And you look miserable, too, and you're not a dick—not like my dad—not yet, anyway—and I just—look. If you want to date my mom, I don't care. I mean, I do care. Don't hurt her. Don't make her sad. Don't use her. Don't take her for granted. Don't be a toadstool. Don't cheat on her.

Don't lie to her. And don't push it, because *I will know*, and apparently I can bring the entire tabloid industry to their knees, so *do not test me*."

Jesus.

This is why I work with kids.

Because they're fucking amazing.

"You doing okay?" I ask her.

Her face twists, and her eyes get shiny. "You know my dad hasn't called to ask me that?"

I look up at the ceiling and blow out a slow breath so I don't say anything I shouldn't say in front of June.

"I mean, I told him he was dead to me, but I thought parents were supposed to fight for their kids or something." She laughs shakily. "He hasn't even issued a statement on the news, like, calling out the stupid gossip sites for saying mean things about me. Like I said. He's a dick. But I don't think you are. And even if it doesn't work out with you and my mom, I want her to decide that for her. Not because of me."

I have to swallow twice before I can answer her. "I'll do everything in my power to not hurt her."

"Thank you," she whispers. "She's sadder than she was when Gran—when she found out Dad was cheating on her."

"You know I know about your grandma, June."

"It's *Junie*," she mutters. "And, like, so does half the school."

I lift my brows.

She scowls at me. "Okay, fine, I started to tell Vivian one time, and I chickened out, because so many of my friends back in Cedar Rapids turned into cuntnuggets when—what? I can say *dick*, but I can't say *cuntnugget*?"

I'm still wheezing in shock. This is a new one for me. "Exactly that."

She's wearing the same mischievous smile that Maisey had on the day she informed me my puzzle piece was wrong last week and made me take off my third sock.

Yes, I'm a man who comes prepared to a strip-puzzle game.

Which is not an experience I expect to have again for well over another year, and I'm okay with that.

It's also something I need to stop thinking about in front of Junie.

"Anyone here give you grief over the gossip sites last week?" I ask her.

She shakes her head, and I believe her.

"Pretty sure they won't care about what your grandma did either. You didn't do it. And besides, you have the Tony-and-Gingersnap factor working to your benefit."

"Can you tell me more about them?"

"Yep."

She waits.

I let her.

"Now?" she prompts.

"Oh. No. Not now. I'm saving those for family dinners with you and your mom."

She blinks at me twice to hide her eyes going shiny, and I have to swallow hard one more time myself.

I've always said I went into teaching because I remembered how hard this age was. And Kory isn't wrong when he says I love building them up and letting them go so I don't get attached.

But I'm attached.

I'm attached, and I have zero regrets.

Chapter 36

Maisey

That damn bear is back.

"Aren't you supposed to be hibernating?" I ask Earl as he loafs under my bedroom window.

He pauses and looks up at me like I'm the problem here.

I grunt at him.

He grunts back.

"Shoo, or I'll make you. Junie's getting home soon."

It's Friday.

One very, very long week down since I flew to Tampa to get Junie. With soccer over, she's been riding the bus home, and yes, she grumbles every day about the long walk up the driveway.

Like she doesn't run around soccer fields for fun.

And like she doesn't willfully walk even longer on the nights she gets dropped off at Almosta Ranch up the road to help Kory with his animals now that she has more time.

God, it's good to have her home, even if faking all my cheerfulness has been a total pain in the ass.

I pull out my phone and shoot her a quick text. Earl's here. He's under my bedroom window. Be aware.

Earl snuffles around eating something on the ground.

I squint.

Whatever it is that has his attention, I can't see it. "Don't make me get the hose, Earl. It's too late in the year for sprinklers."

He snorts at me once again, then plops his rump down right there, right outside my bedroom window, and buries his nose in the ground.

My phone dings.

Well, that's unexpectedly convenient, Junie has replied.

I reply with a side-eye emoji.

Teenage sarcasm isn't my favorite this week.

I finish folding my laundry and glance out my window again.

Earl's freaking *taking a nap*.

Right there. Right outside my bedroom window.

I sigh. "If you're planning on hibernating outside my bedroom, Earl, you're about to have the worst winter of your life."

My phone dings again.

It's Junie. Again.

I was thinking we should donate a statue of Gingersnap to the town. You know, like, in honor of your uncle Tony and all the stuff he and Gingersnap did for the people here. Like this one.

She includes a picture of a bronzed cow, and despite my mood this week, I still find a smile.

That's a really sweet idea, I text back.

And once again, I get a near-immediate response. Glad you think so, because I invited the cow-statue committee over to hash out details at five.

"*What?*" I say out loud to my phone.

It dings again like Junie heard me. Don't worry, Mom. Everyone's bringing food. They know you've been under the weather.

I rush out to the living room. We've been eating like frat boys this week. Take-out food, frozen meals, sometimes just microwave popcorn, all of it while sitting in front of the television watching Junie's favorite shows.

She suggested *The Princess Bride* early in the week, but when I burst into tears, she dove for the remote and turned on *Bob's Burgers* instead.

She didn't ask.

I didn't explain.

But I know she knows there's more to the story than *I went on a couple of dates with the high school soccer coach.*

And now she's bringing friends over to talk about how to erect a statue for the old cow that Flint helped us bury on our first day here, and I'm not okay.

But I will be.

Oh God, not again, Junie texts as I'm halfway through a quick clean of the kitchen.

She should be here soon. She should be *walking up the driveway.*

Alarm bells go off. Not what again? I ask. Oh no. Is Earl in your way?

I dash to the bedroom to see if the bear has moved, and—

Oh my God.

He hasn't.

But he's about to.

Because there's a man on a horse charging full steam at him.

I fling open my bedroom window.

"*Shoo*, you ugly beast," Flint yells at the bear.

I gape.

And I gape some more.

And then I blink back the heat in my eyes and tell myself it's Kory coming to my rescue, just dressed up like Flint, which is basically the most ridiculous idea I've ever had—they look nothing alike—but no.

That's Flint.

Galloping our way on Parsnip, Uncle Tony's old horse, and disturbing the bear.

"What are you doing?" I yell at him.

He flashes me a grin from under his baseball cap as he pulls the horse to a stop a few feet from the bear and me. "Got a note that Earl was bothering you again. Try not to get me thrown off my horse this time, yeah?"

How the *hell* is he so happy?

"C'mon, Earl," he says. "Don't make me get out my air horn. You know you can't hibernate by the house."

The bear snorts.

Flint flips his cap backward. "I'll do it," he tells Earl.

And I can't watch anymore.

I let the window shut, and I walk through the house, going up to the front, facing the other way.

Junie flies through the front door. "Mom. *Mom.* Mr. Jackson's chasing Earl away again."

"I'm sure he'll do a great job." I'm flustered and cranky, and *I don't want to deal with this.* "How many people are coming over? When did you decide to make a *statue*? How are you going to raise money for it? Is the town council okay with this? Where will you put it? Who's in charge? Did you volunteer to be in charge? Because you know if you—"

"*Mom.* Maybe try to breathe a little here? It's Friday. Time to let it all go and pretend we have no worries. I've got this, okay?"

"Junie—"

She tosses her bag on the couch I just picked up, then grabs me by the hand. "Come on. Let's go see who wins."

"*Juniper Louise.*"

She ignores the reprimand and pulls me back down the short hall to my bedroom.

Flint's still on Parsnip.

Earl's shaking his whole body as he climbs to his feet, shooting dirty looks at man and horse the whole time.

Junie pushes my window up, letting in a blast of cold air. "He's being stubborn today, isn't he?" she calls to Flint.

"Winter bones must've settled in," Flint replies. He's in a dark-yellow jacket that I know for a fact is super warm and super soft, and I want to reach out and touch him. Or have him pull me up on the horse in front of him and take me for a ride.

But *I can't.*

"That's the dumbest thing I've ever heard," she tells him.

He cuts her a look that calls her out without saying a word.

"Third dumbest?" she says with a grin.

"Were we in the same classroom for an hour a day every day this week?"

Wait.

Wait *what?*

"What's going on here?" I ask, looking between them.

Junie gives me the fakest innocent look I've ever seen in my life. "Mr. Jackson's chasing the bear away. Again."

"Juniper Louise Spencer, *that is not what I meant.*"

"Your daughter's a good one, Maisey," Flint says. "Even if she's completely useless when it comes to chasing bears away."

I look between them like they're playing a silent tennis match, not sure who to ask what next.

"Would it help if I jumped on Mom's back again?" Junie calls.

"*You set this up?* What? Why? *Did you feed the bear under my window?*"

"Nobody feeds bears," Flint says.

Parsnip whinnies in agreement, then snorts.

Earl grumbles out a huff and takes two moseying steps away from my window.

"This is what we call *nice timing*," Junie says, once more seemingly agreeing with Flint. "A fed bear is a dead bear."

"Did you—are you—*what is going on?*"

"If you have to date someone, at least you picked someone who's a thousand times better than Dad."

"Get, Earl," Flint growls.

Parsnip yells at the bear too.

And Earl finally gets the hint, glaring at all of us as he moseys back toward the creek.

I look at Junie.

"*Phew*," she says. "I didn't have to climb on your back this time. That's a relief."

"Junie."

She looks out the window at Flint, who's watching the bear meander back toward the old cabin while stealing glances at the two of us through the window. And then she looks back at me. "You should be happy. Even if it's only for a little while."

"Thanks, June," Flint says.

She rolls her eyes, but my cranky, lonely, angry teenage daughter is smiling as she does it. "I know you've done worse for a lot longer," she adds to me.

"You—you know you come first," I stutter.

"Mom. I'm sixteen. And sometimes dumb. And sometimes ridiculous. But I'm still less than two years from being able to run away for real. If I can leave you in good hands, then I want to. Also, you *do* know it's really stupid to keep telling me I come first when you never put yourself first, don't you? Which lesson am I supposed to learn here? Do as you say, or do as you do?"

"This is not the speech she told me she was going to give," Flint says through the window.

Junie smiles at him again. "I'm improvising."

Flint shakes his head, then he looks at me. "You wanna go for a ride?"

"*Now?*"

"Better now than after it gets dark."

"Go on," Junie says. "At least decide for yourself instead of for me. But I really don't want to ever call anyone *Dad* again. For the record."

I grab her in a hug and squeeze her tight. "Do you have any idea how amazing you are?"

"A little bit," she replies. "Go on. But don't fall off, or I really will run away again so I don't have to live with my sperm donor."

"*Junie.*"

"I get time to deal, too, Mom. This is today's method."

She shoves my boots and a coat at me and shoos me out the door, and honestly, she doesn't have to shoo very hard.

Flint and Parsnip meet me around front. He dismounts just off the front porch and holds out a hand. "Help you up?"

"You're here."

"Been down the driveway all week."

"Junie—"

"Is a smart, kind, determined tribute to having a really good mother."

Here I go again, getting all wet in the eyes for the umpteenth time this week.

But these tears feel like hope. Like forgiveness. Like a fresh start. Like a new life.

He twitches his fingers, and I take his hand. The minute our skin connects, an electric current zaps its way up my arm and straight to my heart. "You remember how to do this?" he asks softly.

"Get on a horse or take a leap?" I ask.

It will never not be a treat to have his smile aimed at me. "Yes."

"Not so much on either one."

He helps me up onto the horse, then easily swings up behind me. I'm pretty sure the saddle's not built for this, but he assures me Parsnip's a sturdy old girl, and we're not going very far.

"And I've got you," he murmurs.

He does.

His body is lined up behind me, his chest to my back, his thighs to the backs of mine, his arms around me, his hands guiding mine to help hold the reins.

I lean back into him. "I've missed you," I whisper as we head toward the bluffs that are taking on the deep-orange hue of sunset.

His arms tighten on either side of me, and he kisses my head. "I was working out how to ask Junie's permission to date you when she walked into my classroom last night and offered it to me."

"You—she—are you serious?"

"Kids are smart. And yours—yours is pretty fucking amazing."

"She told you that you can date me." I shouldn't be surprised. She really is a great kid.

"She also asked to announce in homeroom this morning, to the whole school, that her grandmother is a jailbird for embezzling money through fake homeowners' associations, so you might want to be prepared for a bunch of texts and calls this weekend."

"Oh my God."

"She says this way, if you stay here and run your retreat for wayward moms when she goes to college and you succeed in convincing your mother to move into the old cabin, she won't take anyone else for a ride."

It takes a moment for that to sink in, and when it does, I tip my head back into Flint's shoulder and laugh.

And I laugh.

And I laugh some more.

Not because it's crazy.

But because I suddenly feel so *free*.

"The whole town knows?" I ask.

"If they don't yet, they will by morning."

"How'd the kids take it?"

"There were a few who told her they couldn't loan her lunch money, and a few who wanted to know if she'd been to prison to visit and could describe it—mostly the Dungeons and Dragons crowd, don't worry, no jailbird wannabes—but overall, they were very supportive and told her anyone who'd judge her for her grandmother's law-breaking ways were . . . actually, it doesn't matter what names they used. That's a problem for someone above my pay grade."

"She truly is remarkable."

"She comes by it naturally."

"Are you flattering me, Mr. Jackson?"

"I'm trying to tell you that I'm madly in love with you, Ms. Spencer, and want to be part of your life and your daughter's too."

My breath catches.

He fists the reins in one hand and wraps his other arm around my belly. "I don't fall, Maisey. I refuse. But with you—I can't help myself. You're nothing that I expected you'd be and everything I've ever wanted but never thought I'd find. We can go slow. We *should* go slow. But I can't walk away from you. I want to be on this journey with you. Ups and downs. The hard times and the easy times. I want to be the man right beside you as you keep reaching for your own stars, and I want you to be the woman holding my hand while I take a few leaps of my own. I always thought I'd be happy being alone, but that was before I knew what it was like to be with you."

"Flint," I whisper.

I can't find words beyond that.

"I love the way you say my name," he says, low and husky in my ear.

The sky is turning a soft orange over the butte in the distance. Wind swirls around us. Earl is nowhere to be seen.

And I'm safe and warm and *loved*, on the back of a horse, in the middle of a place that was my escape when I needed it in my teenage years and is my *home* now.

"Is this real?" I whisper.

"Very, very real."

"Are you scared?"

"That I'll fuck up sometimes? Yes. Of loving you? No."

I twist in the saddle, trying to kiss him, and something lurches wrong.

"Oh God," I gasp.

But he laughs.

Laughs, and quickly dismounts from Parsnip before we fall, pulling me down into his arms when I flail without him behind me.

Parsnip snorts.

Flint pulls me close, one hand looped around my back, the other holding the horse. "I love you, Maisey Spencer. And I will love you no matter how many horses you get me thrown off of, no matter how many times you tell me Junie comes first, no matter how badly you cook, or how often you demonstrate that you can fix a leaky pipe and paint a wall faster and better than I can."

Tears are turning into little slushy icicles all down my face, so I bury my head in his chest, listening to that strong, steady thump of his heart while I wrap my arms around his waist. "I didn't want to love you," I confess. "I didn't want to love anyone. But I can't help myself. Not when you're so much more than I ever expected you to be."

"Young and hot?" he murmurs.

And now I'm laughing too. "Yes. Young and hot. And kind and generous and attentive and so, *so* good to my daughter. When you told her she was the heart of the team? I couldn't fight it anymore. I just couldn't. You're everything she deserves and nothing she's ever had."

"She has you."

"And she deserves *more*."

"I hope I'm everything *you* deserve too."

"I wanted to find me"—I whisper—"and I think I did. In you."

"So you'll give me a chance?"

The hope and the fear lingering in his voice hit a sensitive part of my heart that knows exactly how he's feeling.

Scared. But hopeful. Knowing you deserve love, that you deserve to *be* loved, not for who someone wants you to be but for who you are.

I lift my head and take his scruffy cheeks in my hands. "I love you so much," I tell him. "I thought I wanted—that I *needed*—to find me by myself. But finding *us* will be the greatest joy of my life."

He drops the reins holding Parsnip, lifts me, and twirls me in a circle that ends with more proof that Flint Jackson is the world's best kisser.

But more?

He's *my* best kisser.

And for the first time in years, I know that everything—for me, for Junie, for Flint—won't be *fine*.

My life, my future, my family—it will all be so much better.

Epilogue

Flint

For the second time in my life, I'm giving a eulogy for a cow.

Difference is, today I'm standing in front of a newly unveiled bronze statue of her inside the doorway of the newly rebuilt barn at Wit's End, with the love of my life and the daughter of my heart at my side.

Weather's a little nippy, even for late spring, so June's in a long-sleeved Colorado School of Mines shirt and matching beanie. Maisey's hiding her emotions behind massive sunglasses and a Hell's Bells Demons ball cap.

Most of the town's come out for the dedication to the statue of Gingersnap, and I'm proud to say there isn't a dry eye in the crowd as I wrap up. "So may we all be as fearless and full of life as Gingersnap would've wanted us to be."

Laughter ripples through the crowd, mixed in with the sniffles.

Gingersnap was loved, and she's now the official cow of Hell's Bells. The mayor said so.

Maisey takes my hand and squeezes as I cede the mic to Charlotte, who'll be directing us all to the refreshment tables around the outside of the barn.

"That was beautiful," Maisey whispers. "It almost made me want to get a cow."

"*Mom*," Junie sighs.

"What? You're taking the dog. I'm going to need a new pet."

"You have Flint."

They both look at me.

I try to stifle a snort of laughter, which earns me a look from Charlotte. "Is there something else you'd like to share with the crowd, Mr. Jackson?"

The students situated on the temporary stands hoot with laughter.

I clear my throat. "No, ma'am."

"I thought so."

She flashes the crowd a cheeky grin and gets back down to the business of explaining where we have volunteer students manning lemonade and ice cream tables.

"I still don't understand what's so special about the damn cow that they had to have a whole hullabaloo for it," Maisey's mom mutters behind us.

"Because it's *Gingersnap*, Grandma. Come on. We saved a special seat for you between the sheriff and the mayor."

Yep.

Maisey's mom is out of prison and has moved into the original cabin on the land. We've installed the same software on her computer and phone as they use on the kids' laptops that get distributed through the Hell's Bells school system, so Maisey can monitor her mother's activities.

Junie just finished her senior year and is headed to engineering school just a few hours away. *With* her driver's license. For the record.

I won't say helping her through driver's ed was my favorite part of the past year and a half, but it might be one of my proudest accomplishments.

That, and being in the stands beside Maisey when Junie led the Hell's Bells soccer team to the state championship win this year.

Turns out there *was* someone else willing to take over as soccer coach.

Had no idea that Kory's boo was just as obsessed with soccer as he is with drag, but all's well that ends with a championship trophy.

Maisey's split Wit's End into two parts. The smaller part is a true training ground now for ranchers of the future, which is also useful for letting about a quarter of the high school population blow off steam by helping take care of chickens, goats, and the three horses that we have now. The other part of the ranch had a soft opening last fall when she hired part-time staff to run classes in basically everything that every woman in Hell's Bells wanted to learn or try for a hobby.

It's been an interesting school year.

But mostly, it's been fun.

"Ice cream?" Maisey asks me as the crowd starts dispersing away from the statue of Gingersnap, which will eventually be moved into the park where I cut Maisey out of the swing almost two years ago now.

I slip an arm around her shoulder. "Or we could go make out up in the loft."

She smiles. "We could."

"Unless Junie's planning on kicking any soccer balls that way . . ."

"At least they'd know we went out happy."

I grin at her again and press a kiss to her forehead. "Would your mother or your daughter be more embarrassed?"

She pretends to think about it. "Ooh, tough question."

"What's a tough question?" Opal asks.

"Strawberry or cookies and cream," I answer instantly, which sends Maisey into a fit of laughter.

"That is *not* what you were discussing," Kory says behind her.

I shrug. "And that's a problem because . . . ?"

The two of them team up on us and shoo us out of the barn, not letting us get away with sneaking up to the loft for alone time. So instead, we mingle with our friends and fellow citizens of Hell's Bells, with more stories about Gingersnap and Tony getting told than we've heard in a while.

Maisey's mom is new enough here that she's the novelty now, and every time I check on her, she's telling another story about prison.

Safe to say life won't be boring, even with Junie leaving us for college in a few months.

Gradually, most of the townsfolk head home after we get the refreshments tables cleaned up, until it's just a small group left.

Charlotte and her kids and their dog. Kory and his lovebug. Regina and her kids and *their* dog. Opal. Junie and her boyfriend, who's headed to the Colorado School of Mines with her. Maisey's mom.

The most important people, all gathered around, eating sandwiches we ordered in advance.

I pull Maisey into my lap as she attempts to walk past me. "Hey," I murmur. "Good day?"

She loops her arms around my shoulders and kisses my forehead. "The best. You?"

"Not quite done yet."

"No?"

"Lot changing."

She sighs, and this time, instead of kissing my forehead, she rests her head against it. "There is."

"Think I want one more."

"Day?"

"Change."

She pulls back and frowns at me, like she can sense the way my heart's picking up and my veins are starting to buzz. "What kind of change?"

"A good kind."

Her brows lift. "There's more good change?"

"There is if you marry me."

Her mouth forms a perfect O.

Junie squeals softly. "*He finally did it,*" she whispers to Vivian.

"Oh my God, this is so romantic," Vivian squeals back. "Say yes, Ms. Maisey!"

"I did *not* approve this question," Maisey's mom says.

"Sit down, Grandma," Junie replies. "I did."

Maisey's still staring at me, her eyes going shiny. "Are you serious?"

I pull her hand to my mouth and kiss her knuckles. "You're already my wife in my heart. The woman who makes my soul complete. I want to make it official. Share it with the world. Celebrate. Love you. Forever."

She stares at me a moment longer, and then the brightest, biggest, most beautiful smile lights her entire face. "*Yes!*" she shrieks, and when she throws her arms around me, tackling me in the chair, we topple backward together, landing in the dusty earth with a thud.

"That's not a very auspicious start," Maisey's mom murmurs. "But I suppose if—"

"Don't start, Grandma," Junie says while Maisey peppers my face with kisses. "He's gonna be the one helping Mom pick your nursing home in a few years."

Everyone cracks up.

Charlotte and Regina help us out of the broken chair.

Opal kisses Maisey on the cheek. "I knew you were special the minute I saw you, and I'm so glad to have you in my family."

Junie tackles me in a hug. "She said yes! I'm so proud of you. Look how far you've come."

I hug her back. "Thank you for your permission."

"I wouldn't give it to anyone else." She turns to Maisey. "I'm so happy for you. And I want you to know, I only agreed because he said he'd take you somewhere tropical to elope, and I get to come along."

Maisey wheezes out a laugh. "I'm sure that was your only consideration."

"You two are so cute together. I'm so happy for you."
"You are *amazing*," Maisey whispers to her daughter.
"Because I learned from the best," Junie whispers back.
Yep.
This is my family.
All my family.
And they were all worth the wait.

AUTHOR'S NOTE

Dear Reader,

When my family and I moved recently into our forever home after my hubby's military retirement, our house came with a few unexpected surprises that 100 percent inspired the opening of this book. So this one will forever be close to my heart.

I hope you fell in love with Maisey, Flint, Junie, Gingersnap, Earl, and all the residents of Hell's Bells. As an often-overworked mom myself, I have such a soft spot for mothers, fathers, caregivers, and everyone who has ever sacrificed to put other people's needs above their own.

Always remember that you matter. You deserve time to breathe too. And if you want more single-mom love, I hope you'll dive into my book *The Hot Mess and the Heartthrob*, which is more escapist fun dedicated to all of us who do our best every day, even when it's tough.

Happy reading always, and stay amazing.

Pippa

ACKNOWLEDGMENTS

A massive thanks to Maria Gomez for taking another chance on me, to Lindsey Faber for making me cry in the best way in assuring me that the first draft of this book was so much more than a flaming pile of poo, and to Jessica Alvarez for inspiring me to put my own wildlife experiences into a book.

To my Pippaverse Lady Fireballs, thank you for helping me name Wit's End, Almosta Ranch, Gingersnap, and Helen Heifer. And thank you for being a safe space to say things like "So, the working title of my next book is *The Dead Cow Book*."

To Jodi, Beth, and Jess, thank you for making #TeamPippa run so smoothly behind the scenes. I say it in every book, and I mean it—I couldn't do my job without you.

To the Pipsquad, you are a source of light and joy, and I'm so grateful that you've chosen to spend your time hanging out in our little community, boosting each other, and making one another laugh.

And to my hubby and kids, thank you for supporting me on this roller coaster that is the writing business. You've always been my number one cheerleaders, and it means more to me than I can put into words to know that you're always in my corner.

EXCERPT FROM *THE HOT MESS AND THE HEARTTHROB*

Why does my child have a dying red squirrel in a shoebox?

Also, why is that not the weirdest question I've ever asked myself? I curl my fingers into my palms, then release them before I say something I'll regret. "Zoe, we can take this upstairs, and—"

Levi steps around me and tilts the lid to peer inside. "I know a great vet. Lives in my brother's neighborhood, which is awesome, since my nephew's always finding frogs and gophers."

I try to push the lid closed again. "We can't—"

"When he says she's *the best*"—his bodyguard interrupts—"he means that in all possible ways."

Fantastic.

So Levi's slept with her.

He stiffens next to me too. "Giselle, you might want to reword that before Dr. Murphy's husband gets the wrong idea."

His bodyguard cracks a grin. "Did that come out wrong?"

He ignores her and peeks inside the box again. "You know what he smells like? He smells like this time Tripp and Cash got drunk on apple wine when we were—*aaaah!*"

There's a flash of fur, and he flings himself backward with a furry creature hanging on to his face. *"Drunk squirrel!"*

Giselle lunges for him.

Zoe lunges for the squirrel. *"Skippy!"*

I lunge for all of them. At once.

Levi twists and spins while the squirrel climbs his perfectly mussed hair, then goes down his back and into his jacket. His face contorts, and he makes a strangled noise, and *oh my God.*

Ohmygod ohmygod ohmygod.

Please tell me my kid's rescue squirrel didn't just go down Levi Wilson's pants.

Ohmygod ohmygod ohmygod.

He rips his jacket off and flings it onto the floor, and *oh thank God,* there's the squirrel, racing to the top of the bookshelves.

"I got it," Giselle announces.

Zoe's crying. "But he was sick."

"He's *not sick*! He's *loose in the store*!"

"Drunk," Levi says, wiping his face. "That squirrel is definitely drunk."

"He lost his balance!" Zoe shrieks as I try to hug her and calm her down. "He could've died! I love him, and he doesn't know how to be a wild squirrel anymore."

Levi's eyeballing me, and I don't know if it's reverence or repulsion. "You have a pet squirrel?"

"I have chaos and a guilt complex, and I didn't know we have a squirrel."

Excerpt from The Hot Mess and the Heartthrob, *copyright © 2021 by Pippa Grant*

ABOUT THE AUTHOR

Photo © 2021 Briana Snyder, Knack Video + Photo

Pippa Grant is a *USA Today* bestselling author who writes romantic comedies that will make tears run down your leg. When she's not reading, writing, or sleeping, she's being crowned employee of the month as a stay-at-home mom and housewife trying to prepare her adorable demon spawn to be productive members of society, all the while fantasizing about long walks on the beach with hot chocolate chip cookies.